A Dollar Outta Fifteen Cent 4.5:
Married to the Money

SPECIAL EDITION

CAROLINE McGILL

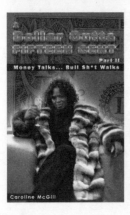

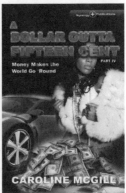

A Dollar Outta Fifteen Cent 4.5:
Married to the Money

SPECIAL EDITION

CAROLINE McGILL

Synergy Publications
P.O. Box 210-987
Brooklyn, NY 11221

www.SynergyPublications.com

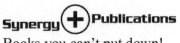

Books you can't put down!

A Dollar Outta Fifteen Cent 4.5: Married to the Money

© 2013 Synergy Publications

ISBN: 978-0-9890253-1-7

Library of Congress Control Number: 2013950554

Cover by: Karoz Newman for Stl King designs

www.SynergyPublications.com

This novel is for my diehard readers.

It is your undying loyalty and support that has inspired me to release this Special Edition.

Thank you all.

PROLOGUE

It was Saturday, the day after Valentine's Day. Although love and happiness were the most prevalent emotions circulating amongst folks, for some there was pain and tears as well. That evening a hysterical woman dialed 9-1-1 to report a shooting at an elite wedding reception in the affluent hills of New Jersey. The operator that took the call asked the woman to please calm down, and quickly dispatched the police and ambulance.

Sirens blared as the emergency vehicles sped toward the crime scene. The paramedics arrived at the carnage that was Cas and Laila's ruined wedding reception, and were met with chaos. The event had been exquisitely decorated in red and white for the holiday, but most of the upper echelon attendees were in pure panic. Lurking in the midst of the turmoil were shameless paparazzi aspiring to break the story first. They snapped random photos and tried to get a statement from anyone who looked like they knew details. Due to the holiday and lovely red floral arrangements about, a young paparazzo had dubbed the celebration-turned-melee the "Valentine's Day Massacre."

The 9-1-1 call had come in for two injured parties – black males – in need of emergency care. The paramedics rushed in anxious to save lives, but the determined bunch quickly discovered that there was only hope for one half of the injured pair. The other half had been beaten to a bloody pulp. Two hopeful paramedics checked the man's wrist and neck for a pulse and realized that there was none. The brother had succumbed to the horrendous fate he had clearly suffered. The dead man had been beaten so badly, he had broken bones, missing teeth, and cuts and gashes so deep that some of his flesh and cartilage was exposed. The man they would soon learn was Khalil Atkins was no longer.

The other gentleman was alive, but clinging to his life. Three young EMTs loaded the victim into the back of an ambulance car. They were on their jobs, trying to save him. Sirens blaring, they whisked Cas away and sped toward the hospital.

As the three young men diligently tended to Cas, he went in and out of consciousness. He kept on forgetting where he was and felt weaker and weaker. He wasn't sure if the paramedics gave him something, or if he was dying.

Cas heard his best man, Jay, and his mother's voices in the distance. They were both telling him to hold on. He wanted to, but it got harder and harder to keep his eyes open. Breathing became more and more difficult. Cas gasped for air and slipped into darkness. He drifted into a slumber so deep it was near death.

The next thing Cas knew, he was floating. There was a flash of light, and then Laila, his new wife, appeared. They stood on opposite sides of a huge field filled with pretty colorful flowers. Cas and Laila called out each other's names, but couldn't seem to get across the field to touch one another. The closer they moved toward one another, the further apart they wound up. It was as if the field grew wider and wider.

Suddenly, the flowers in the field began to wilt and die. The sky turned a gloomy dark gray and then things appeared to be monochromatic. Cas looked down at his hand. Everything had turned black and white, including him. He looked down and saw bright crimson-red dew drops on the flower petals. They matched the blood stains that suddenly appeared on the beautiful dress Laila wore. Cas realized that she was sobbing her heart out. He wondered why she was crying. Before he could ask Laila what was wrong, she turned and fled. Cas went after her but she disappeared as if she had evaporated into thin air.

After Laila disappeared, Cas stopped short, confused. The he saw a rainbow in the distance. It was surrounded by the bluest sky he'd ever seen. The sight was literally breathtaking. Cas was awed and drawn to its serenity. As he was beckoned toward it, he wondered if that was heaven.

Inside the ambulance, Jay and Cas's mother, Ms. B, sat by Cas's side and watched every move the paramedics made. Jay and Ms. B were both terrified. They prayed nonstop for Cas's wellbeing and desperately held on to their faith. Their prayers were almost identical. They each begged God to spare Casino's life.

Ms. B had tears streaming down her face. As she held her son's hand, she traveled down memory lane. Caseem was her only child. Flashbacks of his childhood ran through her mind as vividly as a full color slideshow. She pictured the day Cas was born. His first steps, his first birthday, then she thought of his first fall off of his first bike, his first day at school, his first girlfriend, and his first car, and when his first child was born. Reminiscing was joyful yet painful. She had been a single mother Cas's whole life. Her son was everything to her.

Ms. B squeezed his hand and prayed he would make it. "Come on, Caseem, I need you to pull through, baby," she told her unconscious son. She was an emotional mother in tears. She frantically willed Cas to fight to live. "Your mama needs you, baby boy. Come on, Caseem, you all I got!"

As Jay listened to the anxious pleas of his wounded comrade's mother, his heart was broken as well. Jay sat there and had flashbacks of his own. In his mind he saw him and Cas slap boxing and wrestling as nine year-old kids, then balling nonstop on the court at sixteen, and then copping their first whips and flossing at nineteen. Jay pictured the two of them lighting cigars in celebration of their first born sons, and then Jay thought about the time he was shot in the face. Cas was by his side the whole time. That was his ace and number one crimie. Cas had to make it.

Jay was so worried he asked the paramedics for an update about every thirty seconds. He was willing to let a lot of things go in life, but Cas was not one of them. That dude was a part of him. He was the brother Jay never had. Life without him was unimaginable. "*Please* God," Jay prayed aloud. "Bring my man through. Only You got the power, so *please God.*"

One of the machines they had Casino hooked up to began to beep and blink. The paramedics moved quickly, speaking in medical jargon. Jay and Ms. B didn't comprehend what they were saying but they got out of the way so the trained professionals could do their jobs.

As they waited for the outcome, Casino's mother and honorary brother's hearts raced. They were on the verge of cardiac arrest. Whatever had just happened couldn't have been good. Jay and Ms. B tried hard to be optimistic but they were exasperated. They squeezed hands and sat there helpless. Cas had to make it. Their family needed him.

Meanwhile, Cas was literally having an out-of-body experience. His soul ascended from his dying body and he looked down at himself laying there. He watched as the paramedics fussed over him and did everything they could to save him.

What the fuck? What's goin' on?, Cas thought. He didn't like the sight of himself lying there lifeless. It frightened him to say the least. Cas prayed he was dreaming and tried not to panic. He wondered what had happened. Whatever it was, it looked bad. Cas tried to tell his mother and Jay that he was okay, but they couldn't seem to hear him or see him.

Cas looked down at his attire and realized he was wearing a custom-tailored black suit with no blood on it. He looked okay and felt fine. He ran his hand over his chest. Yes, he was fine. Casino wondered if he was bugging. Confused, his soul moved on.

Next, Cas looked down on a luxury car that was sped down the highway. It was a silver-colored Bentley he recognized. It belonged to Fatima. He could see the vehicle's occupants as clear as day. He zoomed in on the face that belonged to his new bride. Laila sat in the backseat in tears. Portia sat next to her comforting her. Wise drove and pregnant Fatima rode in the passenger seat. Everyone looked upset. Their eyes were red and swollen. Cas yelled out to let them know that he was fine, but no one heard him there either. That really started to bother him.

Casino's wandering soul moved on. He had to find his children and let them know he was okay. He prayed they would be able to hear him. A few seconds later, he got his wish. Cas stood there looking at his only son, Jahseim. The boy was with his grandmother, Mama Mitchell, who appeared to be consoling him. Cas walked up to his son and placed a hand on his shoulder. "Jah, quit crying. Here I am, lil' man. Your daddy's okay."

Jahseim didn't respond and Mama Mitchell acted as if she couldn't see Cas either. The discovery was so disheartening he grew a huge lump in his throat. Being invisible to his son was enough to make his eyes tear up a little. Cas's vision was blurry with emotion but he realized that Mama Mitchell had some of her other grandchildren as well. Cas's baby girl, Skye, and Jay's little girls, Jazz and Trixie. Wise's daughter, Falynn, was also there. All of the kids looked upset.

Cas saw his stepdaughter, Macy, knelt down on the floor crying over what looked like a body covered by a tablecloth. Jay's son Jayquan and Macy's grandmother, Mama Atkins, hovered over her. Cas noticed that Macy's grandmother wept as well. Lil' Jay comforted both ladies like a gentleman.

Everything came back to Casino with a jolt and he finally realized what had happened. He and Laila had just gotten married and were seated at a table at their wedding reception, when her crazy ex-husband stormed in and fired on them. Cas was usually armed, but that nigga Khalil caught him slipping because that was his wedding day. The bullet Cas took to the chest had punctured his right lung.

Cas guessed that sheet covered body on the floor was Khalil. He looked over on the other side of the table. That was where he had laid shot and bleeding, waiting on the paramedics. There was a small puddle of blood on the floor. It had to belong to him. The events leading up to the shooting replayed in Cas's head.

The wedding had turned out lovely. He and Laila had both been happy because it had been a success. They had tied the knot and made it official. Afterwards, they'd all headed to the reception, where Laila resurfaced in another dress that was equally stunning compared to her wedding gown, but just a little more revealing. They had all eaten, and then Jay had proposed a toast to Cas and Laila's future. It was just about time for their last dance.

Right after the toast, that lame Khalil showed up and serenaded them with bullets. Cas remembered quickly moving to cover Laila, who was sitting on his lap at the time. He took a slug to the chest in the process. Cas looked down at poor Mama Atkins. The weeping woman had lost her son because of that nonsense. That dude just couldn't move on. That didn't make any sense.

Before Cas knew it, he looked down at his body in the back of the ambulance again. They were trying hard to revive him because he wasn't breathing. Jay sat by Cas with his arm around his mother, who cried just like Mama Atkins. Cas wondered if his mother would lose her son because of that nonsense as well.

Cas had an unwelcomed epiphany. He wondered if he was dead. Panic set in as he grasped his situation and realized how afraid he was. He was not ready to go yet. He had too much to do. There were lots of people depending on him. He had small kids who needed him. So did his mother and Laila. Cas placed his head in his hands and began to feel defeated.

Cas knew it was time for a change. Just hours before he was shot, he had promised God that he would turn over a new leaf. He meant what he said, too. He was really sorry about killing Jay's trifling baby mother, Ysatis. That had occurred just weeks before. He was sorry for all the other dirt he had done as well. Cas prayed his repentance wasn't a little bit too late. God had to give him another chance.

Casino began to pray. He wasn't perfect but he had always maintained a relationship with God. With no shame in his game, he candidly begged for another chance. "God, I'm sorry for all the wrong I've ever done. Please forgive me for my sins. I'm not proud of some of the things I've done in my lifetime, but I need to stick around, God. I got a family. I got kids!"

Suddenly, a dapper gentleman appeared on Cas's left. The man wore dark shades and smoked a fine cigar. He was dressed in an expensive brimmed hat and a black tailored suit. Cas glimpsed down at the guy's black and white wing-tipped shoes and had to admit, he was pretty clean. It seemed as if he had appeared out of nowhere. Cas was curious about his well-dressed company's identity, so he greeted him with a little suspicious nod. "What up?"

"Hey, pal, how's it goin'? It's good to see you, Casino." The guy had an Italian accent like a mafia wise guy. He reached in his inside cocktail jacket pocket and handed Cas a cigar.

Cas didn't want the cigar but he took it just to be polite. Smoking was the last thing on his mind. He couldn't see the dude's eyes through the dark glasses he wore. For some reason that bothered him. The fact that he knew his name bothered Cas as well. Puzzled, he asked, "Have we met?"

The guy chuckled. "C'mon, Casino, you know me. It's your old buddy . . . Lou." He reached out to Cas for a handshake.

Cas declined. He didn't shake hands with people whose eyes he couldn't look into. "Nah, I don't think I know you, man." Something about that dude gave him the creeps.

The guy chortled and exhaled thick cigar smoke. "Jeez, I gotta beg to differ. I think you know me well, *Killa Cas.*"

Alarmed, Cas took a step back. He had a feeling Lou wasn't the ally he claimed to be.

Lou grinned and blew out more smoke. "Hey, relax there, pal. It's pretty cold out here. You had' a get married in February, huh? I know, for *Valentine's Day*. C'mon, *Mr. Romance.* What'ta you say we head back to my place where it's nice and warm."

Cas backed up another step. He had the urge to put some distance between the two of them. Something told him that guy was bad news. Cas shook his head and started in the other direction without another word.

Lou grabbed Cas's shoulder and stopped him in his tracks. "Hey, where you goin'?" he demanded. "When I said let's go to my place, that wasn't a request."

Cas didn't like to be touched by strangers. He didn't like to feel pressured or threatened either. He was about ready to fuck that nigga up. Cas turned around and barked on that fool. "Yo, back up off me, mo'fucka! Who you think you talkin' to? You think it's somethin' sweet?"

Lou laughed sinisterly, then bellowed, "Mothafucka, you ain't in *'da hood* no more! You know who *you* talkin' to? I own you! You're *mine*! We made a deal a long fuckin' time ago!"

The hairs on the back of Cas's neck stood up. He realized he was in bad company. However, he was determined not to be intimidated by anyone walking on two feet. The fighter in Cas said, "I ain't never been strong armed by *nobody*, nigga! You better check my résumé!"

Lou laughed creepily and removed his hat and glasses. Cas was so startled his jaw dropped. His mouth hung open in surprise. In Lou's eye sockets sat these glowing red orbs. That would spook the most hardcore dude on earth. Cas's instinct said *"run for your life."* But his feet were glued to the spot he stood in.

Cas realized then that "Lou" was short for Lucifer. That crazy mothafucka was the devil himself! Cas grew more frightened then he'd ever been. His knees weakened, but to display fear was to display weakness. He dared not. He made up his mind to fight for his life.

Casino had a mean left hook. He swung on Lou and struck him in the jaw. Determined to knock that nigga out, he gave that punch all he had. Dudes usually respected the Cas's one-hitter-quitter, especially after they were shamed and left sprawled on the ground unconscious. Lou was the exception to the rule. He took that sucker punch like a champ.

After Cas hit him, Lou laughed in his face. He took off his suit jacket and said, "Casino, you bastard! Killa Cas! Is that all you got? Come on, mothafucka, make my day!"

Cas swallowed hard and then removed his jacket too. Although he was undoubtedly intimidated by those glowing red eyes, he had never shied away from a brawl before. He got in a fighter's stance and prepared to go toe-to-toe with the devil.

Lou loved a challenge. He snarled, "C'mon, Golden Gloves, take your best shot!"

Cas swung again but Lou ducked and punched him in the midsection. That gut punch caused Cas to double over for a second. That bastard hit hard as hell. Cas shook it off. Once he recovered from that blow, he threw his hands back up and skillfully bombarded Lou with what was usually a knockout combination. Cas figured that would finish him.

Lou stood there and laughed while Cas gave it everything he had. Cas got pretty frustrated because he just couldn't seem to conquer Lou. Nothing he tried worked. He was involved in the fight of his life. Casino realized then what his mother had been preaching to him his whole life. He couldn't beat the devil without God. Cas was out of breath and in need of some backup. He began to pray. "Heavenly Father, I can't win this without You! Please, God, help me!"

Lou got very upset when he heard Cas's cries for help from heaven. Determined to silence him, he angrily socked him in the midsection. Cas retaliated with a blow and a brief struggle ensued. Lou managed to get Cas in a chokehold and then proceeded to put him to sleep.

Cas couldn't believe how strong that mothafucka was. Lou was straight handling him. Cas hated to admit it but he was no match for his strength. As he sank to the ground, he kept the faith and kept on calling on the Big Homie upstairs. "God, *please* help me! I got somethin' to live for! I need to get back to my kids! Please, God . . ." Cas could no longer speak because he couldn't breathe. He was losing the battle.

Suddenly, he heard the voice of The Almighty. God actually spoke to him. "Son, I've given you so many chances. You've had a good life." The Most High spoke calmly but His voice was so powerful the devil was forced to shield his ears. He let Cas go in the process.

Cas was relieved to be out of that sleeper hold. He struggled for breath and continued to plead. "Yes, I've had a good life, Father, and I thank You for that. But I need more time. *Please!*"

"And what will you give me, son?" asked God.

Cas was completely awed. He knew he had one shot, so he swallowed hard and trembled in his shoes. Stripped and humbled, he got on his knees and threw his hands up. "You can take everything, God," he cried. "All of my worldly possessions. Just let me live! *Please, God.*"

"Son, I'm not sure if I'm convinced."

Cas lost control of his emotions and tears rolled down his face. It was that real. He continued to beg God for mercy. "Life is the most precious gift there is, God. I realize that, and I wanna live right. I'ma change, I guarantee You! Just give me another chance, so I can make things right with my kids!"

Disgruntled, Lou interrupted. He'd heard enough. "*Killa Cas,* you full of shit! C'mon, you gotta be kidding me!"

Cas ignored Lou and focused on God. "I'm begging you to spare my life, God. I know I've done wrong, but I've also done a lot of good! From the heart. Give me another chance, God! Please! *Please!!*"

Lou knew he had no wins with the Big Fellow in the vicinity. It was time to get lost for the time being. "Cas, we'll see about all this *I'ma change* shit. I'm sure we'll meet again soon, *my nigga!*" He cackled evilly and disappeared. His creepy laughter echoed in his wake. It faded away until there was just silence. Darkness fell simultaneously until it was pitch black. Cas's soul lay sprawled out on the ground as still as death.

CHAPTER ONE

"I sing because I'm happy. I sing because I'm free. His eye is on the sparrow, and I know he watches over me..."

A soloist belted out a moving rendition of "His Eye Is on the Sparrow" to commemorate the ending of a burial that left a family brokenhearted. The woman sang with the same emotion the attendees felt. By no means had the deceased lived the life of an angel, but he would surely be missed.

The mood of the service was sullen. It matched the gray skies overhead. Laila stood at the gravesite in tears and overlooked the casket that housed the body of a man she would never forget. It was hard to believe she had buried someone that had meant so much to her. Heartache had overtaken her entire being. Laila was distraught. She could barely breathe. She stared down at the red roses she had tossed on his casket and wished for the ten trillionth time that she could turn back time.

Jay and Portia stood on either side of Laila for support. Jay held a large black umbrella over their heads to shield them from the raindrops that fell ceremoniously from heaven. It was as if God was weeping as well. What had occurred was a tragedy.

In Jay's head, he mentally replayed him and Cas's last conversation. Jay had a huge lump in his throat and blamed himself somewhat. If it wasn't for him, Casino and Laila would've never met. Jay was heavyhearted. Cas was his ace. He really had love for that dude. Thank God, his right-hand man was in the hospital holding on. Cas was hooked up to a respirator, but he had survived.

He was the main reason Jay was there. A week before, Cas had taken a bullet to the chest. The slug had punctured his right lung, but God was good. Cas was recovering slowly but surely. Though the doctors said it wouldn't happen overnight, he had certainly made a lot of progress. It had been seven days since the shooting. It was horrible that it had happened on his man's wedding day. Cas had been unconscious for days. He was finally alert and talking a little. Jay and the fam had stood by his bedside everyday and monitored his progress. Cas wasn't exactly jumping up and down yet, but they took the first hoarse whispers he'd mouthed to be a great sign. He had only come that far by faith. Many people had prayed for him.

The day before, Cas made Jay promise to accompany Laila to her ex-husband, Khalil's funeral. Jay thought that was big of Cas, considering the fact that Khalil had tried to take his life. Jay agreed to go to the funeral for Cas and also out of love for Laila and Macy. They were both broken from their loss.

Jay was a decent dude that had a good heart. Even though Khalil had almost killed his main man, he stood there feeling it. Jay was especially affected by the pitiful state Laila appeared to be in. He was there to offer her the strength she lacked that day. She was like his sister, and he would be there for her no matter what the circumstances were. Though Laila was with Cas now, she had every right to cry. She and Khalil had a long history. From what Jay understood, they had been together since they were kids. They had also made two children together. That meant a lot.

Portia stood there and wept along with Laila. She cried for Khalil, too. They went back pretty far. They had met in the early nineties. He had hooked up with Laila while they were all in high school, so there were lots of memories. It was heartbreaking. Khalil was wrong for shooting Cas at the reception, but regardless of what had happened, a life was lost. There was no pleasure in that.

Laila was thankful for her dear friends' support. She looked around and watched the small crowd at the gravesite disperse. Laila realized it was time to go. She bowed her head and whispered a final prayer that Khalil would rest in peace. When she was done, she looked up at Jay and Portia. Both of their eyes were filled with compassion. Jay and Portia were family. They both had huge hearts.

Fatima was there for Laila that day as well. When the rain had started, Laila had insisted that she go on to the car because she was almost eight-months pregnant. She didn't want Fatima to get sick. It was a frigid February day.

Laila's daughter, Macy, was pregnant as well. Unlike Fatima, she was in the early stage. Laila looked around for her. She saw Macy standing with her grandmother, Mama Atkins. Seeing Macy comforting Mama Atkins caused Laila to snap out of it. She put her grief on a backburner and hurried over to her mother-in-law's side. The poor woman had lost a child. One whose death she had the misfortune of witnessing. Khalil had been Mama Atkins's only child. Though he had moved foolishly when he'd opened fire at Laila's wedding reception, that couldn't have been easy. Laila had lost a child before. Her baby, Pebbles, had been killed and then raped by a sick scumbag, so she knew how dreadful it was.

Although the occasion was sad, a part of Laila was satisfied because they had done just as she'd promised Mama Atkins they would. They had stuck together and put Khalil away nicely. He may have spent his last days alive as a drunken, raving lunatic who let jealousy destroy him, but his funeral ceremony was grand. He was buried with respect and dignity. That hadn't exactly rectified the situation, but hopefully he would rest in peace.

Portia and Jay followed Laila over there so they could offer their condolences to Mama Atkins as well. That was particularly awkward for Jay because he actually felt horrible about the fact that his peoples had murdered her son right in front of her. That was something he would've normally never co-signed. However, the circumstances surrounding that dude Khalil's demise had made his death inevitable. He'd clearly had a death wish.

Jay was a man of good character, so when Laila and Portia were done speaking, he respectfully removed the dark Ferragamo glasses he was wearing and stepped up and sincerely apologized. "Ma'am, I'm truly sorry about the loss of your son. Should you ever need anything, and I mean *anything*, please don't hesitate to reach out to me and my family."

Mama Atkins was a strong, God-fearing woman with a forgiving heart. She could tell Jay was genuine. Before she thanked him, she managed a little smile. "That's very kind of you, son. I appreciate that."

Jay extended his hand for a polite handshake, but Mama Atkins surprised him with a big hug, just as she had given Laila and Portia. Then she looked in his eyes and said, "Thank you for coming, son. Be blessed, darling. And be careful out there. *Please*."

Jay was so moved by her reception he could only nod. There was something about her that reminded him of his own mother. Her embrace was warm and welcoming. She made him feel as if he was in a judgment-free zone. Jay's heart went out to her so much he made a mental note to do something nice for her. Something much nicer than the plant he and Portia had sent her.

Mama Atkins was wise. She didn't blame anyone for her son's death. It was Khalil's own recklessness that had got him put in that grave. It pained her to say so, but he'd brought it on himself. Though she admittedly struggled throughout her ordeal, she was a religious woman who was a firm believer in God's will. If God had intended for her son to continue living, then Khalil would still be alive.

Mama Atkins had no hard feelings against Jay, Laila, or her new husband for what had happened. She wished them all a happy life. She was glad that Cas hadn't succumbed to that bullet hole Khalil had put in him. She prayed for his survival just as she would've prayed for her own son's. Cas was a good man that she knew looked after her grandchild. He was a positive force in Macy's life. Laila deserved happiness, so she and Cas had her blessings.

Mama Atkins had accepted her daughter-in-law and friends' kind words gracefully, but she was indeed hurting. She knew God would give her the strength she needed to get on. She had that type of faith. Mama Atkins was more concerned about her granddaughter's well being. During the early stages of pregnancy that type of trauma could be detrimental. The stress could take a serious toll on the baby's health.

Laila, Portia, and Jay must've all thought the same thing Mama Atkins did, because all at once, everyone looked at Macy and asked her if she was okay. Macy nodded and hugged them all one by one. Though she had lost her father, she was grateful for the guardians she did have in her life. Four of them stood right there. Macy knew she was loved without a doubt. She looked over at Jayquan, who had been by her side the whole time. He had asked her if she needed space to grieve, but she wanted him there.

After the hugs, the gang headed for the limos awaiting them. Jayquan fell in step beside Macy and placed his arm around her waist protectively. Macy sighed wearily and leaned on his shoulder. She knew Jayquan really cared about her. That was why she loved him so much.

CHAPTER TWO

That evening, Portia and Jay were in their bedroom winding down from their busy day. After they had attended Khalil's funeral earlier, they had gone to pick up their kids. Their three little ones, Jazmin, Trixie, and Jaylin, and also Casino and Laila's baby girl, Skye, had all been at Jay's mother's house. Mama Mitchell had been a saint as usual. She babysat the whole bus load with no complaints.

After the kids were tucked in bed, Portia called the hospital to check on Cas again. Satisfied that he was okay, she told Jay what the nurse she spoke with said. "Baby, Cas is doing fine. They said he's resting right now."

Pleased with the news, Jay nodded. "That's what's up. P, now you should call Lil' Jay and see what he up to."

They were on the same page. Portia had already dialed Jayquan's number when Jay made the suggestion. She smiled, "I was just calling him, boo."

Jay grinned back at her. A few seconds later, he stood there and watched her grill their son about his whereabouts. Portia was always on her mommy shit. She was a great parent. Jay loved that about her. When she asked Jayquan about Macy, Jay knew they were together. Those two were always together. It was still hard to believe they were having a kid. He and Portia were going to be grandparents, and so were Laila and Cas. Considering the fact that they were all still so young, it just seemed surreal.

Portia told Jayquan to be careful, and then she hung up. "Jay, he said he and Macy are grabbing a bite to eat, and then they're coming home."

Jay nodded. He pulled off his shirt. It had been a long day so he looked forward to relaxing. Still thinking about the "grandparents" thing, Jay laughed out loud. He was only thirty-eight years old.

As Portia made another call, she eyed Jay lustfully. She had to check on Laila next. She stared at Jay's chiseled chest approvingly and listened to the phone ring. Her husband was a good looking man. There was no question about that.

Poor Laila was beat. She had been spending the majority of her time at the hospital with Cas. She'd also been running around to assist Mama Atkins with Khalil's funeral arrangements. Laila was so worn out they had insisted that she go home and rest that night. She picked up on the fourth ring. "Hey, P. What's good, sis?"

Portia was glad her girl was okay. Laila sure sounded tired tough. Portia smiled, "Hey, boo! You good?"

"I'm good, P. Just up in here thinking too much. You know how that shit goes."

Portia sighed. "Yeah, sis, I know. Just try to get some rest."

"Yeah, I am. So I can go to the hospital in the morning. I was still gonna go tonight, but Cas told me to stay home. Last night he said I looked tired. You seen these damn circles under my eyes? These shits as big as Birken bags."

Portia laughed. "You good, boo. You're still pretty. Just plug in and recharge a bit."

"Thanks, boo." Laila sighed. "I guess I'd better, because a bitch is *beat*. How my girls doing? I gotta call Mama Mitchell and thank her for keeping the baby for me."

Portia smiled. "She knows you appreciate it, sis. Skye is asleep now. Macy and Lil' Jay went out to eat. I just called them. They'll be in soon. I just checked on Cas, too. The nurse said he was doing fine. She said he was resting. So try to relax a little, baby girl. The worse is over now. Things will be looking up in no time."

Laila smiled into the phone. That was the first time she'd smiled all day. Portia was truly a gem. She always found a way to make things seem better. Thank God for friends. "I called up there when I got in, so I got a chance to speak to my hubby wubby before he fell out. He's been sleeping a lot. You know they got him all drugged up and shit."

"I know," Portia said. "And you know Cas's ass is totally narcotic-free, so it's affecting him even more."

"Umm-hmm," Laila smiled. Cas wouldn't even take Tylenol when he had a headache. "P, I still can't believe this shit happened. I'm just so glad he's gonna be okay. God is so good! I don't know what I'd do without him, P. Real talk."

"I know, boo. But God is good all the time!"

Laila responded, "And all the time, God is good!" The girlfriends agreed to talk the following morning and then they got off the phone.

Portia smiled at her husband again. Jay looked particularly attractive at the time. She just wanted to be held in those big strong arms. In need of a reason to cuddle, Portia suggested they watch a movie. "Jay, let's enjoy this little bit of quiet time we got. You wanna watch a flick?"

Jay shrugged. "If you want to."

Portia grinned and put on her cozy hot-pink slipper booties and matching robe. They peeked in on the kids again, and then headed down to the theater on the second level of their spacious home.

"Baby, what you wanna watch?" Portia asked.

Jay had a naughty thought and raised an eyebrow. "How 'bout a little porn?"

Portia made a face at him. "Really?"

"Well, you asked. I was just being honest, Kit Kat."

"Well, I'm not in the mood for that right now. How about a romantic comedy? A few laughs would lighten up the mood. That funeral left me kind of depressed."

Jay shrugged. He wasn't really into romantic comedies like that. However, those days he was doing pretty much everything Portia asked him to. When he had come home with little Jaylin, the outside child he made on her with that crazy bitch, Ysatis, Portia had embraced the baby. She had regally insisted that they keep Jaylin and raise him with the rest of their children. Jay knew he was married to a queen. Portia was a class act. She had handled that situation with such grace it was unbelievable. As far as he was concerned, she was Wonder Woman.

Portia wanted to watch an old classic favorite of hers: "Pretty Woman" with Julia Roberts. That was a movie Jay had heard of, but had never seen. He only agreed to watch it for P. Whatever she wanted was okay by him. He had come to realize that when you had a happy wife you had a happy life. That statement was cliché but Jay could testify that it was true.

He figured he would just pretend to enjoy the movie for his wife's sake, but Jay had to admit it turned out to be not bad. The film was about a rich businessman who picked up a hooker that he winded up ultimately falling for. Jay felt a little corny associating himself with the likes, but it sort of reminded him of the way he and Portia had met.

Halfway through the movie, Jay thought about mentioning his observations to Portia. After he saw the part where the guy paid the hooker to stay with him longer because he enjoyed her company, Jay had to speak on it. "P, who does this movie remind you of?" He could see Portia smiling in the dark.

She giggled, "I don't know, boo. Who?"

Jay knew she was trying to front. "C'mon, P. Us!"

"Yeah, I guess." Portia made a face and then hesitated. "No doubt. But don't front, nigga. I didn't look as cheap as Julia Roberts looks in that blonde wig though."

"Hell no," Jay laughed. "I would've never hollered at you lookin' like that."

"Jay, if I recall, you didn't exactly holler at me. You was on your thug shit that night. I saw you lookin' at me and try'na front, so *I* pushed up on *you*. Remember?"

Oh shit, P was right. Jay laughed. "Be quiet and watch the movie."

"Okay, daddy. It's chilly in here. I'ma sit in the chair with you. You mind?"

"Nah, c'mon." Jay moved over and made room. Portia snuggled up under him and he held her closely from behind. They continued to watch the movie in silence.

Jay was quiet but his body language spoke loud and clear. His erection poked into Portia's backside. She smiled to herself and backed her ass up against him a little more. That big, soft rump had Jay so turned on, he wanted to explore more. He reached under the Ralph Lauren sleep shirt she wore and rubbed on those chocolate milk jugs. Jay was delighted to discover that Portia was bra-less. He cupped her left breast and fondled it until her nipple stiffened. Pleased that her body responded to him, Jay continued his conquest.

Portia blushed in the dark and laid there and enjoyed it. Her husband groped her like a high school freshman copping his first feel. She loved when Jay paid attention to her breasts. Portia couldn't front, she had held back on her feelings a bit. Deep inside, she couldn't help but still feel a little resentment about that baby situation. She felt betrayed and she was hurt by the way Jay had fucked up their family structure. His stupidity had forced her to have to fabricate a story to their daughters. Jayquan was too old to fool, but they told Jazz and Trixie some fairytale bullshit about the way they gained their new baby brother. Their little girls fell for it, and all of the kids accepted Jaylin as their baby brother. There were four of them now, and that was that.

Although Portia forgave Jay because she loved him from the depths of her soul, she could not forget. She lay there in the theater being caressed by her handsome and attentive spouse, and the issues she'd been harboring began to melt away. Lying there in his arms, nothing else mattered.

Jay was freshly showered and smelling good. He wasn't wearing any cologne but his spicy masculine deodorant tickled Portia's nostrils and drove her mad. She wanted him. Right that instant.

As the movie played, she stood up and unbuttoned her nightshirt. Jay was pleasantly surprised. He stared on attentively. That was exactly what he'd been thinking. He wanted Portia out of those clothes. She stripped down to her lavender lace boylegs and then Jay stood up and wrapped his arms around her. His wife was sexy and voluptuous. He pulled her close and caressed her. Portia felt good. She was as soft as cashmere and she smelled like cotton candy. Jay was ready to feast on that.

Jay had noticed a little change in Portia. She acted like everything was good all the time, but she had been holding back on him. She really surprised Jay when she initiated intimacy that evening. He knew he had violated her when he made a child on the side, so he understood that she had issues with him. Jay knew it would take time. He would be patient, because Portia was a hell of a woman. He loved his Kit Kat.

Jay was ready to taste that cocoa, but Portia surprised him again. She looked in his eyes and sensually bared her soul. "I need you to hold me and make love to me, baby."

Jay didn't respond with words; just body language. He pressed his hard-on against Portia to show her how willing he was to fulfill her needs. Jay pulled down her lavender lace panties and simultaneously squeezed her ass. A drop of pre-cum formed on the tip of his dick.

Portia was eager to feel him inside of her. She took the liberty of pulling down Jay's gray Polo pajama pants. His soldier sprang out and saluted her. Rocky was ready for combat. "Hello there," Portia murmured. She traced his length and felt the pre-cum that had escaped. Jay must've wanted it as bad as she did. Overcome with intense sexual desire, Portia sat back on the plush reclining theater seat. She was ready.

Jay stepped out of his pants and boxers. Portia sat up and massaged Rocky. She leaned in and swirled her tongue around his head a few times, and proceeded to swallow him. Jay stopped her in the act. "Nah, P. Wait." He was ready to get straight to it.

Portia read his mind. She leaned back in the spacious reclining chair and spread her legs. Jay breathed deep and tried to shake off some of his overexcitement. He wanted their lovemaking to last, so he could please his woman. He knew that would be a task, because Portia's pussy could be overpowering. He mounted her and slowly slid inside.

For a minute, Jay just laid there. Portia caressed his back and squeezed her sugar walls around him. Jay kissed his wife on her sweet-smelling neck and slid in deeper. She was so moist.

"Jay," Portia murmured. "I love you. I *love* you. Don't ever leave me. You hear me?"

The notion of him leaving Portia was absurd. It was insane of her to believe for one second that he could ever do such a thing. She was talking foolish, but the thought of her needing him so much was pretty sexy. Jay responded with a passionate kiss and stroked that pussy slowly, from side to side.

Portia caressed her husband's back and enjoyed making love to him. Their sexual connection was bananas. There were still fireworks between them, after all those years. She was still in love with Jay. She couldn't get enough of him.

CHAPTER THREE

That night Wise and Fatima lay intertwined on their king size bed. Fatima was an emotional wreck. As she lay across Wise's chest she was almost in tears. She was vulnerable and needed to be held by her husband.

Wise knew Fatima's hormones were the reason she was especially melancholy. She'd gone through the same symptoms during her first pregnancy. He smoothed her hair and assured her that everything was going to be okay. "Tima, we *good*. The worse is behind us. So why you buggin'?"

As Fatima's voiced her fears, her lips trembled. "I dunno. I'm just scared, baby. I don't wanna lose you again." Tears brimmed in her eyes and threatened to spill over.

Wise realized she was tripping over Cas's shooting again, and shook his head. That situation had shaken his wife up pretty bad. Fatima had been particularly clingy since it happened. Wise took her face in her hands and looked in her eyes. "You not, Ma. I ain't goin' no where. Relax." He kissed her on the forehead.

Fatima sighed. The bloody crime scene that had started out as Laila's lovely wedding reception had been a wakeup call. When Cas got shot, it brought back some bad memories. The incident was reminiscent of the day she thought she'd lost Wise forever. A couple of years prior, Wise had been shot in the neck in a shootout that he, Jay, and Cas had with some revenge-driven maniac in the hospital parking lot. They'd all been at the hospital because Laila had gotten into a terrible car accident that had left her temporarily paralyzed. Fatima couldn't stop thinking about it. She was so frightened she didn't want to let Wise out of her sight. She was afraid that something else horrible would happen to him. "Okay, baby. I'm good," she lied.

Wise actually enjoyed all the love Fatima had been smothering him with. It was great to be cared for so deeply. Being loved like that was indescribable. Fatima was the best thing that ever happened to Wise. The baby she carried had put a lot of things into perspective for him. Family came first.

Wise grinned every time he thought about it. He would soon have the son he had always wanted. He and Fatima had their princess, Falynn, already, so now they would have the perfect family. Cas's survival was the icing on the cake. Life was good. As far as Wise was concerned, things couldn't get any better. He was grateful. He placed his hand on his wife's bulging belly and winked up at God and sent up a little prayer of thanks. Fatima smiled and placed her hand on top of his and guided it to the baby's movement. Wise felt his son kick and grinned from ear to ear.

Just then, Wise's cell phone rang. Only a few people had his number, so he looked at his caller ID. He didn't recognize the number so he wondered who it belonged to. Wise continued rubbing Fatima's belly and answered his phone. "Hello?"

"What's good, Chulo? I miss you, baby. I haven't heard from you."

Wise recognized the voice immediately. It was Lily, the nurse that had saved his life after he was shot in the neck and declared dead. With the assistance of Lily and his mother, he had faked his own death after the shooting. He later resurfaced, but only to his family and closest friends. Wise was caught off guard by Lily's call. Without thinking, he pushed Fatima off him and stood up. "What up, L? What's good?"

Lily beamed into the phone. She was glad she had finally gotten up the nerve to call him. "You what's good, boo. I need to holla at you, face to face. As soon as possible."

Wise made a face. "Word?" He wondered what she wanted to discuss. He didn't want to talk in front of Fatima, so he cut it short. "A'ight. Well, it's a family night, so I'll holla back at you. Later." He ended the call without another word.

Lily realized Wise hung up on her and got very disappointed. She sat there and frowned at the phone for a moment. Wise had brushed her off like she was nobody. He was obviously around someone he couldn't speak freely in front of. Lily got a pang of jealousy. Her gut told her that Wise was with his wife. Wise had talked about his wife and his daughter a lot during the time they had spent together, so Lily figured he would go back to them. She just didn't like it. She had fallen for Wise.

Wise sat back down on the bed and feigned nonchalance about that phone call. Fatima didn't buy it. She had peeped the way he had jumped up and moved away so she wouldn't hear his conversation. Fatima knew her husband. That was a bitch on the phone. Pokerfaced, she composedly questioned Wise. "Who was that, baby?"

Wise knew his wife well. Fatima's calm exterior belied the reaction she would've normally given him in that scenario. He hesitated for a moment, and then he decided to be honest. "That was my nurse, Lily. She just called to say what up. She said she had to holla at me."

Fatima swallowed. Why was that damned girl still calling her husband? Uneasy, she asked, "About what, boo?"

Wise shrugged. "I dunno, Ma." He didn't want to talk about Lily, especially given the fact that he still sexed her occasionally. Lily was cool but she had been acting as if she was catching feelings. Wise quickly changed the subject. "So, Tima, what we gon' name this baby? My lil' man will be here before you know it." He reached over and rubbed Fatima's belly again.

Fatima wasn't stupid. She saw right through Wise. He'd tried to switch it up on her. She didn't feel like arguing so she let that one slide. At least for the time being. She wasn't fond of that nurse bitch but that night she just wanted to enjoy her husband's company. "Boo, you don't want him to be a junior?"

Wise made a face and shook his head. "Nah, not really. I don't wanna name him William. It's too traditional. We can do better than that."

"Okay, so lemme think about it, boo. Maybe something else that starts with a W, like Wakim? Or maybe an F name, like Fahid or something." Fatima knew Wise would beef with the latter suggestion. She timed him.

Before she could count to three, Wise protested just as she'd predicted. "Nah, come on, you already got an F name with Falynn. This one is mine."

Fatima giggled. "Yeah, but *you* named Falynn. Remember?"

Wise grinned. "Yeah, I named her after you because she was so pretty when she was born. So now you gotta do the same thing for me. That would be the noble thing to do."

Fatima's eyes lit up. "Ooh, I like that. Babe, how about we name him Noble. Let's think outside of the box. He'll be our little noble prince. Shit, let's name him Noble Prince!"

Wise scratched his chin and thought about it for a second. "I like Noble, but I don't know about the Prince part. Fuck around and have my son runnin' around here try'na cut the ass out his diapers, and shit."

Fatima didn't get it. She looked at Wise like he was crazy. Then a light bulb came on. "*Oh*! Like Prince, the singer. Word, Wise? You so damn stupid." Fatima laughed for a moment. "But I guess you right, boo. We don't want the baby to fuck around and be like *'move, mommy, I don't want no titty! I want daddy to feed me!'*"

"Hell no!" Wise didn't find that joke funny. "See, you play too fuckin' much. Why would you even say some shit like that? What is wrong with you?"

Fatima snickered. "You started it! But I know, right? What kind of mother am I? That was sick, right, boo? Lord, forgive me for my sick mind. I ain't got no sense. And, ooh, God forbid." She looked at Wise again and started cracking up.

Wise tried hard not to, but he joined his silly wife in laughter. That was one of the reasons he and Fatima had clicked. She had a sense of humor.

CHAPTER FOUR

The following morning, Macy was awakened by the sound of the song "Dear Mama" by Tupac loudly playing on her cell phone. She had programmed the chorus as the ringtone for her mom's incoming calls.

"Lady.... Don't you know we love you? Sweet lady. Dear mama. Place no one above ya, sweet lady. You are appreciated."

At the time Macy was in Jayquan's bedroom lying in his arms. She rolled over and grabbed her iPhone from the nightstand. Before she addressed her mother, Macy cleared her throat and tried to sound alert. She looked at the clock and realized it was just after eight, so she relaxed. Her mom was up early as usual. "Morning, Mommy."

"Hey, baby girl! How're you feeling?"

"I'm good. Still sleeping."

"I fell asleep last night before speaking to you. Why didn't you call me and lemme know you were okay? And how's the baby?"

"When we got in, Auntie Portia told me you were resting. I didn't wanna disturb you. And the baby's fine." Macy unconsciously rubbed her belly.

Jayquan heard Macy talking on the phone and opened his eyes. He looked at the time on the cable box and then rolled over and hugged her from behind. "Good morning," he whispered in her ear.

Macy smiled to herself as Jayquan pressed his stiff morning hard-on against her buttocks. She liked when he woke up feeling horny. His hands found her breasts, and Macy cut her conversation with Laila short. "Ma, you alright?"

"Yes, baby. I'm getting ready to head over to the hospital to see about Cas."

"Okay. Lil' Jay and I plan to stop by there to see him, but don't tell him. We want it to be a surprise."

Laila smiled. "Okay, that's what's up!" At the mention of Lil' Jay, Laila thought to ask about him. "Where is Jayquan now?"

"In his room, I guess, probably asleep," Macy lied. Her mother knew that she and Jayquan were expecting a baby, but Macy didn't want to give Laila the impression that Portia and Jay just let them sleep together like adults.

Laila was satisfied with Macy's answer. "Okay, rose petal, get some sleep. That baby is growing." Laila smiled into the phone. Her poor daughter had been through a lot over the past week.

Macy beamed at Laila's soothing words. "Okay, Ma. I'll call you in a little while. When I get up." The second she hung up the phone, Jayquan was on her. Macy laughed out loud. "Damn, wait a minute, thirsty! I gotta pee first. Be patient, wit' your lil' horny self."

Lil' Jay grinned sheepishly and watched Macy get out of the bed. She was clad in a pair of his pajama pants and a pink sports bra. He stared at her booty appreciatively as she switched into his private bathroom.

After the bathroom door closed, Jayquan stared up at the ceiling deep in thought. Macy's father had been buried the day before. She was holding up well but Jayquan knew it had affected her. He wondered if he'd been insensitive when he groped her. Sex with Macy was always great but he didn't want to treat her as if she was a piece of meat. She wasn't just some jump-off. She meant a lot to him.

After Jayquan heard the toilet flush, he got up and went in the bathroom behind Macy. They were so close he didn't bother to knock. Jayquan headed straight for the toilet, where he took a leak and farted in the process. Macy brushed her teeth at the sink and wrinkled up her nose at Jayquan in the mirror. That wasn't the first time she'd heard him pass gas. The pair had shed their innocence and became lovers that had ultimately conceived a child together, but they were still best friends. Their baby was due in October.

Jayquan walked up beside Macy and reached for his toothbrush in the medicine cabinet. Macy purposely backed up and rubbed her derriere against him to spark a reaction. Jayquan just played along and didn't say anything. The two rub-a-dubbed flirtatiously and slay their morning dragons with Colgate Total.

With a mouth full of toothpaste, Jayquan asked, "Mace, are you good? How you feelin'?" His words were full of concern.

Macy smiled at him in the mirror. "I'm sure I'll have my days, but right now I'm good. I'm just glad the funeral and everything is over."

Jayquan stared at her for a moment with the serious expression Macy adored. She loved when he made that face. She found lots of little things about Jayquan attractive: the way he walked, the way he talked, and the cute little way he stuck out his tongue when he went for a basket while playing ball. The list went on. Macy especially liked the way he had cradled her in his arms the night before. He had held her until she cried herself to sleep. Jayquan had a sensitive side that she was mad about.

Macy put down her toothbrush and rinsed her mouth. When she bent over she shyly eyed Lil' Jay's torso. He was clad in a wife beater, light blue Polo boxers, and navy Nike basketball shorts that sagged just below his waist. Jayquan gave off quite a bit of sexy. Macy stood up and raked her French-manicured nails across his washboard-like abs. Tiny sparks shot through her body. That happened almost every time she touched him. Macy smiled to herself. Jayquan was an athletic young man so he was nice and fit. Macy lifted his shirt and traced along his waistline.

Jayquan maintained a serious face in the mirror. Inwardly, he smiled from ear to ear. Macy knew that was his spot. She had him ready to beat. After Jayquan was done brushing and rinsing he grabbed Macy and spun her around to face him. They shared a minty morning kiss.

When they usually spent the night together, Macy would sneak back to her bedroom before Jayquan's parents woke up. Jay and Portia had sort of given them a pass ever since her father was killed. The juvenile lovers didn't hear any signs of movement yet, so they figured everyone else in the house was still asleep. Their little sisters, Jazz, Trixie, and Skye, got a kick out of banging on their bedroom doors every morning to "scare" them; so they would certainly know if they were up.

The young couple quit kissing and exchanged knowing looks. There were no words needed. In seconds, they were half-naked on the bed entangled in lust. Macy kept on her sports bra but Jayquan pulled it up and exposed her ripe breasts. He caressed the magnificent mounds gently and then circled them with his tongue. Macy gasped in pleasure. Her nipples had been particularly sensitive lately. Jayquan knew that because Macy regularly filled him in with details about the changes she noticed in her body since she got pregnant. Jayquan took his time on her breasts until she was literally creaming.

Though Macy was his first, Jayquan had been taking notes. He'd learned to pleasure her skillfully. That was unusual for a boy his age but he had a few mentors in that department. His uncles, Cas and Wise, had schooled him on some things. His father had also.

A moment later, Jayquan was deep inside of Macy's wetness. She clawed his back and breathed hard. Soft moans escaped her throat ever so often. She and Jayquan's bodies moved together as they enjoyed each other as quietly as possible. Neither wanted to get caught.

When the two young lovers were done, they lay there in one another's arms. About ten minutes later, they showered together, and then got dressed. Afterwards, Macy said she was hungry. She suggested they cook some breakfast. Jayquan agreed and they headed downstairs.

Macy assigned him to making the pancakes, which he was pretty good at. She made the rest of the food herself and made Jayquan promise to wash the dishes. He only agreed because he simply had to load the dishwasher. When the food was done, they feasted on pancakes, scrambled eggs with cheddar cheese, and turkey bacon until their bellies were full.

When they were done eating, Lil' Jay went upstairs to sound the chow alarm. When he got up there, Jay was in the shower and Portia was in their bedroom changing baby Jaylin. Jaylin was a handsome little fellow. He was growing and had a good appetite. "Good morning, pretty lady," Jayquan greeted Portia.

Portia smiled when he walked in the room. Jaylin laughed and started making noise. Jayquan went over and kissed Portia on the cheek and then he played with the baby a bit. "Me and Macy made breakfast," he informed Portia. "Pancakes and stuff. There's enough for everybody."

Portia grinned from ear to ear. She loved when her son stepped up and acted responsible. Jayquan was the oldest child she and Jay had. It was important that he knew how to look after the little ones, God forbid something should happen. He would soon be a father himself, so it was also good practice. Portia proudly commended Lil' Jay on his efforts. "Thank you, darling! A man needs to know how to cook so he will never have to depend on anybody - especially a woman - to take care of him. Ever!"

Jayquan laughed and rolled his eyes. Portia had given him that "independent-responsible man" talk a thousand times. "I know, Lady P. You taught me well. I know."

They smiled at one another. Lady P was what Humble, God bless the dead, used to call Portia. She and Jayquan reflected on Humble's memory for moment. "God bless his soul," Portia said.

Lil' Jay looked up toward heaven. "Humble, rest in peace, my nigga! Never forget you, bro!" He smiled fondly and walked off to go get the Terrible Three for breakfast.

To Jayquan's surprise, the brats were in a pretty sweet mood. Jazz, Trixie, and Skye all got up and showered him with kisses. None of them had brushed their teeth yet, so he grinned and pretended to wipe their kisses off. "All of y'all got dragon breath!" Jayquan ordered them into the bathroom and armed them with toothbrushes and toothpaste. After the girls were done brushing and washing their faces, they put on their robes and followed him downstairs.

About ten minutes later, Portia went downstairs for breakfast with the baby on her hip. She watched as Jayquan and Macy supervised the Terrible Three while they ate at the dining table like little ladies. Macy cut up the little ones' pancakes for them and Jayquan put apple juice in their training cups. Portia thought that was so cute.

Portia put Jaylin in his highchair and had a seat at the table with the kids. A minute later, she was served breakfast with smile. "Why, thank you very much. A girl could really get used to this." She grinned at Macy and Jayquan and then bowed her head in grace.

A few minutes later, Jay came down. He greeted his family with love. All of the ladies, including his nieces Macy and Skye, got a kiss on the forehead. The girls all blushed at the affection. When Jay kissed little Jaylin, he made these happy noises. Jayquan was excluded from the kisses. Jay gave him a pound instead.

Macy and Jayquan seated Jay and gave him the same service they gave Portia. He grinned and thanked them, and then he blessed his food and dove in.

While they were done eating, Portia told the kids that she and Jay were going to the hospital to see Cas. Macy offered to babysit the brats while they were gone. Portia smiled and took her up on the offer. They were a close family. They always stuck together and held each other down.

CHAPTER FIVE

Across town at the hospital, Laila sat at Casino's bedside and stared at him as he slept. Cas was grand, even in slumber. Laila loved him so much it overwhelmed her sometimes. She thanked God for the zillionth time that her husband was alive and well.

Cas must've felt her presence because he opened his eyes. Laila knew that was no coincidence. Their connection was that strong. She smiled at her husband brightly.

When Cas saw Laila standing there smiling he gave her a little grin back. Her attendance was always welcomed. Seeing her was a reminder that he was still there. Cas hadn't told anyone about the out-of-body experience he had after he got shot yet. He'd kept it between him and God so far, but that was something he would never forget. He had been approached by the devil himself, but he had called on God and beat him. That was the biggest wake-up call he'd ever had. Cas couldn't put it into words, but he had promised God he would change for the better. A little bit of change never hurt anybody.

Cas was glad he had got another chance. Now he was concerned about his lovely wife. Laila had been there for him when her well being was at stake as well. "What up, sunshine? You a'ight?"

Laila beamed at him. Even as Cas lay in the hospital recovering from a collapsed lung, he was checking up on her. The respirator he was hooked up to didn't damper his spirit one bit. "Good morning, handsome," Laila said gleefully. "I'm *good*, baby. How are *you*? It's good to see a smile on your face." Laila leaned down and kissed him on the lips.

Cas needed a haircut and a shave but Laila made him feel good. He unconsciously stroked his chin. Then he stared at the I.V. stuck in the back of his hand. It reminded him that he couldn't get up and walk out of there. His barber visit would have to wait. His strength wasn't at its' peak yet, so he figured he'd better take it easy.

Laila sat in the chair by Cas's bedside. She asked him when the last time was he had seen his doctor.

"Not today yet," Cas said.

Laila was glad to learn she hadn't missed the doctor yet. Cas was still hooked up to a bunch of machines and wires, so she had some questions.

Cas hummed along with an old-school song that was playing on the small radio Laila had placed by his bedside. *"Just to be close to you, girl. Just for a moment..."*

Laila had figured the music would be therapeutic. It seemed to be working. She smiled and hummed the lyrics of the old school song along with her hubby. Then she gave him the rundown on the funeral the day before. Cas listened attentively and then asked her how Macy was doing.

A few minutes later, Casino's mom strolled in. Ms. B was dressed up as usual. When she saw her son awake and sitting up, she broke into a smile that lit up the room. "Caseem! Hey, baby! Thank you, Lord Jesus! Look at my boy!"

Cas grinned like a big kid as his mama rushed to his side and showered him with kisses. "Hey, Lady," he laughed. "How you doin'?"

"I'm doing fine, son. Even better now!" Though Ms. B was jovial with Cas as usual, when she greeted Laila her enthusiasm level dropped substantially. "Hey, Laila," she said. It came out flat and dry.

At first, Laila had this big grin on her face because she was happy to see her mother in-law. Ms. B's arctic greeting made her feel like an idiot. That cold reaction to her presence indicated that there was a problem. *Oh boy,* Laila thought. *Here we go.*

Ms. B wasn't the phony baloney type. She always shot straight from the heart. She did have a problem. Laila was on her shit list. Ms. B had seen the way she had cried and prayed over Cas after the shooting, so she didn't doubt that Laila loved her son. Ms. B just had some issues with the fact that it was Laila's ex-husband who had shot Cas. She was too classy to make a scene at the hospital, but she and Miss Laila would definitely talk.

Laila felt extremely uncomfortable. The situation was pretty awkward. She excused herself and took a walk so Ms. B could visit with her son without any interference.

$$$$$

Jay and Portia showed up at the hospital about two hours later. When they arrived, Ms. B was just leaving. Cas had insisted that she go home and relax. She had been at the hospital a lot since he got shot too. It was Sunday, so she should've been at home catching up on her rest.

Jay greeted Ms. B with a hug and then looked at his right-hand man with concern. "Yo, what up, Cas? You a'ight man?"

Cas chuckled at him. "Yeah, son, I'm good. Stop lookin' at me like you all scared and shit. You're worrying too much. Jay, relax, man."

Portia laughed and kissed Cas on the cheek. "Hey! You get some rest, bro?" she inquired.

Cas's chest hurt when he laughed too hard, so he just grinned at her. "Not really. That nigga Wise called me about seven hundred times last night, talkin' about he just checking on me. It seemed like every time I dozed off, my phone rang again."

Jay laughed. "Damn, I ain't call because I wanted you to get some rest. But I might as well have joined in on the party line." He reached over and rubbed Cas's head affectionately. "It's good to see you, man. You look good, son."

Cas beamed and gave his best buddy some dap. "Put the word out, man. Your boy been down, but he ain't out."

Jay co-signed and seconded the motion. "I couldn't have said it better, son."

CHAPTER SIX

Kira woke up early Sunday afternoon in the huge, luxurious home she had inherited in her divorce settlement. Though she had everything she wanted, she was all alone. Kira yawned and stretched, and then she looked around her lavishly furnished bedroom and thanked God she'd had the opportunity to catch up on her rest. She had slept nine hours straight and felt rejuvenated. Eager to get her day started, she sprang out of bed. Kira wore nothing but the pajamas she was born in. She usually slept in her birthday suit.

On her way to the bathroom, Kira stopped to turn the heat up a few degrees. There was a chill in the air that made her headlights come on. She rubbed her hard nipples and decided to play the record she had listened to over and over the night before until she fell asleep. She pressed play on her iPod and then listened to herself. She rapped through the speakers over a hot ass track that Five and Vino had produced. The three of them had recorded that the other day. The music filled the bedroom and made Kira dance. She shook her hips to the beat and admired her naked body in the full mirror on her bedroom wall.

Kira had been working with a personal trainer and the results were visible. The Pilates had paid off. She was absolutely stunning. She had her basketball body from high school again. She was just a hell of a lot sexier and more confident this time.

"Who wakes up *this* cute?" Kira asked herself. She laughed and then thought about her son, who was even cuter. Jahseim was at her mother's house that weekend. Kira winked at her reflection and blew herself a kiss. She struck a chic pose like there were cameras on her and then she giggled and headed to the bathroom. She loved being silly.

Kira wondered what her baby was doing. Jahseim was getting older now, so Kira was trying to raise him right. Her mom was a huge help and thank God, his father was always on his job. Jahseim was away because he had gotten annoyed by the cameras that were always around lately. During the past two weeks, Kira had been filming a pilot for her new reality show. With the invasion of the film crew and equipment, their household had basically been turned upside down. All of their privacy had gone out the window. At first, Kira had believed it would be amazing to be the center of attention on her very own show. Now it was getting on her nerves as well.

In fact, just two days ago Kira had sent the camera crew and producers packing. She got pissed off because they had tried to exploit the fact that her wealthy, music executive ex-husband, Casino, had been shot in the chest. They wanted footage of Kira crying, comforting her upset son, and even going to the hospital to visit Cas. Though Kira could be a mess when she wanted to be, she did have some integrity. She flat out refused to do it. Those bastards didn't respect that though. They pushed and pushed until she snapped and told them to go to hell.

Those mothafuckas' inconsideration had made Kira feel violated. They had actually tried to film her crying about Cas. At the time, she had just received the news about him being shot. She thought it was real bad. All she could think about was the fact that her son could be fatherless.

Those bastards only cared about ratings. True, Kira had signed up for all of that. She wanted to have a top-rated show but there were limitations in life. There were certain boundaries you just didn't cross.

After Kira spazzed on the producers, they had the nerve to throw a contract clause in her face. That only made her flip worse. They tried to film that as well. Kira shoved the camera out of her face and bombed on the cameraman. "My ex-husband's money is paying your salary, asshole! You gon' fuck around and not have a job tomorrow! Keep pushing me, mothafucka!"

The production manager, Sean, shot the pushy camera guy a warning look because there was truth to that statement indeed. Cas and Jay were behind-the-scenes executive producers of the show. They had backed off filming for a few days, but Sean had been calling Kira every day. She had deliberately sent his phone calls to voicemail. He left several messages saying he was sorry and anxious to get back to work.

Kira wasn't that pissed at them. Her priorities had just shifted. She had taken a few days off to be there for her child so she could help him get through his father's shooting. Jah was nine years old now. He had lots of sense and he demanded straight answers.

Jahseim had a few nightmares about the situation. He was at the wedding reception when his father was shot. The boy was traumatized. Now her baby was afraid of being left alone. When his father was wounded, he clung to Kira for emotional support. Jahseim had been in her ass like a wedgie. She didn't mind either. She loved being a mother. Kira was still trying to make up for the time she had missed in his life when she was locked up. She made sure her son knew he came before work and everything else. Jahseim was her reason for living.

Kira brushed her teeth and then showered. When she hopped out of the shower, she air dried and called the love of her life. She knew her mom had taken Jahseim to church that morning. Her son wanted to go to the hospital to visit his father, but he had to settle for speaking to Cas on the phone because there were no small children allowed in the hospital unit he was in. Although Kira was sure Cas would be thrilled to see his son, it was out of her hands.

Kira smiled to herself. Cas was a great father. A lot had happened between the two of them, but Cas was by far the best baby daddy she could ask for. They had smoothed over their once irreconcilable differences and she had finally accepted their breakup and moved on. Not that Kira had any other choice. That year-long bid she did in prison for torching Laila's crib was pretty sobering. Kira had used the time to grow up. Now she had a new perspective on life.

After she called and spoke with her mother and her son, Kira walked around her huge house and realized just how lonely she was. Though she was tough, deep down inside she wanted someone to wake up with sometimes.

Kira stepped into her gigantic walk-in closet and searched for a figure flattering outfit that would turn heads. She was going to see Vino that day and she wanted to entice his sexy ass. Kira looked over about two hundred pairs of ridiculously fabulous shoes, and finally decided on a pair of spiked Red-Bottoms. You could never go wrong with Louboutins. Kira paired the fierce shoes with a simple outfit: some black Cavalli skinny jeans and a low-cut purple V-neck sweater. She accessorized with a wide Gucci belt, huge earrings, and a dangling necklace and matching bangles. Kira picked out a purse and a stylish patent leather motorcycle jacket she had just copped. It was the end of February and still cold out, so she picked out some chic leather gloves as well.

When Kira looked in her mirror to fix her hair she noticed that her vanity mirror was dirty. She frowned in distaste. She hated smudged glass. Kira didn't have a live-in housekeeper, but she had a cleaning company come in part-time. She made a mental note to call them so they could come out and clean up the following day. She cooked sometimes but she didn't really like cleaning. Her house was just too big.

When Kira was dolled up to her satisfaction she headed downstairs. She made another mental note to get herself an assistant. She was currently looking for a new manager, so she would add that to her to-do list as well. Down in the kitchen, she fixed herself a bite to eat. As Kira waited on her whole wheat toast to brown, she dialed Vino on her cell phone.

Vino picked up on the fourth ring and sounded agitated. "Yo, what's good, Kira? I'm here waitin' on you. I thought you said twelve noon."

Kira thought he had the cutest Californian accent. She had the dumb face. "Umm, I did, boo. My bad, I overslept. I'll see you in about twenty minutes. I'm leaving as soon as I'm done eating this toast."

"If you ain't here in the next thirty minutes, I'm outta here. Later, man." *Click*

Kira smiled into the phone. She liked Vino. The fact that he hadn't hesitated to check her made her like him even more. Kira loved to get a reaction out of a dude she was into. She didn't like guys she could just walk over. Vino got points for standing up to her.

Over the past few weeks Kira had been shamelessly flirting with Vino. She knew he got the signals she threw at him and he had to be attracted to her. Who wouldn't be? He just wouldn't follow her lead for some reason. Something about that had to change. Kira wasn't trying to hear that.

Twenty-six minutes later, she walked into the studio where Vino was. He was swagged out as usual in a crisp white tee and blue denim Levis that fit him just right. The matching Levi jacket hung on the back of his chair. Vino had a navy blue bandana tied around his wrist. Kira knew that identified his lifelong Crip affiliation. She didn't have a problem with that; she loved street dudes. Kira eyed the tattooed sleeves on Vino's muscular forearms and stopped herself from drooling. She stuck out her hip and gave him the hottest, most flirtatious greeting she had. "Hey, boobie! What up?"

Vino was upset about Kira's lateness so he feigned disinterest and looked straight through her. She looked good but that sexy shit didn't faze him. He was no sucker. He glimpsed at his watch and spoke to her in an unexcited monotone. "What up, Kira? You had four minutes left. You better be on time from now on. On some real shit. Now let's get to work."

Kira smiled demurely and apologized. "My bad, baby. Sorry about that. I won't be late again." She reached out and touched him on the arm. Vino quickly moved out of her grasp. That brush-off was unwelcomed but it only made Kira want him more. She was determined to bag him. She made it one of her short-term goals.

Vino hadn't meant to be rude. Kira just came on a little too strong for him. He ignored the eye contact she gave him and sat down at the mixing board. He wanted her to listen to a new track he'd worked on over the past weekend.

He played the music without a word and watched her reaction from the corner of his eye. Kira bobbed her head to the beat and smiled. She broke into a little two-step and swayed her hips. She appeared to be feeling it, just as he had hoped. At that point, Vino pretty much knew what her vibe was. There was no denying that their rapport was harmonious.

Vino and his partner, Five, were an up and coming music-production team from Los Angeles that Jay and Cas had commissioned to work with Kira. They were a hot and happening duo whose signature bass lines made the clubs jump from coast to coast. The fellows had signed on for Kira's project and were so dedicated they had switched coasts during the coldest months of New York winter to accommodate her, just so she could stay close to her son. The bosses, Jay and Cas, had made the offer sweet enough to counteract the inconvenience. Kira promised Vino and Five they wouldn't regret it. She assured them that they would all make what she predicted to be a part of hip-hop history.

Professionally, Vino respected Kira. She was a dope emcee. She had what it took, and had proved it. She had earned hers, so he and his partner were honored to work with her. The dynamic duo had been creating tracks for Kira's album non-stop, until Cas took a slug to the chest. When that happened, they had respectfully taken a few days off until the big homie was better. They had agreed to resume recording on Monday, so Five had flown home that weekend. He had a three-month old baby back in Cali, so he went home whenever he could. The only reason Vino was at the studio that Sunday was because Kira had called him the night before and said she was ready to get back to work.

Then she had the nerve to be late. Vino was a prompt person, so he wasn't going for that.

The other issue was that Kira kept on flirting with him. Though Vino found her to be very sexy, he had scruples. He knew she used to be with Cas, so he didn't want to violate like that. It was fucked up enough that he had slept with Jay's wife, Portia, that time she and Fatima came to California. He wasn't trying to bang everybody's broad. He wasn't that dude. Furthermore, shit like that could get a nigga diced up. He didn't need the drama. He was good.

Truthfully, what had happened between Vino and Portia was a little different. That shit just happened. He and Portia had swept it under a rug, but she was married to Jay, so Vino definitely regretted it. Jay was a real good dude. He and Cas both were. Vino liked how those guys moved.

Therefore, it was strictly business with Kira. She was pressing him and throwing signals like she wanted to fuck with him, but that could get ugly. Vino knew that Cas had remarried, but who was to say he wanted another man touching something that was his. That was a chance Vino wasn't willing to take. Business was good at the time. He couldn't deny that Kira was sexy. He could definitely envision those long shapely legs wrapped around him, but he preferred bread over bitches. He was married to the money.

CHAPTER SEVEN

"Unnngghhhh! Damn, you got some good dick! Don't fuckin' stop!" Melanie cried out in sheer bliss. She and her lover's relationship was fairly new, but that afternoon they were in the middle of some old-school sex. Eighty lay on top of her missionary-style pounding away at her insides.

The hardcore fucking occurred in the bedroom of Melanie's cozy condo, which had been financed by the hush money Wise had paid her for the "rape" she'd threatened to destroy his rap career with a few years prior. Melanie loved her crib and referred to it as her dollhouse. It was laced with elaborate red leather Italian furniture and state of the art fixtures and appliances. Mel and Eighty had sex christened every nook and cranny of her place.

The couple went at it hard, hot, and heavy. Eighty's tongue hung out of the side of his mouth, his toes were curled and his ass cheeks were clenched. He was dead focused on trying hard not to cum. Melanie had some good ass box. He really enjoyed that pussy. Eighty went deeper and she hollered and squirmed away from him. "Shut up and quit runnin', girl! Take this dick!" he commanded.

"Okay, baby! Gimme that shit, nigga," Mel cried. Eleven strokes later, they both exploded. Eighty grunted and Melanie screamed at the top of her lungs. Afterward, he lay inside of her panting. Melanie nibbled his ear and sucked on his neck. The giant orgasmic wave they had just surfed had Eighty super sensitive at the time so he stopped Mel from kissing on him and withdrew from her wetness.

When Eighty rolled over Mel stared down at his dick appreciatively. She was overcome with the animalistic urge to suck him off. She grabbed a tissue from the nightstand and pulled the cum-soaked condom off. She balled up the tissue and tossed it into a small red wastebasket next to her queen-size bed. Melanie was a man-eater that didn't play any games. She took Eighty's semen glazed shaft in her hand and smiled at him naughtily.

Eighty was spent. He started to stop Mel because he didn't believe he had another round in him at the time. Then she bent down and twirled her tongue around the head. Eighty was surprised when his joint stiffened. The next thing he knew, Mel held a big sturdy piece of hardwood. She smiled up at him sexily and continued servicing him.

Mel wanted to see how many licks it took the second time around but girlfriend got impatient and swallowed him. She almost choked on his immenseness but she got it together. If there was one thing Melanie could do, it was suck a mean dick. She made lust-hooded eye contact with Eighty and rocked his world.

Eighty lay there with his eyes rolled back in his head. Mel had spoiled him with sexual favors lately. She'd just about sucked him bone dry. She wanted it all the time, night and day. Melanie's sexual appetite was insatiable. Eighty would be damned if he'd let a chick outdo him, no matter how freaky the bitch was. So he gave it to her little ass every chance he got.

Eighty couldn't front; Mel had put it on him so good he had caught a few feelings. He knew she was fast because his mans had pulled his coat about her promiscuity. She had also been honest and told him what she was into. Eighty knew Mel was a little porn starlet but he wasn't intimidated by her occupation. He actually liked how forward and open she was about sex.

He also liked how Mel moved. He knew about the take she did on Wise with those bogus ass rape charges she threatened him with. Wise was his man, but Mel had caught that nigga slipping and came up. Eighty preferred the strong-arm method as opposed to Melanie's more subtle approach, but he could tell that he and she were cut from the same cloth. The way he saw it, they were both opportunists. Melanie had taken Wise for a ride, and Eighty had taken money for a living most of his life. He couldn't knock the hustle.

Eighty was a thorough dude that could tame any bitch he chose to. He wasn't sure if he'd wife Mel or anything, but it was safe to say he had a thing for shorty. He grabbed the back of her head and guided her up and down on his meat. Eighty talked dirty to Melanie and took his time and fucked her pretty face until he exploded and shot hot cum all over her.

Melanie loved to have a good time and she could be very silly when she wanted to. She pretended she was on camera and struck a sexy pose and smiled for the money shot. Then she stood up and took a bow.

Eighty grinned lazily. Melanie was nasty as hell. He was a nasty nigga himself so he liked that about her. He actually liked quite a few things about her. Eighty was no idiot. He wasn't some dumb mothafucka who got open over some hoe. He was a business man with aspirations to get rich or die trying, so when Mel told him about her goals to start up a porn production company he listened with open ears. Melanie had experience in the business and Eighty saw her vision. The sex business was a billion dollar industry. Pussy would sell when cotton and corn wouldn't. He wanted in.

Mel giggled and headed for the bathroom to clean up her messy face. She turned on the shower and yelled out for Eighty to join her. She didn't get any response so she peaked in the bedroom to see what he was up to. Mel discovered that her lover was fast asleep. "Awww... Look at my poor baby," she cooed. She had clearly drained him. Mel laughed and commenced to shower alone. Eighty may as well have stuck his thumb in his mouth. He was sleeping like a baby.

As Melanie scrubbed her taut skin with a Dove body wash soaked loofah sponge, she mulled over the connection she and Eighty had. She had started to catch feelings for him as well. He had the three things she desired the most in a man. Eighty had good dick, he was rich, and he knew how to handle her. Mel felt like he could really be the one.

She and Eighty had met at a birthday party that Portia and Jay had for their little girl, Jazz. Melanie's first encounter with Eighty had been a little awkward because he was sort of mean to her. Mel didn't shy away because she loved no-nonsense dudes. She smiled in the shower like a fool in love and thought about their first meeting.

Melanie had batted her eyes flirtatiously but Eighty didn't even blink once. Mel laughed out loud at the memory. She was caught off guard at first, but Portia had warned her that Eighty was hard. Mel had stood her ground. When Eighty realized she wouldn't give up, he stopped being so hard on her. Mel broke him down and got his phone number. She'd called him two days later and they took it from there.

Now they were an item of sorts. Although Eighty was aggressive and a thug by all means, he kept Melanie in her place. That was the part of him that she found irresistible.

CHAPTER EIGHT

Laila smiled at her husband appreciatively. "Awww... Baby, I appreciate that." She got up and leaned over and pecked Cas on the lips. "But us missing it was no big deal. As long as I got you here with me safe and sound, I'm good. That's the best wedding present I could get."

Cas shook his head. "Nah, we still goin'. We gon' roll out as soon as I get better, Ma," he assured Laila. He was referring to the honeymoon they'd been forced to postpone. They had originally planned to go to Rio.

"Okay, if you say so," Laila laughed. "I'll go with you anywhere, baby. But just so you know, the only thing you could have done to disappoint me is not be here."

Laila always knew the right thing to say. Cas was touched by her sentiments. He was a lucky man. He had married a woman that was also his friend. He enjoyed talking to Laila. He realized the importance of having a spouse you could communicate with. The two of them had been through a lot during the time they had been together.

Cas and Laila sat in Cas's private hospital room engaged in a heart to heart. They had been discussing all of the things Cas wanted to do when he got better. They were newlyweds, so Cas figured that their honeymoon should be on that list. Laila deserved the star treatment. Especially after he saw the way she had stood by his side while he was down. Cas had done the same thing for her back when she'd been involved in that terrible car accident that had left her comatose and paralyzed. He had learned that Laila was pregnant at the time and had made the bold decision that she would keep the baby despite the odds against her. As a result, they had their lovely daughter, Skye. That was Cas's little princess. Cas would be there for Laila again and again if he had to. The fact that she was there for him as well made him love her even more.

Cas thought about the kids a lot since he'd been in the hospital. They were all at the wedding reception when he got popped. His children were there, Jay's kids, and Wise's little girl, too. The children should've never had to witness something so brutal. That could destroy their innocence. They'd seen Cas get shot and then also seen Khalil get beaten to death. There was no way that should've happened. Cas felt horrible about it. He prayed they were all okay. He was a father before anything. He couldn't wait to get home to his kids. That was the main reason he wanted to get out of the hospital. He had to regain their trust in his ability to protect them.

Cas thanked God that every day he felt better. His physical strength wasn't at a hundred percent yet but he was getting there. Cas's libido, on the other hand, was better than ever. His sexually appetite was voracious. He had requested that Laila show up some days wearing easy access clothing like skirts and dresses with no panties on. She had been a sport and catered to his wishes.

Laila looked forward to her and Cas's little sexcapades as much as he did. She had purposely worn a dress that day. She sat in a chair at Cas's bedside and waited for the signal. As if on cue, Cas threw her a look that said he was ready. Laila knew him like a book.

Laila was right. Cas was thinking naughty. "Lock the door, Ma. Then let me get a lil' peek at that thang."

Laila smiled and followed his directions. She locked the door and then sat back down and spread her legs. Cas's face lit up like a kid in a candy store. He looked at her for a second and then couldn't help himself. He placed his hand between Laila's legs and played with her pussy until her eyes rolled back in pleasure. "Ooh baby... Yes, right there," she encouraged.

Cas had a hard-on you wouldn't believe. Laila was soaking wet. He fingered her juice box and rubbed his thumb across her clit. Damn, his dick was throbbing. He licked his lips and fantasized about sliding up in it.

Though Cas was in the Intensive Care Unit, his room was private. With the door locked and lights dimmed, the newlyweds were oblivious to the busy hospital surroundings. Laila sat there posed like a Hollywood diva in a pair of fabulous high-heeled YSL boots. Being touched by her new hubby felt so great she wished she could feel Cas's manhood inside of her. She wanted to make passionate love to him.

When they had first begun their shenanigans, Laila was reluctant because she was afraid the arousal might hurt Cas in his condition. One of his lungs was punctured and he'd been hooked up to all those machines, so she didn't want him doing anything that would trigger heavy breathing. He wore a breathing tube, for God's sake. However, Cas was laid up in that hospital bed with no other choice, so when he desired a strip tease, asked for a hand job, or a blow job, she willingly fulfilled his wishes. The first time Cas ejaculated, Laila was scared he would bust his stitches open or something. Thank God, everything had gone fine. Laila enjoyed pleasing Cas in his predicament and now she truly believed the TLC was good for him. So it had become their ritual. Laila came to the hospital prepared.

Cas had been enjoying the hookups Laila had been giving him. He had even gone down on her a couple of times to repay her. He genuinely got pleasure from pleasing his wife. He watched as she moaned and bucked her hips as if she wanted his fingers deeper inside of her. Her body said she needed more. Cas needed a little more that day, too. Pussy was the sweetest joy there was. He was ready to take it there. That peach looked so ripe and tasty he thought about having Laila sit on his face. Cas decided they would save that for when he got home. Right now he just wanted to beat. "Damn ... I want me some of this," he thought aloud. He believed he was finally up to it.

Laila eyed him seductively. "That's exactly what I was just thinking. I miss feeling you inside of me. Baby, I would love to give it to you."

Cas fought back a smile. That was the right answer. "Yo, I'm 'bout to wear yo' ass out."

Laila's face lit up. Then she had second thoughts and looked worried. "Baby, you sure?"

Cas nodded. "Hell yeah."

"But I'm scared to get on top of you."

Cas said, "Nah, I'ma get on top." He sat up and removed the nasal cannula that delivered oxygen through his nose and then he swung his legs around the side of the bed. Laila stopped him before he got up and made sure his I.V. was in tact.

When Cas stood up, Laila grinned. A big erection poked out in front of his hospital gown. She looked down at it and licked her lips, and then she unzipped her dress. Her coral-colored lace bra peeked out and teased him. Laila unconsciously looked over at the door.

The room door was locked but Cas still sensed her reluctance. He refused to make his wife uncomfortable, no matter how horny he was. He respected the ground Laila walked on. Cas nodded at the bathroom.

Laila looked pleased with his suggestion. "Okay, boo, let's go in there."

Cas started toward the bathroom and she followed him. Along the way, he held the hospital gown he wore closed in the back. Laila teasingly reached over and pinched him on the bottom. Cas made a face at her like he didn't approve of that. Laila laughed and pushed his I.V. to the bathroom.

When they got inside, they shut the door and embraced for a moment. Laila stood on her tiptoes and planted a soft kiss on Cas's lips. He ran his hands along her curves and caressed her. Laila smiled to herself. It had been a long time since she'd been in her man's arms. Cas had stitches across his chest so she was careful not to press against them.

Laila stepped out of her dress and eyed him naughtily. Cas motioned for her to spin around so he could get a good look at her. When she twirled around he gazed at her lustfully and shook his head. "I'm hard as a mothafucka."

Laila smiled, "I see. Hmmm… Lemme see if I can help you with that." She lifted Cas's hospital gown up and pulled down his boxers in the front. His stiff dick sprung out and saluted her. Laila gasped in delight and greeted him with a handshake and a wet tongue kiss. Then she swallowed as much of him as she could.

Cas happily enjoyed the bird's eye view of Laila deep-throating him. He was well endowed so she had a mouth full. She gagged and coughed a little bit, and then she cleared her throat and got right back down to business. He noted Laila's perseverance and laughed to himself.

Cas enjoyed the head but he was ready for the bonus. He pulled Laila to her feet and bent her over the sink. She was considerably shorter than him but her high heels boosted her up a few inches and put her ass directly in front of him. Cas gripped her ass and slid in it from behind. He breathed deep and slowly exhaled. That stuff was right and tight. He groaned and pushed deeper inside until he'd filled her to capacity. Cas palmed her titties and stroked that pussy. Laila threw it back on him as if she was hot and ready. They went at it passionately like the newlyweds they were.

Laila bucked and writhed and called out her husband's name. "Cas! Baby, it feels so good!"

Cas sensed the urgency in Laila's lovemaking. She reacted as if it was crucial. He knew she really needed it. Cas held her hips and gave her that dick. They caught eyes in the mirror and Laila looked at him through lust-hooded eyes like she appreciated it. She squeezed her pussy muscles and threw it back. Cas groaned in pleasure, overwhelmed. "Be still, Ma. You gon' make me cum." He grinded his teeth and fought to regain control.

"Okay, baby," Laila said breathily. She relaxed and gave Cas the reins. He pounded her with passion and hit the right spot again and again. Laila enjoyed it so much she was on the verge of tears. It was delightful and gratifying. Each stroke pushed her further toward her peak. Her eyes rolled around in her head as Cas fucked her silly. Laila's body began to jerk involuntary. As she shook uncontrollably, her eyelids fluttered and her lips trembled. Cas had positioned her in a way that she felt every inch of him. It felt so good she almost blacked out.

Cas felt Laila cumming. Her legs were shaking and that pussy was literally quivering. That did things to him he couldn't explain. Cas clenched his teeth and drove it to the finished line. He grabbed Laila's hips and buried his last strokes deep inside of her until they exploded together.

After they were done, Cas and Laila took a moment to catch their breath. They stood there in silence and heard a knock at the room door. The couple quickly scrambled out of the bathroom like two teenagers caught making out under the bleachers.

Cas thought about it and stopped short. He laughed and slapped Laila on the butt. "Ma, you know how much I'm paying for this room? I'll screw in this mothafucka if I want to."

Laila laughed and agreed. If they wanted to get their rocks off that was their damn business. They were husband and wife. Cas sat on the bed and she hooked his nasal cannula back up. After he was straight, she scurried to get her clothes back on. A moment later, Laila opened the door as innocently as if she and Cas had been having bible study. She greeted the nurse standing there with a smile. "Hello there."

The nurse that Laila granted access to was named Luann. She was an attractive, fit, thirty-something Asian sister dressed in aqua-colored scrubs. Luann wore Fendi glasses and her blonde-streaked hair was pulled back into a ponytail. "Hello, I'm fine, thank you. How are you?"

"I'm good, thanks. Come in."

The nurse smiled and walked in and greeted Cas. "Good day, Mr. Brighton. You look very happy today. How are we doing?"

Cas smiled and thought about the quickie he and Laila just had. He was happy indeed. "I'm feeling a lot better. I'm ready to get up outta here."

The nurse chuckled and commenced to check Cas's vital signs. "Dr. Sanji will be joining us in a minute. Perhaps he has some good news for you."

Just then, the doctor walked in. Dr. Sanji was a tall, slightly graying, Indian gentleman with a thick accent. He was wearing a white coat over a light blue shirt and navy tie. He looked at Cas closely and said, "Good afternoon, Mr. Brighton. How are you feeling today?"

Cas responded with the revere he'd been shown. "Doc, I'm well, thanks. How are you doing?"

"Oh, I'm feeling pretty okay. Thanks for asking." The doctor smiled politely and then looked over something on a chart he was holding. "Mr. Brighton, you are a very lucky young man. The tests we ran this morning came back squeaky clean. There is no infection anywhere. The damaged lung is getting strong. You're in very good shape, young man. You're healing fast. So I am going to do you a favor. I'm going to send you home soon. I want to run one more test in the morning and I'm also ordering another MRI. If all goes well, you will likely be released tomorrow sometime."

That was great news. Cas smiled at the premise of being a free man soon. "Thanks, Dr. Sanji. And thank God." He was ready to blow that depressing joint and get home to his kids.

CHAPTER NINE

That evening, Jay stared out of his office window at the New York City skyline. He felt pretty good about the phone call he he'd just ended. It spawned from a good deed he'd done earlier that day. While he was at Street Life's headquarters catching up on some work, he'd had his assistant book some travel plans for Macy's grandmother, Mama Atkins. Mama Atkins had just called him to thank him for the gift.

It was Portia's idea to present her with a vacation voucher, so Jay got one on their behalf worth three thousand dollars. It was payable toward the destination of her choice. Mama Atkins said she was surprised, but very happy to be thought of. She told him their timing was perfect because she could certainly use a pick me up.

Jay was glad it had turned out good. He'd wanted to do something nice for her for a while, but he didn't want to interfere with her grieving process, so he gave it a few weeks.

Just before Jay left the office, he got a call from his main man, Cas. Jay answered concernedly and hoped he was okay. "Son, what's good? You a'ight, man?"

Cas grinned into the phone. "Yeah, son, I'm good. Just called to let you know they might be releasing me tomorrow."

Jay's face lit up. "Word? My nigga! So that's what it is, son. Keep me posted."

"You already know, man. I'll scream at you later."

"A'ight." Jay hung up with a huge grin. The good news about his man's progress put him in an even better mood. Jay gave Robin, his assistant, a list of things he needed done the following day, and then he decided to make a little detour before he went home. He was going to stop by his man B.J.'s spot for a drink. The Honeycomb was a new and happening New York City nightspot that had recently opened. Over the last months the joint had become pretty popular. Jay was glad for B.J. because the Honeycomb was officially on the radar.

Before Jay left the office, he had Robin call down to parking to have his car brought out. He drove the Ferrari that day. When he got downstairs his car was waiting for him. The parking attendant was a young white dude with a Mohawk haircut. Jay tipped him for his promptness and then he hopped in the whip and drove across the city.

He maneuvered through traffic for about twenty minutes before he arrived at the spot. B.J. had taken Jay and Cas's suggestions and established an agreement with the parking lot down the block, so now the Honeycomb provided valet parking. The club brought the parking lot lots of business, so it worked out for both parties. Jay hopped out and turned his car over to the uniformed middle-aged Latino dude that waited to assist him. He tipped the guy a C-note as an incentive to take care of his whip. The guy smiled appreciatively and thanked him.

Jay slid through the VIP entrance on the side of the building and was ushered to a table by a hostess in a sexy bumblebee inspired black and yellow striped uniform. The girl was a slender but shapely redbone in her twenties. She smiled when Jay was seated and asked, "Can I get you something to drink?"

Jay went with his usual. "Lemme get a double shot of Henny."

The girl nodded. "Coming right up, sir." She smiled and walked off.

Jay looked around to see if he spotted his mans Eighty and Handy Andy, who both held positions at the Honeycomb.

B.J., the proprietor, came out of his office and was informed by his staff that Jay was in the building. He grinned and headed over to his table. B.J. walked up on Jay's left and surprised him. "My nigga Jay! What's the business, baby? You been a'ight, man?"

Jay grinned and stood up. He dapped B.J. and gave him a man hug. "I'm alive, man. That's all that matters."

B.J. nodded in agreement. He knew just what Jay meant. The men shared an epigrammatic moment because they had a lot of friends that weren't there anymore. Life was truly precious. B.J. said, "You look like you had a long day, Jay. Let's have a drink, man."

Jay nodded. "Shit, I just ordered me one."

"Then it's on the house. How's my nigga Cas?"

"Much better, man. The doctor said he might be coming home tomorrow."

"Shit, that's what it is! Then let's have another drink! For my nigga!" B.J. grinned.

After his second drink, Jay felt pretty good. He was in the mix chumming with his mans and currently had no worries. Eighty had joined Jay and B.J. at the table. Eighty was head of security so he had seen Jay on camera and came out to say what up. Jay felt good chilling with his peoples. He hadn't seen any of them since they had murdered that dude Khalil for clapping Cas at the reception. They had called Jay to check on Casino's condition but none of them had gone up to the hospital. Jay understood the reasoning behind that, and so did Cas.

A Billionaire Black Russian and another double shot of Hennessy later, Jay was pretty mellow. The evening was reminiscent of happier times. His mans Cas and Wise weren't there at the moment but they were both alive and well. They had all gone through so much recently that any little occasion was joyous.

Jay was in such a good mood he smiled back at this broad who kept making eyes at him. The girl was pretty and brown-skin and she wore a gray blazer. She sat in VIP as well. She was two tables over with two equally attractive sisters. All of the ladies seemed refined and sure of themselves. Jay recognized and gave it up. He caught himself smiling but it was too late. Homegirl took the little grin he gave her as a signal and sent him a drink.

The cute redbone hostess who had seated Jay walked up to him carrying another Billionaire Black Russian. The hostess said, "Pardon me. The lady over there in the gray asked me to refill whatever it was you were drinking." She pointed at the girl who had been flirting.

Jay raised an eyebrow and paused for a second. It would be rude to send it back, but he didn't want chicks buying him drinks and shit. He was a man. What did he look like? He accepted it but he wasn't about to be clowned by a table full of bitches. Simply motivated by his foolish male pride, Jay said, "Thank you. Send her a bottle of your finest champagne."

B.J. knew where that was coming from. He was a jokester by nature so he got ready to tease Jay and break his balls.

Eighty beat him to the punch. "This nigga Jay got bitches buying him drinks and shit. I ain't mad, son. At least you know you still got it."

"Nigga, I'ma always have it," Jay stated cockily. They all laughed. "Who is that broad anyway?" he asked. "Y'all know her?"

Eighty shrugged. "Not like that. Her and her homegirls come in around twice a week. They usually do the little after-work thing. They got good jobs, too. They work over at NBC. I believe she's some type of executive over there, or something. Head bitch in charge."

No wonder she seemed so sure of herself. She was a shot caller. Jay changed the subject to something else. A minute later they saw the hostess take the ladies the champagne Jay had sent over. The bubbly sat in a fancy silver bucket of ice. The women looked pleasantly surprised. You could tell the hostess had told them Jay sent it over because they all looked his way. Jay could've sworn he saw the broad that sent him the drink wink at him. He remained pokerfaced and pretended he didn't see her. Eighty had to go make his rounds and B.J. was wanted in another section, so they left Jay alone at the table for a moment. When they got up and walked off, homegirl saw a window of opportunity. She got up and sauntered Jay's way.

When she got to his table, she smiled and introduced herself. "Hi, I'm Breylan. Do you mind if I join you for a minute?"

Jay glanced at his watch and then shrugged and gestured for her to have a seat. She had taken the initiative to come over, so he would be polite and hear her out. Breylan was dressed in a fitted, double-breasted, gray St. John blazer and a pencil skirt with a turquoise camisole underneath. She was built nicely and looked pretty tall in the stylish high-heeled boots she wore. A few of her jacket buttons were open to expose a little cleavage. Jay guessed that was her afterhours look. He would bet that blazer was buttoned up during the day.

Jay didn't like pushy women and he wasn't in the mood for small talk. He had only come out to unwind a little. He wanted to say get lost but he didn't want to be rude. He regretted sending over that bottle service because homegirl had taken it the wrong way. Jay guessed there was no harm in talking. That wasn't a sin. Suddenly a vision of Portia popped in his head. He dismissed the notion that he had anything to feel guilty about.

Breylan smiled and took a seat. "I'ma be honest. My girlfriends bet me that I wouldn't come over here and talk to you. They claim I need to get out more and date. They seem to think I've lost it, and I *may* have... But I'll be damned if I lose this bet! It's for a hundred dollars."

Jay couldn't help but smile. "A hundred dollars? Living life on the edge, huh?"

Breylan laughed. "Yes, I am. I don't gamble! If you play along, I'll give you half!"

"I'll play along so you can win, but you can keep that."

"Are you sure? In this economy fifty dollars isn't chump change. It can buy dinner and a drink. Or a tank of gas!"

Jay laughed. "That's depending on what you drive."

Breylan nodded in agreement. "True, but I drive a hybrid Lexus, so it would last me for a while. Here in the city anyway."

"Well, I assure you that fifty bucks won't fill up my vehicle. Maybe about halfway."

Breylan grinned. "Damn, what do you drive? An aircraft?"

Jay nodded solemnly. "Boeing Jet. 757."

She looked like she believed him for a moment. Then she laughed. "Oh, you got jokes, huh?"

Jay actually owned a private plane, but he didn't mention it because he wasn't the fronting type.

Breylan felt relaxed from the champagne she'd been sipping, courtesy of Jay. "What's your name?"

"Jay. What's yours?"

"Breylan. I told you that already."

"My bad. I guess I wasn't listening before."

"So I have your attention now?"

"Yeah, I guess."

Breylan smiled across the table at Jay with a pair of dimples that made it impossible for him to not smile back. She seemed decent and genuine so he felt like he was in good company. Jay suddenly had another vision of his lovely wife. He wondered if that was his conscience or if Portia was talking about him.

CHAPTER TEN

Portia was at the house with the kids that evening. She was in the kitchen preparing dinner for her family. As she cut up the vegetables for the salad she was making, she talked on the phone with Fatima.

"Tima, hold on a second before I be done chopped off my finger. Let me put you on the speaker." Portia hit the speaker button and stood the phone up on the counter. "Okay, boo. Now, as I was saying, things have been so good between me and Jay. We finally got pass all the bullshit. I can honestly say that. I forgave him, and we are okay. We been through some things, but I know I have a good husband."

"You sure do. Jay's a gem, sis. I'm glad y'all good. But girl, lemme tell you about my piece of shit." Fatima was in her bedroom, kicked back in a comfy recliner. She was eating peanut butter and pickles to satisfy a sweet and sour craving she had. She noisily smacked in Portia's ear and gave her an account of the unwelcome phone calls her husband had been receiving. "P, Wise's ass is really starting to fuckin' annoy me. That nurse bitch keep on calling, and he swears he ain't fuckin' her. The shit that gets me mad is the fact that he keep lying." Fatima stuck a pickle spear into the peanut butter jar and chomped on it. "Just tell the truth, dummy! N'ah mean, P?"

Portia agreed. "Yeah, sis, I feel you. I'm so glad me and Jay got our little trust thing back."

Fatima sighed. "I thought *we* did. But I guess not."

Portia glimpsed at the clock on the microwave and wondered where Jay was. He should've been home by then. She had called headquarters and spoke to Robin, so she knew Jay had left the office already. Though Portia didn't want to say it out loud, she felt like Jay should rush home every night to help take care of the baby he'd made on her. Portia didn't want to be small and throw that in his face; especially not after she'd accepted Jaylin into their family. She just didn't want to be taken for granted.

In Jay's defense, he had suggested that they hire another nanny so Portia wouldn't be overwhelmed by responsibilities that she didn't sign up for. Portia didn't want to hire any help because she felt like that would be alienating the baby. He needed a mother, not a sitter. Portia loved all of her kids, including Jaylin, but some days she felt like she needed a break. Her baby, Trixie, was barely two years old, and now she had to do it all over again. Jay could participate a little more. Portia didn't think she was asking too much. She realized Fatima was still talking about her and Wise's issues and zoned back to the conversation.

"P, I'm tired of getting my feelings hurt. Wise thinks he so slick. Sometimes I just wanna hurt that bastard back. But I can't get even right now, because who the fuck gon' want me with this big ass belly?"

Portia laughed, "Oh, somebody will. Trust, boo. There're dudes out there that love pregnant stuff. Somebody will beat that big old wolf pussy up right now, Miss Pearlie!"

Fatima cracked up. "Bitch, fuck you. My shit is nice and tight. And if having this baby destroys that, I'ma get that reconstructive cootchie operation Cher got."

Portia laughed. "You so silly. You ain't gon' need that. Baby number two didn't mess up my twat. I'm good."

"Yeah right," Fatima teased. "I heard your shit is like the Holland Tunnel – straight through."

"Oh, you tried it, bitch," Portia giggled. "But trust me, dudes get beat by this box."

"I know that's right." Fatima chuckled mischievously. "I *should* tell Wise I fucked his lil' man Five when we went to L.A. that time. I know he wouldn't appreciate hearing *that*. I know that shit is mad old, but that's all the dirt I got, P."

Portia started rolling. "Girl, you so stupid. Hell no! I *know* Wise wouldn't appreciate that. Don't even play, Tima. We gotta keep that little secret 'til the day we die. We gon' take that one to our graves. *Right*?"

Fatima giggled. "Right, P. Bitch, I ain't stupid. That nigga would probably kill my ass. Even though I thought he was dead at the time, Wise would kill me. And I ain't even gon' talk about what Jay would do to you if he knew about Vino! There would be some smoke in the city!"

Portia almost choked. "O.M.G.! Jay would kill me, Tima! He'd probably empty the clips out *both* hammers on my ass!" Jay carried two guns everywhere he went, so that wasn't an overstatement.

Fatima was so silly. She sighed, "I know, P. You would have two different sets of holes in your ass. So don't worry, girlfriend. I would *never* tell that shit." She and Portia shared a good laugh.

$$$$$

Wise stood outside of him and Fatima's bedroom door with his mouth hanging open in shock. He was totally stunned. He had just overheard his wife cop to giving up some ass. Dear Lord, his pussy had been tampered with. Fatima thought she was so slick. She was a sneaky bitch.

The only thing that stopped Wise from barging in that room and slapping fire out of her ass was the fact that he was mad enough to really hurt her. Fatima was over eight months pregnant, so Wise was too concerned about his baby boy's safety to wild out. That bitch was lucky. He knew her little whorish secret though.

From what he'd heard, perfect little Portia was a hoe as well. Fatima said she had done some dirt too. Wise heard it loud and clear. He knew Jay wouldn't like the idea of his wife fucking around, but he felt obligated to tell him. Jay was his man. He was like Wise's brother. If the shoe was on the other foot, Jay would've told him about Fatima. They didn't keep secrets like that from one another. That was what those sneaky ass broads did.

"Fuckin' hoe," Wise mumbled. He had come home to make nice after an argument he and Tima had, but that was out the window now. Fuck Fatima. Wise didn't blow it up yet, but that shit wasn't over. He was upset so he left in a hurry. In his haste, Wise didn't realize he dropped his iPhone. It landed on a plush rug at the top of the hardwood stairs, so he never heard it hit the floor. Wise left the crib as quietly as he came.

$$\$\$\$\$\$$

About ten minutes later, Fatima got up to go use the bathroom. On her way, she heard what sounded like Wise's cell phone ring tone. The music came from outside the bedroom, so Fatima figured he had just arrived. She walked in the hallway to greet Wise. To her surprise, she didn't see him. Fatima called out, "Wise? I know you in here. I just heard your phone ringing."

There was no response, so Fatima got the creeps. She decided to check the security monitors and see where in the house he was. Just then, the phone rang again. She followed the music and found it lying on the floor. It appeared that Wise had dropped his phone. Fatima had gone downstairs at least three times since Wise left the house earlier. If that phone was just lying there like that, she would've seen it. It was impossible not to. Wise had just come home. She wondered if he was there now.

When Fatima picked up the phone it stopped ringing. She checked the incoming call log and saw that the same person had called several times. It was as if Wise had either missed or had been ignoring the calls. Just then, the phone rang again. It was the same number. It must've been pretty urgent. Fatima answered coolly. "Hello?"

The caller was stunned when they heard a female voice. They remained quiet.

"*Hello*?" Fatima repeated.

Lily regained her voice and cleared her throat. "Who is this?"

Fatima was thrown off by the premise of some rude bitch questioning her on her husband's phone, but strangely she was calm. Over the past years, she had been through a lot of shit with Wise. She'd even been led to believe that she'd lost him forever. So it took a lot to get to her now. Fatima took a deep breath. She knew it was that nurse bitch calling. "This is his wife, honey. I'm sure you know he's married. So what's the problem?"

Lily didn't know what to say. So she didn't say anything. She wanted to speak to Wise but she guessed he wasn't taking her calls that day. His rejection really stung because they'd become quite close while Lily had nursed Wise back to health. For a while they'd been really happy, but then he had this urge to return to his family. They had parted as "friends" but Wise left Lily under the impression that they could have a future together. Especially since they had continued to talk on the phone regularly, and had also hooked up a few times for dinner and "dessert." That was no longer enough because Lily had fallen in love with Wise.

Fatima saw that Wise's little girlfriend was intimidated. It was important that that bitch understand that she didn't have a chance with Wise. "Stay away from my husband. Wise doesn't love you, he loves *me*. We have a beautiful family. Our daughter's gorgeous and we're expecting a son in just weeks. Thank you for what you did for us, Lily. Now it's time for you to move on, honey, and find a man of your own. When you mess with a happily married man, there's no such thing as a happy ending. Please don't call this number again." *Click*

After Wise's wife hung up on her, Lily sat on the other end of the line dumbfounded. That reality check was unwelcome but sobering. Of all the stuff Fatima said, the thing Lily remembered the most was the revelation that Wise was having a baby soon. That was the knockout punch. Lily had been pregnant by Wise as well. He had insisted that she abort. Lily was floored by Fatima's news but she wasn't going out without a fight.

CHAPTER ELEVEN

"Who the fuck is this, paging me at six in the morning? Now I'm yawning. Wipe the cold from my eye, see who's this paging me, and why. It's my nigga Don from the barber shop, told me he was in the gambling spot, heard the intricate plot..."

Wise's music blared as he turned down Jay's long winding driveway. He had intended to call and announce his arrival but he couldn't seem to find his phone. He figured he had dropped it somewhere, probably outside his house. He would try and locate it before the night was over. Wise knew that someone was at Jay's crib because it was a school night. Wise pulled up out front and parked, and then he hopped out and rang the bell.

Lil' Jay opened the door and greeted him with a hearty pound. "Uncle Wise, what up?" Jayquan had some music that he'd recorded and wanted Wise to listen to. He had been writing lots of lyrics and honing his delivery skills so he believed he was nice enough to record something in the big studio. Excitedly, he said, "Yo, I got some shit you gotta hear."

Wise grinned and walked inside. The little dude was the spitting image of his old man. Lil' Jay was getting tall as hell and he was also growing a mustache. Wise was so tickled he broke his nephew's balls. "Ahhh, this little nigga got a mustache! Oh shit!" Wise laughed. He faked a few jabs at Jayquan.

Jayquan was on point like he'd been trained to be. He skillfully blocked the punches. "Come on, Unc, you ain't Mayweather or nobody, so chill!"

Wise laughed. The boy had a slick mouth like his pops. "Ain't it a school night, man?"

Lil' Jay looked at him like he had cursed. "So what? Lemme tell you somethin', Uncle Wise. I'm a grown ass man."

Wise shook his head. That little dude was a trip. "Where your pops at?"

"I don't know. That dude ain't get home yet. You called his phone?"

"Nah, I think I left my phone at the crib. Call him for me."

Lil' Jay sighed. "Hold up, man, my phone upstairs in the rec section. Be right back."

"A'ight, I'm 'bout to fix myself a drink," Wise informed his nephew.

Jayquan shrugged like he couldn't care less. "I don't give a rat's ass. Help yourself."

$$$$$

Jay was still at the Honeycomb chatting with Breylan. She had been smiling during their whole conversation. Jay enjoyed conversing with her as well. He looked at his phone and then sat it on the table next to his glass. Oddly, it had been as quiet as a church mouse. Just then, the phone vibrated. Jay looked down at the caller ID and saw that it was his son, Jayquan, calling.

"Excuse me for a second," Jay told Breylan. Then he addressed his son. "What up, lil' man? You a'ight?"

Jayquan said, "I'm good. Pop, what up? Where are you?"

"I'm on my way now. Everybody good?"

"Yeah. Uncle Wise is here. He wanna holla at you."

"When, now?" Jay asked. "Or when I get there?"

"Hold on." Jayquan poked Wise to get his attention. "You wanna speak to Pop now?"

Wise said, "Nah. Just tell that nigga to get home as soon as possible."

Jayquan nodded and relayed the message. "Pop, he'll see you when you get here, but he said hurry up. Be safe, man."

Jay held back a smile. Jayquan sounded like he was the dad. "A'ight, thanks lil' man. I'll see you in a little while. Love you."

"Love you too, Pop. See you soon." Jayquan hung up.

Jay took that call from his son as a sign to take his black ass home. He smiled politely at his new acquaintance. "It was nice talking to you, but that was my cue. I'd better call it a night. I'm pretty sure you won that bet by now."

Breylan gave Jay a winning smile. "I believe I have. Thank you for your assistance."

"The pleasure was mine. Congrats on your win."

"I'm glad I won the money but the conversation was even better. We should keep in touch." She slid her business card across the table and stood up. Breylan smiled and wished Jay a good evening.

"You have a good one too." Jay watched Breylan strut away and noted what a pretty smile she had. Another vision of Portia popped in his head. That time it was her and the kids. That meant it was time for him to go. Jay put the card Breylan slid him in his jacket pocket. He had no intentions on calling her; he just didn't want to be rude. She seemed like a nice girl but Jay had a great family life. He wasn't willing to sabotage that for anybody. After all that he and Portia had been through, there was no margin for error.

$$\$\$\$\$\$$

That evening Kira lounged at home in cream colored silk Chanel pajamas. She sipped her signature cocktail, a Kira Kahlua, and smiled to herself. She'd had a meeting earlier that day with the producers of her reality show. Kira informed them about her decision not to involve her son in the project, so they decided to make some changes to the concept. They were also debating on a new title. *Vi-Kira-ously*, (pronounced vicariously), was in the air, but it wasn't in stone yet. The idea was to give the viewers an up close and personal look at Kira's life.

The production crew had even filmed her at a couple of the mandatory anger management sessions she'd been ordered to attend. Kira had served a year in prison for torching the house of her ex-husband, Cas's new girlfriend at the time, Laila. She had heartlessly set the house ablaze in the middle of the night, while crippled Laila and her baby were inside. Kira still cringed when she thought about it. That was the dumbest thing she had ever done. As a condition of her release from prison, the judge had ordered her to attend anger management sessions for six months.

The changes of plans for the show included bringing in a love interest. Kira looked at that part as an opportunity. She agreed on the grounds that she would be able to pick out the guy herself. She had the perfect person for the job.

Vino was her first pick. Kira and he were already musically involved, so it made sense. She pretended it was all business but that was what she had hoped would come to pass. She was really feeling Vino. She had it bad. The attraction was almost animalistic.

Kira decided to call Vino and ask him what the deal was. Her cell reception sucked in the house sometimes, so she dialed him on her land line. Kira was as nervous as a freshman on a first date.

Vino was en route to his penthouse, eager to shower and relax, when his phone rung. He checked the mirrors of the Beamer he had recently copped to get around in, to make sure there were no pigs in the vicinity, before he looked at the phone. He assumed it was Five's baby mother, Rochelle, calling him with another message from Five. His partner got snatched up when he went back to Callie, so they had been communicating through her. It was a fucked up time for Five to be incarcerated, when so much was happening for them. But there had been a warrant for his arrest, so it was beyond his control. At first they thought it was something petty, but now the pigs were questioning him about a murder. That shit was serious.

Vino didn't recognize the number on his cell phone. He had Kira's cell phone number saved under her name, so no name popped up. He considered sending it to voicemail, but then decided to see who it was. "Hello?"

Kira smiled as if there were cameras on her. *Cheese.* Vino's voice did it to her every time. "What up, baby? What you doin'?"

"Who's this?"

Kira frowned at the phone. "It's me, Kira."

"Oh, what up? Is this a new number?"

"This is my house number. You should save it. What you up to?"

"Nothin'. I just left the studio. I finished up that mix, so I'm on the way to the crib. I been up workin' for about two days."

"Aawww, you poor baby. Listen, how long before you get home? I need to holla at you."

"Holla at me about what?"

"Well... I got a proposition for you."

Vino hesitated for a moment. He wondered what she was up to. With Kira, there was no telling. "I guess I'll be home in about a half."

"Okay, I'ma meet you at your house in an hour."

Vino was thrown off by her forwardness. "*What?*" Who did Kira think she was?

She stood firm. "I'm comin' through to holla at you. Unless you try'na come to my crib." Vino didn't respond. Kira chuckled. "Yeah, that's what I thought. I'll see you then." *Click*

Vino looked at the phone and shook his head. She didn't even ask him if she could come over. She just told him she was coming. That girl was a trip. Nevertheless, Vino smiled to himself about the special attention she always showed him. He knew Kira could have any dude she wanted, so he couldn't front, it was flattering. He wondered what she was up to now.

Vino focused his attention back on his new girlfriend, the burgundy BMW 760Li Sedan he had just copped. She was lovely and she handled magnificently. Any man would be proud. Vino grinned. The vehicle was nothing spectacular, compared to the exotic cars his business associates, Jay and company, drove, but that pre-owned Beamer was the finest car he'd ever owned. It only had six thousand miles on it.

Vino wasn't the fronting type. He stayed in his lane. He was getting money, but not quite like team Street Life. Not yet, anyhow. So he intended to stay humble. And he intended to put his mother in a better house before he bought a Lamborghini. He was planning to build her a lavish new home soon, so he couldn't allow himself to be sidetracked. He was in New York for a reason. He'd come to chase those pesos.

Vino dipped through traffic and hurried to his temporary east coast home. He wanted to jerk off and take a shower before Kira showed up. The ritzy apartment he was renting was the finest crib he'd ever occupied. He liked his new life. He prayed his man, Five, would get home soon to reap the benefits as well.

CHAPTER TWELVE

Kira was in hip-hop mode, as usual. As she picked out a matching set of La Perla underwear so she could take a shower, the rapstress made up a little freestyle about the apple of her eye – Vino.

> *"So tired of being alone, just got off the phone -*
> *Dude could be worthy of sharing da' throne*
> *Bright lights, big city, she got a master plan -*
> *'Bout to get real pretty, goin' to get her man*
> *Five-inch heels, sex appeal,*
> *What you gon' do, boo? Shit is real..."*

On the way to her master bathroom, she stopped short and decided to run a quick security scan. Being in that huge house alone was scary sometimes. She and her son lived there together, but Jahseim stayed with family lots of the time. Kira was home alone a lot, and lately she hated it. Jay kept insisting that she needed some live-in security, but she didn't want any strangers in her house. Kira depended on three things to keep her safe: God, security alarms on every window and door in her crib, and the small collection of guns she had strategically placed throughout the house – just in case. She secretly wanted to fill her house with a family. There was plenty space for a good quality dude and a couple more kids. She hurried to check the security monitors so she could get ready for Vino.

After Kira made sure everything was good, she turned up her stereo and headed to the bathroom. The music bumped through the speakers in there while the rap diva showered. She spit lyrics the whole time. When Kira was done, she dressed in fitted sweats and a short, belly-revealing hoodie. Kira stepped into a pair of black sequined Uggs and brushed her hair back into a side ponytail. Her flawless skin afforded her the opportunity to go without makeup when she wanted to. She didn't want Vino to crash before she got there so she skipped the primping. She wasn't in the mood anyhow. Kira applied translucent gloss to her pouty lips and admired her reflection in the mirror. Other than a little lip gloss and her usual eyelashes, she was au naturale. At least her face was. The Indian Remy hair extensions on her head were a different story. Kira laughed to herself and called to make sure the car she had hired was on schedule.

Forty minutes later, a black suit clad driver opened the back door of the princess's Cadillac carriage in front of Vino's ritzy apartment building. He helped Kira get out and escorted her inside the lobby. Kira stopped at the front and tipped him. "Thanks, I got it from here."

The middle-aged, dark-haired, Turkish gentleman adjusted his necktie and smiled. "It was my pleasure. Thank *you*. I shall call in two hours to see if you wish to return to your residence, as we agreed. Have a good night, madam." He nodded curtly and returned to his vehicle.

The doorman, was a sandy-haired, white boy about twenty-two that worked nights to finance his hip-hop pipe dreams. He had dropped out of college in his sophomore year in pursuit of fame. The market was oversaturated with kids with the same dream, so he gotten a reality check soon after. He recognized Kira as soon as she flounced in. He grinned and blurted out, "Oh shit! What up, Kira? I fuckin' *love* you!" he caught himself and grinned sheepishly. "Err, your music. I love your music. Pardon me." He laughed uneasily.

Kira was flattered by the recognition. She smiled at her fan and touched his arm. "Nah, you're okay. Thanks, boo. What's your name?"

His face lit up. He looked down at Kira's hand on his arm like it was the most spectacular thing since the Mona Lisa. "Jeez, I'm not gonna wash this arm for six months!" He looked embarrassed the moment he said that. "Did I say that out loud?"

Kira smiled and nodded. "Umm hmm."

"Christ, I'm sorry, it's just that you're so beautiful. Oh man, there I go again. I'm a freakin' idiot."

"It's okay, hon," Kira laughed. "What's your name?"

He was thrilled that she even cared who he was. He took a deep breath and shook off his nervousness. "My birth certificate says Daniel Moynihan, but I'm an emcee by day," he said proudly. "They call me Day Glo. You probably never heard of me, but I'm on my way." He nodded like he really meant that. "My dad got me this gig so I work it nights. But there's no way I can see myself retiring as a doorman like the old man. Screw the benefits he's always raving about. You know?" He laughed.

Kira nodded and smiled. Then she waited for him to hand her a CD or tell her his Facebook page or website where she could hear his music. She got that a lot. It seemed like everybody was trying to get on.

Day Glo said, "You know, I'd be honored if you would give me your autograph."

"Sure. No problem. Where do I sign?"

He rolled up his sleeve and exposed his pale, milky white forearm. "Right here." He reached inside his inside pocket and grabbed a pen. Kira took it and signed:

See you at the top, Day Glo! Good luck... Kira. Smooches!!!

He read what she wrote and beamed. "Wow, thanks! This is awesome!" Then just as she had predicted, he produced a CD from the back pocket of his uniform pants. "I'm not gonna hold you up any longer... But if you could listen to a couple of my songs, I would be honored."

Kira took the CD and stuffed it in her purse. "I will. I will also critique it honestly, so I hope you have tough skin." She grinned and walked off toward the elevator. Kira didn't bother to look back. She didn't turn around until she stepped into the open elevator doors. He was still staring. She winked at him through the closing doors.

Kira rode up to the top floor where Vino's penthouse condominium was. The elevator was pretty fast. Her stomach felt like she was on a roller coaster. A moment later, she stood in front of his door. Kira took a deep breath and rang the doorbell. Then she waited patiently for her man to answer.

When Vino opened his apartment door, Kira smiled innocently. *She looks younger without all that makeup on,* he thought. He also noted that she wasn't as tall as he'd originally thought. Vino stood six feet high. In the high heels Kira usually wore, she looked like she had him by a couple of inches, but he was actually taller than she was.

Kira greeted him brightly. "Hey, Vino!"

Vino was wearing a crispy white T-shirt, a pair of navy-blue Polo sweats, white socks, and black Polo slides. He fought back a smile. "What up, Kira?" He stepped aside so she could enter his domicile.

Vino's t-shirt wasn't tight but it fit his muscles nice and snug. Kira's imagination ran wild and she pictured herself savagely ripping it off him with her teeth and devouring him. She was so turned on by his manliness she wanted to bite him. She took a deep breath and refrained. She didn't want to frighten Vino with her animalistic urges so she opted to just undress him with her eyes. Kira stared at his biceps and pectorals appreciatively. Vino was all kinds of sexy. She gathered herself and walked inside. When she passed him, her knees weakened. *Be strong, bitch, be strong,* Kira told herself.

She looked around the state of the art loft-style condominium and smiled. "Nice place."

"Thanks," Vino said humbly. "I ain't been here that long yet."

Kira removed her black sequined Adrienne Vittadini motorcycle jacket and handed it to him. "I know, West Coast. You've barely been here two months. I'm thirsty, boo. What you got to drink?"

Vino shrugged and pointed to the kitchen. Kira started that way and he went the other way to hang up her coat. When Kira opened the stainless steel double refrigerator all she saw was Dasani bottled water and club soda. When Vino joined her in the kitchen she broke his balls. "Damn, you don't got nothin' in here but water and seltzer water. And there's *nothin'* to eat in here."

Vino fought back a smile and shook his head. Kira was so outspoken all the time. "Nah, I been eating out every day. I been so busy, I'm hardly ever here."

Kira gave him a little flirtatious smirk. "You mean you ain't got no little girlfriend that can run to the store and pick up a few things for you every now and then?"

Vino maintained a straight face and shook his head. "Nah. You the first female that ever been in here." He regretted saying that as soon as it came out. That was none of Kira's business.

Kira made a face and raised an eyebrow like she didn't believe him. "Yeah right. A young and handsome bachelor like you? Please."

Vino stopped her right there. "True, I *am* a bachelor, but I'm not into bringing random chicks where I rest my head. I don't really know anyone out here well enough to feel that comfortable yet. I'm usually working, so I haven't really had time to get to know nobody." Vino wasn't lying. Though he'd beat a couple of bitches since he'd been in New York, it was just casual sex. He took the biddies to a hotel. None of them was worthy enough to bring to his spot. Vino didn't trust bitches. He wasn't trying to wind up being a statistic. All he had on his mind at the time was success and the money it would bring.

Kira nodded like she understood. "Tell me about it, boo. I'm so busy I can't tell my head from my ass some days. My social life has been desert dry. So trust me, I feel you."

Now it was Vino's turn to exhibit disbelief. "Come on, I'm sure you got niggas beating down your door try'na see you. High profile niggas."

Kira smiled coyly. "I wish. Nobody that I'm interested in anyway. I been celibate since I came home from doin' my little bid."

Vino didn't comment but his expression said he didn't believe her. Kira was the aggressive type. She probably had a boy toy that serviced her at the snap of a finger. Vino envisioned her in black dominatrix getup and held back a laugh.

Kira wanted to assure him that she was being truthful. "I saw that little look on your face. I'm dead ass serious. That's word on my son."

Vino was convinced after she said that. "And how long you been home again?"

"Almost four months," Kira sighed. "I came home right before the New Year came in. Almost four long ass, lonely ass months. So add that to the year I did and then do the math. We talking sixteen months and still counting." She laughed and shook her head.

Vino got quiet for a few seconds. He was contemplating whether or not he should say what he was thinking.

"What? I'm serious, Vino!"

"Nah, I hear you. I was just thinking. Even if you set aside your status and popularity, the fact that you're so pretty makes that hard to believe."

Kira blushed at the compliment. "Thank you, darling. But I'll pass on the groupies. There are too many STDs out here. I ain't about *that* life." She paused for a moment before she continued. "You know, it ain't even just about sex though. They make toys for that if it gets that serious. Trust me, I own a couple." Kira chuckled naughtily.

Vino tried to delete the image in his head of her playing with sex toys. He willed the big hard-on that stood up in his pants down, and didn't comment. He was glad when she moved on and kept on talking.

"I'm looking for somethin' real. Nothing too heavy, 'cause I'm so busy with my career, I don't have time to be anybody's wife right now. It'd just be nice to have a special friend. Someone I can look forward to seeing." Kira paused. She hoped she hadn't said too much. She didn't want to scare him. "That's pretty much where I am in my life right now. She just wants to be happy." She shrugged and feigned nonchalance.

Vino noted that she had referred to herself in third person. "I feel you. Everyone deserves a chance at that."

Kira took two bottles of water from the fridge. "Yeah, well, I guess when it's meant to be, it's meant to be. Until then, I'm M to the M – Married to the money! Now let's drink to that." Kira handed him a bottle of water and laughed.

Vino tried not to smile but was unsuccessful that time. He took the water and twisted the bottle open. Kira seemed so human, he was surprised. Vino had heard a lot of stuff about her, some good and some bad, but she gave him a different impression than he expected. In the studio she always came across as so pushy. He wondered now if that was just a part of her bad girl image.

Kira was thrilled when Vino smiled. He was usually curt and on edge with her. It seemed as if he had put his guards down for a change.

Vino said, "Look, I was just about to order something to eat. You hungry?"

"Yes! I'm starving. What you got a taste for?"

"Well, I only know a couple of places to order from. I'm still pretty new here."

"I'm not really picky eater, so it's whatever."

"I got the number to this Chinese joint that makes some pretty good food. You like Chinese? Or pizza?"

Kira shook her head. "Chinese. Take charge and order for me. I'ma make myself comfortable, if that's okay with you."

He shrugged. "You good. You smoke?"

"You mean weed?"

"Shit, I ain't talkin' about crack."

Kira laughed. "Sometimes."

Vino tossed her a sack of loud and fished through his phone for the number to the restaurant. Kira took off her shoes and sat on the sofa Indian-style and began to roll a blunt. After Vino ordered the food, they sat on his sofa and smoked and talked about the industry and the new sound Kira wanted for her new album.

Vino couldn't front, he enjoyed Kira's company. When the food arrived, she showed off by eating her lo mein with chopsticks. She tried to teach Vino how to but he couldn't seem to get it. After Kira rubbed it in, she laughed and passed him a fork.

Kira caught herself blushing a lot that night because she found everything Vino did so adorable. She even liked the way he chewed. She really dug him, and the affection wasn't just sexually charged. They were having a good time.

After Kira and Vino were done eating, she excused herself and went to the bathroom. As she reapplied her lip gloss, she mulled over the fact that she and Vino had bonded somewhat. They had actually clicked. Kira liked everything about him so far. Vino could be the one to fill that empty space in her heart.

Kira remembered the reason she had come. She had to talk to him about coming on the show. She knew she could get just about any guy she wanted to play that part, but she wanted to work with Vino. She had to. She marched back out there in time to see Vino rolling another blunt. He looked up and asked if she minded.

Kira giggled. "Nah, not at all. And even if I did, this is *your* house. I'm just a guest, you make the rules." She decided to wait until he sparked up before she brought up the business she came about.

Vino was a mind reader. "Not that I ain't enjoying your company, but what are you doing over here, Kira?"

Kira grinned. "I just wanted to see your face when I revealed this business proposition I have for you. It's an opportunity to make some extra bread."

Vino was cucumber cool. He passed her the el, and said, "I'm listening."

Kira took two pulls and continued. "Okay, you know the reality show I'm working on, right?"

Vino remained expressionless. "Yeah."

Kira blew out a cloud of smoke and kept on. "Well, we're sort of back in the developmental stage. We got a lot of footage of me doing just about everything from going to my anger management meetings, to taking my son to the zoo. The producers think it would be more interesting if we touched on my love life too." She took another pull and passed him the el back to him. "So, long story short, I need a love interest for the show. And I was hoping you'd be interested."

Vino looked at Kira like she had called him out of his name. "Interested in what? Being your *love interest*? Are you serious?" That girl was out of her mind.

His initial reaction stung but Kira wouldn't give up. "Wait, not like that. I don't mean you really have to *love* me. Just on television."

"So you want me to pretend to love you on TV for money? What you think I am, some type of prostitute? Are you crazy, Kira? Hell no!"

"Wow, you make it sound so bad. Vino, let me explain. They wanted to interview some guys for the role. Then they thought about filming me going out on dates with some guys and getting to know them, like I'm looking for Mr. Right and shit. But I wanna cut to the chase and bring you in."

Kira stared at the floor for a moment. She wasn't proud of the accomplishment she was about to share with him. "Vino, the fact that I burned down my ex-husband's new girlfriend's house is the thing that landed me this show." Saying it out loud made it sound even worse. "But I wanna turn that around. I got a lot of hate mail about that situation. A lotta people got the wrong idea about me, so on my show I wanna be portrayed as a once-bitter, but now focused successful woman who will find love again." She perked up and grinned. "I told the producers I believe that a romance that transpires in the studio between me and my music producer would add a flare to the show. They *loved* the idea! So if you wit' it, we can use the show to cross promote the new material we working on. I want the show to be more about the music. That would be good exposure for me and you both. And we look good together, baby! America would eat that shit up! We'd be one of TV's cutest couples."

Kira let that sink in for a second. Vino didn't say a word but he looked uptight. When Vino's face relaxed a little bit, she kept on. "Like I said, Vino, it would be all about the music. Think of it as an acting gig, boo. That's all reality TV is anyway. Acting. Most of that shit is scripted."

Though Kira had pitched the idea like it was the greatest thing since the invention of sliced bread, Vino was leery. He didn't respond because he felt funny about doing something like that. The idea of Kira paying him to act like her little boyfriend didn't sit well with him. He was a man. And he was no fucking actor. He wasn't with it. Vino shook his head.

"Please," Kira begged. "I could get anybody to do this, but ..."

"So get somebody else," he scoffed.

"I don't want nobody else! I like *you*! For the part, I mean."

Who was Kira trying to fool? Vino knew she liked him. He realized that night that he liked her as well. But they couldn't take it there. And definitely not on camera. She was Casino's ex-wife. He had to turn her down. "Look, Kira, I'ma haf'ta pass on this one. I ain't no actor. And I doubt if Cas will like your little idea anyway. Your brother probably won't either."

Kira made a face. She couldn't believe Vino said that. "What?! Cas don't give a fuck about what I do. He's married again, Vino. And *he* divorced *me*. So that's the least of our worries, trust me. And my brother knows I do what I want. As long as I stay outta trouble, Jay don't care either. And they *both* know you good people. They told me that before I even met you. So don't base your decision on neither one of them. Base it on us... And the success of this new album we're working on. Say you in, boo. This is a paid opportunity; you will be compensated for every episode you're in. And fuck acting, just be you. The guy I met tonight."

Kira stared at him with hearts in her eyes, so it was hard to say no. Vino felt like he had no other choice. "I'm sorry, but I can't."

"Why, are you scared you might really fall for me, or somethin'? Is that what it is?"

Vino sucked his teeth. "What? Nah!"

"So say you're in. Just say yes. *Please*."

"I don't know. I guess I'll think about it."

Kira's eyes filled with hope. "Okay. That's all I ask. Just think about it." She grinned at Vino like he'd just signed on the dotted line. Kira wanted to hug him, but refrained. She was dying to find out how it felt being in his arms, but she contained herself.

CHAPTER THIRTEEN

Jay rode along en route to his not-so-humble abode in silence and thought about his kids. The conversation he'd had at the Honeycomb with Breylan was innocent, so he wondered why he felt a tad guilty. He had an impulse to toss Breylan's business card out of the car window. He started to, and then a police cruiser with its sirens blaring came up behind him. Jay assumed he was about to get pulled over and cursed. "Shit!"

He was both surprised and relieved when the pig went around him and sped on about his business. Jay took that as a sign. He didn't take any chances littering after that. It would be just his luck to get stopped for something dumb like that. It was bad enough that he was a black man driving a half million dollar vehicle. It seemed as if driving while black, also known as DWB, was a crime in itself. Jay left the business card in his pocket and drove on.

A ringtone sounded off on his phone and notified him that he had voicemail. Jay pressed one on his keypad so he could listen on his Bluetooth. He grinned when he discovered that there were two messages from his little girls. Jazmin and Trixie had called him that evening to inquire about his whereabouts and find out what time he was coming home. Jay's smile was so big you'd have thought he'd hit the lotto. The sound of his daughters' voices had lifted him up high. His angels Jazz and Trixie were something. Jay was a proud father.

Jay felt another guilty pang about the time he'd spent conversing with that chick, Breylan. After all the bullshit he'd gone through with that crazy ass broad, Ysatis, he knew better. Ysatis had caused all kinds of drama in his life. Thanks to his man, Cas, she was no longer a problem, but that was something Jay would have to live with forever. If that situation had taught him one thing, he'd learned to keep it in his pants.

When Jay got home, he saw Wise's black Maserati parked out front. He parked in his multi-car garage and headed for the crib. As he walked away, the automatic garage door shut behind him. He entered the house he and Portia had made a home.

Jay had had a long day but he burst into the castle full of energy. The first thing he noticed was the smell of apples and cinnamon, which indicated that Portia had baked a pie or something. The second thing Jay noticed was the toys that littered the floor of the otherwise palatial atmosphere. The little car and dolls was a pleasant reminder of his progeny's presence. Jay smiled and walked inside his home. He loved the fact that he was surrounded with comfort when he walked through the door. The house was gigantic, but there was a warm welcome feeling inside that only a blessed home contained. A home that was full of love.

Jay didn't see anybody, so he went in the kitchen. He didn't see anyone in there either. He looked at his diamond flooded Hublot watch and realized it was after midnight. He figured Portia was upstairs with the kids. Jay walked to his study and began to disrobe so he could relax. The first item he removed was the custom-made double shoulder holster he kept his hammers in. Jay locked the weapons in the hidden gun cabinet in the library and then he sat at his presidential mahogany desk for a minute. The study was one of his favorite rooms. It was probably the least used room in the house because he was so busy. His classic art combined with Portia's entire wall lined with classic leather-bound books gave the room a rustic feeling he enjoyed.

Jay leaned back and put his feet up. He crossed his arms and took a moment to admire one of his framed art pieces on the wall. The painting had cost him a grip, but now it was worth twice as much as he'd invested in it. Jay appreciated fine art, largely because fine art appreciated. He prided himself in the ability to pick 'em. His art collection was sick. Jay grabbed a cigar from the box of Hoyo de Monterrey Double Coronas sitting on his desk and chewed on the tip for a moment. He started to light it, but he changed his mind.

Jay sat there and wondered where his son was. Jayquan had called and said that Wise wanted to holler at him, so he should be in there somewhere too. Jay took a remote control from his desk drawer and used it to open up a secret compartment in the library. After Jay typed in the code, two of the wood panels parted and revealed a huge state of the art security monitor. It showed what was going on in every part of the house. He had upgraded the security system in and around his estate after that prick Smoke had broke into Wise's house and tied up his wife and daughter, Fatima and Falynn. Cas and Wise had beefed up their security as well. They had the same systems installed. None of their family members would ever become victims of a home invasion and robbery again.

Jay zoomed in on the studio, where he figured Jayquan and Wise were. He hit the nail on the head. His son and his bro were in the studio bobbing their heads as if they were listening to something hot. Lil' Jay had recently expressed an interest in making music, so Jay got him everything he needed to make it. He honestly didn't want his boy trying to be a rap star, but he wasn't into dream-killing either. As long as he went to school and did the right thing, Jay would give him anything he wanted. Lil' Jay was actually getting good at making beats. He had let Jay listen to some stuff he'd made and it wasn't half bad.

Jay grinned at how engaged Jayquan appeared. Maybe they were on to something. He got up from his desk and headed that way. As Jay neared the studio he heard a bass line bumping. He'd had the walls soundproofed but you could still hear a little bass when you got close. Jay opened the door and walked in. The twosome grinned and each got up and gave him a pound.

After his father came in, Jayquan started to turn the volume down. Jay stopped him because he wanted to listen as well. He knew his mini-me was showing off for his uncle, but he wanted to see what his offspring had to offer.

When the track cut off, Jay and Wise both gave it up. That was pretty good for a kid who had only been producing for a few months. Jayquan beamed at their praises proudly and stood up a little taller. It was obvious that the young man valued being respected. Jay beamed at that proudly. He was trying to raise a man.

Jay, Wise, and Jayquan lingered in the studio for a while and talked about the business. They discussed the "posthumous" album Wise was dropping soon, and then headed for the kitchen. Jay looked in the microwave for the plate he knew his wife had fixed him. It was there just as he'd predicted, covered in aluminum foil. Portia was always on it. Every time she decided not to cook she gave him a heads up before he got home. As Jay heated his food, he asked Wise if he had heard from Cas.

Wise grinned. "Yeah, my nigga said he supposed to be released from the hospital tomorrow. If all goes well, God willing."

When Jayquan heard that his face lit up. "Uncle Cas comin' home? Yes!"

Jay nodded happily. "Word! My dude comin' home. Wise, man, you hungry?"

Jayquan excused himself. "I'm out, y'all. Good night." He gave his dad and uncle a pound before he broke out. His father grabbed him and kissed him on the forehead. "Yeah, yeah, love you too, Pop."

Jay laughed. "Love you more, baby boy. Go to bed."

Jayquan ignored his father's last sentence. He went upstairs to tell Macy the good news about Cas. She was upstairs watching television. She and her baby sister, Skye, had been staying there since Cas had been in the hospital.

After Lil' Jay left, Wise thought of the best way to tell Jay about the dirt he had on their whorish wives. Jay would probably lose his appetite when he found out, so Wise decided to let his bro finish his meal before he spilled the beans.

Jay washed his hands and then he sat on a stool at the island counter and prepared to dig in. He noticed that Wise kept on looking at him. It was obvious that he had something on his mind. "Son, what's going on?"

Though Wise was tempted to talk, he contained himself so Jay could enjoy his food. "Eat, man. I'll wait until you done."

Jay raised an eyebrow. "What's wrong? Everybody good?"

Wise didn't mean to alarm Jay in that way. He quickly dismissed the notion that someone was sick or hurt. "Yeah, man, it ain't nothin' like *that*."

Jay peered at Wise for a second and then he bowed his head and said his grace. When he was done, he looked at Wise again and began to chow down. Jay didn't realize how hungry he was until he tasted the pineapple-glazed grilled salmon, brown rice, and broccoli Portia had prepared. He'd had a hearty lunch earlier that day but the drinks he'd had at the Honeycomb had burned up all the food in his stomach.

Wise was silent while Jay dined, but he had some loud and disturbing thoughts running through his head. The sound of Fatima's sex moans reverberated in his ears. He could see her and hear her getting slammed fucked by Five. The godforsaken visions were so vivid in his mind, Wise literally tried to shake them out.

Jay watched as Wise shook his head and wondered what the hell was going on. He could tell something was bothering him, so he urged him to speak on it. "Man, what you lookin' all constipated for? Go ahead and say what's on your mind."

Wise sighed and got up and started pacing back and forth. It looked like he was really stressed about something. Jay got impatient with him. "Son, what the fuck is going on?"

Wise sighed exasperatedly and shook his head. "Man ..." He groaned in agony and commenced to share his pain. "Son, I overheard this bitch Fatima on the phone with Portia talkin' 'bout how she let that nigga Five beat that time her and Portia went to L.A."

Jay made a face. That was the last thing he had expected Wise to say. "What? Are you kiddin' me?"

"Nah, I'm dead ass." Wise was visibly upset. "This bitch don't even know I heard her. I goes home to surprise her – you know, rub her feet and shit, like she be complaining I don't do. And I hear this bullshit." He shook his head. "Hoe ass bitch!"

Wise had Jay thinking. Portia and Fatima went to California together. If Wise was right about Fatima fucking with Five, Jay wondered where Portia was while it happened.

Wise stood there and fought another series of hallucinations of Fatima sexing a bunch of random guys. The horror played in his head again and again, clear like HDTV. It was so painful, Wise thought about killing that nigga Five. He took a deep breath and attempted to regroup. "Jay, man, this shit got me so tight I'm ready to put foot to that bitch ass! Tima lucky she pregnant, son. Word." He nodded for emphasis.

Jay felt Wise on that, but he had to be fair. "I understand that you mad, but in Tima's defense, she thought you were dead at the time. You can't blame her for moving on eventually. And it must've just been a onetime thing because I never even heard nothin' about that."

Wise shrugged. He gave what Jay said the benefit of a doubt. "A'ight, maybe Tima *did* think I was dead. I'll give her that. I hate to piss on your parade, but what about Portia?"

Jay put his fork down and looked at Wise. "What? What about her?"

"Fatima said Portia fucked with Vino. She said she would never tell on Portia because you would kill her if you found out."

Jay kept a straight face but he was so shocked he couldn't speak for a moment. Not on no sucker shit, but he felt faint. It was as if the wind had been knocked out of him. What the fuck was Wise talking about? Not his wife.

Jay thought back to the time he'd seen a late-night text Fatima had sent Portia. That happened a while ago. That night he and Portia had just returned from having dinner with Vino and Five. In the text, Fatima had asked if she and Portia were "safe." Jay had wondered at the time what Fatima meant by that. Now it all made sense.

Jay was seething. Though the news Wise bore was a pretty hard gut-punch, the main reason he was pissed was that he had paid Five and Vino some racks to look after the girls. Portia and Fatima had gone out to L.A. to line up that foul chick, Callie, who had stolen Fatima's identity and money. They didn't know anyone out there, so Jay had figured they could use a couple of allies. He felt nauseous. The notion that he had paid a nigga to run up in his wife was disheartening. He almost lost his supper. If Wise was correct, Portia was a fucking slut.

Wise could tell his speechless homie was upset. Over the years they had been friends, they'd grown to know one another well. Wise knew Jay's fury was usually the silent kind. That characteristic made him a dangerous man. Wise said, "Look, my bad for messin' up your mood, son. I just thought you should know."

Jay nodded. Contrary to his raging emotions, his exterior was pretty calm. "Wise, you better know what you talkin' about. Don't get this bitch killed for nothin'. Are you sure, man? Exactly what did you hear?"

Wise took a seat. "I know what I heard. Fatima said …" He switched to a high-pitched mock-female voice. "Portia, I ain't even gon' talk about what Jay would do to your ass if he knew about Vino. You'd have two different sets of holes in your ass. So don't worry, I would *never* tell on you."

Jay sat there silent for a minute. It was probably true. He felt like a damn fool. He had actually financed the couple-fucking those bitches did.

Wise looked like he was disgusted. "Son, I don't put nothin' pass a bitch. Women are way slicker than we are."

"You absolutely right," Jay agreed. He maintained a poker face but the twitch in his jaw muscles and the vein popping out of the side of his head and neck indicated that he was fuming.

Wise was upset about that bullshit but he didn't gain any pleasure from making Jay miserable as well. For a second, he regretted telling him. Wise got up and announced his departure. "Jay, man, I'm about to slide off and get me some head, or something. I guess that's better than me taking my frustration out on my pregnant, hoe ass wife."

Jay stood up as well. He dumped his half-eaten plate in the trashcan in the corner. After getting that news, his appetite was a thing of the past. "Man, you need to change your itinerary and take your ass home."

Wise made a screw face and spat, "Nah, I might do somethin' to that bitch, son."

"So, just chill over here then." Sometimes Jay worried about the way Wise moved. He didn't want him to be recognized by someone.

Wise sighed and shook his head. "I'm good, man. This shit ain't nothin'."

Jay walked him to the door and gave him a pound. "Be safe, man, wherever you headed."

Wise said his thoughts out loud. "I should go home and grudge-fuck the shit outta Tima. Smut that bitch out, since she wanna be a fuckin' hoe!"

Jay shook his head. Wise was a mess.

Wise looked at him closely. "Son, you seem to be handling this shit pretty well. I know you tight, though. Don't fuck around and flip out in this mo'fucka tonight."

Jay stuck his hands in his pockets and didn't respond. He wasn't going to make any promises.

CHAPTER FOURTEEN

When Wise left, the first thing Jay did was fix himself a stiff drink. He sat at the dining table and stared off into space while he replayed Wise's words in his head. Though Jay was pretty much convinced that Portia had been with Vino, a small part of him was in denial. She couldn't be that foul.

Jay knew he was married to a good woman. Portia was a classy broad that had always been a great wife. She was an excellent mom and she played her part as the matriarch well. No one could fill her shoes. Portia had made Jay's life easier and better, ever since way back when Jayquan's mother, Stacy, had passed away. Portia had stepped up and helped him raise his son. Jay loved her for that. His children loved her too; all four of them.

Jay poured himself another drink and sat there in silence. No music, no television, no nothing. All he heard was his thoughts, which were loud and clear. Portia could've been leading a double life the whole time they had been together. He met her in a strip club, so he knew she was loose. Hell, maybe she would always be a hoe. Perhaps he'd put too much trust in her.

Jay had worked hard and built a castle-like home for his family and had established an empire. He felt he had earned the right to call himself a king. There was no doubt about that. But he wondered now if he had chosen the right queen. There was no way he would stay married to a bitch that would screw one of his associates. Especially one that he'd compensated to look after her.

That shit hurt every time Jay thought about it. Literally. He attempted to numb himself with another shot, but the pain in his chest and abdomen still overpowered the top-shelf liquor. How could he stay married to a woman who had done him so dirty? He was ready to lay hands on Portia and then shove a gun in Vino's mouth. Jay was hopping mad but he took a deep breath and tried to remain levelheaded.

After much thought, he came to the conclusion that he would give his wife the benefit of a doubt. He should at least ask Portia about the situation before he assumed she was guilty. They had been together for over ten years. Ten good years. Jay finished the shot he'd poured and then headed upstairs to him and Portia's bedroom.

He walked in and saw Portia in their king-size four poster bed fast asleep. Their youngest three children were all in bed with her as well. Jaylin slept in the crook of one of Portia's arms and Trixie slept in the crook of the other. Jazz lay beside them. Jay glimpsed at the clock on the nightstand. It was after two AM.

Portia wore pink polka dot pajamas. She looked so cute and innocent, she pissed Jay off. She was laying there looking like Suzie Fucking Homemaker. Jay got angrier and angrier by the second. He considered choking Portia out in her sleep, but his kids laying there with her made him think twice. He didn't want to do anything stupid, but he had to question Portia and make her tell him the truth.

Jay tapped Portia on the foot so he wouldn't wake the kids. She moved a little bit but she didn't open her eyes. Portia had her hands full all day, so Jay knew she was tired.

He wouldn't have disturbed her rest under normal circumstances, but the subject matter at hand was pretty damn urgent. He had to know if she had fucked around on him. He tapped her on the foot again, harder that time.

Portia opened her eyes and looked up at Jay. She sleepily blinked a few times and then she looked down at the little ones. When she realized they were all okay, she carefully removed her arms from under Trixie and Jaylin so she wouldn't disturb them. Portia looked alarmed. She sat up and asked, "Baby, what's wrong? Is Jayquan alright?"

"Yeah, he's in his room." Jay took a deep breath and sighed. "Get up, P. I need to talk to you."

"What's wrong, baby? What's going on? Is everybody okay, Jay?"

"Everybody's fine. Just get up, P. Now!"

Portia was worried so she whispered a prayer as she got up. She hoped that nothing bad had happened, but she didn't ask any questions. Portia knew not to be too inquisitive from the time she'd met Jay. He'd been involved in some unethical activities, so she had learned early on. Portia rubbed her eyes and waited on Jay to clarify all the confusion. He just glared at her like he wanted to slap her and pushed her toward the bathroom. Portia wondered what she had done.

In the bathroom, Jay looked at her and spoke sternly. "P, I'ma ask you somethin'. I want you to think very carefully before you answer me. And don't lie to me. Under no circumstances. You understand?"

Portia didn't know where Jay was going but she nodded in agreement. "Okay."

"When you and Fatima went to L.A. that time, did you fuck around on me?" Jay looked in Portia's eyes to analyze her reaction.

Portia was completely surprised. She prayed she had heard Jay wrong. "What? Jay, what are you talkin' about?"

The thought of another man sexing Portia was crippling, but Jay had to know. "Did you mess with Vino, Portia? Answer the question."

Portia stood there dumbfounded for a second. She wondered how the hell Jay knew that. Fatima couldn't be that damn careless. Vino neither. No one else knew except Five. Portia wondered if he was the culprit.

When Portia didn't respond, Jay knew it was true. He bit his lip and shook his head in disbelief. "Damn, you ain't even gon' try to lie? Not even attempt to, huh?"

Portia's good sense kicked back in. "Jay, are you serious? You gotta be kidding me. I ain't mess with no damn Vino! That's what you woke me up for? Who put this crazy shit in your head?"

Jay was so mad it hurt. "Oh, *now* you gon' lie. I know you did it, P. Tell me the fuckin' truth!"

Portia's wanted to get down on her knees and tell him how sorry she was, and then beg for his forgiveness, but there was too much at stake. There was no way she would cop to that one. "Jay, I'm not even gonna entertain this crazy shit. I ain't mess with *nobody,* so I don't know what you talkin' about!" Portia put up a cool front but her heart beat had tripled. It wasn't a game. She could be staring death in the face, because the look in Jay's eyes said he wasn't all there.

Portia would go down with the ship before she surrendered and told on herself. She knew Jay would never forgive her, so she stuck to her guns and didn't admit shit. Jay didn't look like he was in his usual state of mind. Portia sensed that he was about to strike her so she instinctively backed away from him.

When Portia started inching toward the door, Jay took that to be disrespectful. He wasn't finished with her. He grabbed her by the neck and chastised her as if she was an unruly child. "Where the fuck are you goin'? You don't *ever* walk away from me! Don't you fuckin' dare! Didn't I tell you not to lie to me, Portia?"

Portia couldn't believe Jay had choked her. Her husband had gone mad. She pried his hands from her throat and yelled, "Jay, get off me! Have you lost your mind?"

Jay was so vexed he saw red. He forgot who Portia was and violently shook her by the shoulders. "No, *bitch*," he spat venomously. "*You* done lost your fuckin' mind! You think I won't fuck you up in here? Just 'cause I was so fuckin' good to you all these years?" He wrapped his hands around Portia's neck again and squeezed harder.

Portia gasped for air. She was really frightened. She desperately searched Jay's eyes for some type of mercy, but there was none. His soul windows had the shades pulled down. He was so cold Portia didn't even recognize him. "Jay, please, I can't breathe! Let go of my neck!"

"Shut the fuck up, I should kill yo' ass!" Jay threatened.

Portia struggled to free herself from his death grip and kept on pleading with him. He had turned into a raving maniac. "Jay, stop before you do something you gon' regret! Are you *crazy*?"

Jay stuck his finger in her face accusingly. "Bitch, I regret marrying your ass! You a trifling ass trick. I should've left you in the fuckin' club!"

As Portia fought for air, her husband offered no apologies. Jay had clearly blacked out. Portia didn't believe he would intentionally kill her with their children in the next room, but she couldn't seem to get through to him. Her only option was to knock some sense into him. Portia drew back her arm and went upside Jay's head with an open-handed slap.

Portia hit him so hard he could taste it. Jay let go of her neck and looked at her like she was out of her mind. That slap just made him angrier. Jay drew back his fist and started to punch her in the fucking face. Portia cringed, closed her eyes, and covered her face with her arms. That punch would've probably taken her head off so God granted her mercy. Jay opted to hit the wall instead. His fist slammed through the thick sheetrock as if it was newspaper.

Portia stared open-mouthed at the big hole Jay had knocked in their bathroom wall. She thanked God that wasn't her face. She tried to run into the bedroom but Jay grabbed her and shoved her. Portia stumbled and fell against the wall. She hurt her shoulder and cried out in pain.

Jay was unsympathetic about her injury, so Portia ran into him swinging. Jay grabbed her and tried to subdue her, but she wasn't having it. The couple started tussling. In the process they knocked down a few things, including a shelf full of toiletries. During their struggle they winded up on the floor.

Jay and Portia woke up the kids with their noise. Portia heard Jaylin screaming in the bedroom. The next thing they knew, Jazz and Trixie stared at them in the bathroom doorway. Both little girls were upset. Trixie was crying her little heart out, and Jazz hollered, "Daddy, stop it! Get off my mommy! Please!"

Next, Jayquan came running in there. When he realized Jay and Portia were fighting, he looked shocked.

"Pop, chill! You wildin' in here!" He rushed over and pulled his parents apart.

When his son grabbed him, Jay spun around and grabbed him by his shirt. "Go somewhere and mind your business, boy," he snarled. "Take your sisters and get outta here."

"*What*? Pop, are you *serious*? You violatin'! That's my mother!"

Lil' Jay hit a spot when he used the "m" word. Jay was so heated he wasn't thinking straight. He got in his face and said, "You know what, son? Your mother's a whore! Don't marry a fuckin' hoe!"

Jayquan looked at Jay like *"really?"* His father's words cut him deep. He shook his head in disbelief. "Don't ever disrespect my moms like that. You disrespected me and my little sisters as well, so I'ma ask you to apologize, Pop. That was totally unnecessary."

Jay looked at that little dude like he was crazy. Who the hell did Jayquan think he was talking to? Jay knew there was some truth to his words so he paused for a second to decide how he should handle it. Everybody else in the bathroom got quiet as well. You could've heard a pin drop in there. Jay knew Portia and the kids were waiting for him to react. The tension was so thick you could've sliced it like a pie.

Jay looked around at his kids. They each stared at him like they were terrified. They must've thought he'd gone stark raving mad. Although Jay didn't appreciate the fact that his son had challenged him that way, he calmed himself down. Being pissed off at Portia had taken him completely out of his character. Jay glowered at his traitor-for-a-wife and then he just walked out of the bathroom without another word.

He glanced back and saw the kids crowding around Portia. They were comforting her and asking if she was okay. Portia was trying to hush and calm them all down. Jay heard Jazz say, "Mommy, what's wrong with Daddy? Why was he so mean to you?" He heard Jaylin crying as he left the bedroom.

Jay had walked off so he could cool down. He was in his feelings entirely too much. He didn't usually display emotions that way. Jay felt like a real creep for the way he'd behaved in front of his children. He was generally a laidback dude who took pride in being a good example for his kids, so the fact that they'd seen him so irate bothered him. He didn't parent that way.

Jay realized where he had gone wrong. He had approached Portia when he should've been on his way to step to that little nigga Vino. If he had handled the situation that way, he would've avoided appearing like a monster to his kids.

All Vino had to do was take that money and look after Portia when she went out there. He had contravened the direct orders Jay gave him with a direct slap in the face, so now that mothafucka needed to be dealt with directly.

Infuriated, Jay made his way to his gun cabinet. He would never let a nigga violate him that way and get away with it. It was time for him and Vino to have a little Q & A session. Depending on the answers Jay received, there could be some spanking in order. Or bloodshed even. It was just that serious.

CHAPTER FIFTEEN

Loud sirens blared in the distance and echoed Jay's mood. He was turned up. But as he drove through the darkness en route to confront the backstabber he had trusted with his wife, he was consumed by a quiet rage. The thought of another man inside of Portia drove him mad. As much as Jay hated to admit it at the time, Portia was one of his most prized possessions. That shit had him ready to hurt something.

If Vino had slept with his wife, he had some balls. That mothafucka may as well have spit in his face. Jay thought about the fight he had with Portia before he had left the house, and frowned. He was ready to air that shit out. He unconsciously patted the black .45 in his waist.

Jay was doing over ninety on the highway. He knew he was speeding but at the time he didn't care. The alcohol he'd consumed and the fury he felt had disabled his better judgment. He flew through the night in his black Ferrari like it was a battle bound chariot. A few minutes later, he pulled up outside of Vino's crib.

Ms. B had arranged for Vino to rent the condo that Cas had purchased when he and Kira split up. Jay knew it was late but he wanted to speak to that dude so bad he was ready to snatch that nigga up out the bed. He pictured himself shoving a hammer in his mouth.

As Jay was in the process of parking his car, he glanced up and saw a girl coming out of Vino's building. She reminded him a lot of his little sister. The resemblance was so uncanny he sat up and looked closer. He realized it really was Kira. "What the fuck?" He wondered what she was doing over there.

As angry as Jay was, one thing he absolutely would not do was involve Kira in his business. Not in his marital affairs anyhow. There was no way. He guessed a little part of him wasn't sure if he and Portia were done. He didn't need Kira to make the drama brewing boil over. Regardless of what had happened, Portia was still his wife.

Vino had no idea but he owed Kira a lot. When Jay saw his sister come out, he peeled off. Jay couldn't explain the reason Kira was there any more than he could explain a UFO sighting, but she had stopped him from reacting irrationally. He had to use his noodles when he confronted Vino. He was angry and inebriated at the time. He didn't move like that. Acting out of emotion usually led to repercussions. Such mindless behavior could get a man killed.

$$$$$

The following morning, Wise drove along the highway home. It was such a bright and sunny day out, he had squinted eyes. The sunlight was probably blinding him so much because he'd gotten white boy-wasted the night before. Most likely, his pupils were still dilated.

Wise made sure he drove right, though. He constantly reminded himself that he was supposed to be deceased, and made it a point to avoid any police contact. He had all the necessary items to prove his new identity: a driver's license, birth certificate, social security card, you name it. But he still had no desire to interact with any law enforcement. He was playing it safe. It would be just his luck that he would get pulled over, and someone would recognize him. He had been successful thus far in keeping a low profile, thank God. He intended to keep that up.

It had been a long night. Wise knew he was dead wrong for going home after sunrise, but he had done so intentionally. He was pissed off at Fatima for fucking around on him. Adultery was unacceptable and unforgivable. Never mind that he'd cheated on Fatima so many times. That was different. He was a man.

To repay his loose wife, Wise had spent the wee hours of the morning getting his balls licked by his side chick – Nurse Lily. He knew that was immature but he had been so pissed off he had to do something. That was supposed to be his get-back at Fatima but it didn't make him feel any better. Lily had pressed him to leave home every chance she got, which got on his nerves. Especially when all he thought about was Fatima.

Wise had been preoccupied with thoughts of Fatima's infidelity the whole time he was driving home, so he hadn't noticed the car that was following him. Oblivious, he turned down the private road that led to his property. He stopped at the security gate that surrounded his estate to punch in the code of entry. Wise had had the gate installed after Fatima's homegirl Callie had set her up for her boyfriend. That creep had got into the house and tied Fatima and Falynn up and robbed them. He would've killed them if Wise hadn't have showed up from the "dead" and rectified the problem.

As Wise punched in the access code, he replayed the way he had crept up on that lowlife and popped him in the dome. Wise had disguised himself in a dreadlock wig and got there just in time. His heroic efforts had saved his daughter's life. The gate lifted with ease and Wise continued down his driveway. He watched the gate close in his rearview mirror. The car that had been tailing him drove past his road and made a u-turn. The driver parked a few hundred feet down the road.

When Wise walked in the house, Fatima was getting Falynn ready for school. She had been waiting on Wise to come home all night, but she bit her tongue until her daughter left. Once Falynn got on the school bus it was on. Wise had the gall to come in smelling like perfume and liquor. Fatima couldn't wait to let him have it.

She and Wise saw their baby off to school like perfect parents, and then Fatima bared her fangs and dug her claws into her monogamy-challenged husband with no mercy. "Welcome home, you bastard! You didn't even have the decency to try to beat the sun. You smell like booze and ass, Wise. You stink! And you left your phone home last night, *idiot*. Your *bitch* called. And I put her in her fuckin' place!"

Wise smirked at her. "Yeah, she told me." He said that just to be an asshole.

Fatima screw-faced him and demanded, "And how did you speak to her?" A light bulb came on in her head and she realized that was an admission of guilt. Wise had spoke to the bitch in person. Fatima glared at him and went off. "Nigga, you been with that bitch all night? You smell just like after-sex, you disrespectful mothafucka!"

Wise wasn't sorry one bit. He scoffed, "You better be glad I went out. I started to come back here and kill yo' ass!"

"Excuse me? You crazy, cheating piece of shit, you got mental problems. I can't stand your ass!" Fatima shook her head as if he was pathetic.

Wise felt guilty for a second and then he got angry. "What? You're the fuckin' cheater! I can't stand *you*! You cheated on me and fucked that nigga Five! You ain't think I knew that, did you?"

Fatima was so surprised you could've knocked her over with a feather. "What? Boy, you don't know shit! Where you get *that* from?"

"I heard you say it, that's where! You told on yourself, stupid ass!"

Fatima had the dumb face for a moment. That bastard had overheard her on the phone with Portia. Wow. She was caught so she opted to plead the fifth. She had given up enough self-incriminating information.

Wise glared at Fatima and shook his head contemptuously. "Look at you lookin' all stupid. Yeah, that's what the fuck I thought, hoe! I know about your homegirl Portia too. And I already let my bro know."

Fatima's eyes popped at his last sentence. "Wise, are you fuckin' serious? How could you do that? You try'na get my friend killed, nigga?"

Wise looked at Fatima like she was from another planet. "Bitch, is you crazy? You got the nerve to try to make this about *that*? Y'all hoes ain't have no business out there throwin' pussy no way!"

"You don't know *what* happened out there!" Fatima asserted.

Wise didn't back down. "I know what you *said*! I know what I *heard*!"

"You don't know *shit*! What the fuck you tell Jay that for? That ain't even true! Portia didn't mess with nobody!"

"You up in here defending Portia. What about you, hoe? I see you ain't denying fuckin' that nigga Five. I wonder why that is? You fuckin' *hoe*! Damn, is that my baby?"

Wise may as well have spit on Fatima when he said that. She gave him the eye of death. "Look, I was letting you vent, but you starting to talk stupid now. Why would you even say that?"

"Why would you fuck that nigga?"

Fatima sighed. "I was wrong about that, but don't forget I thought you were no longer here, Wise. So that's not fair. Technically, I did not cheat on you. I thought you were dead at the time. Marriage is 'til death do us part, and I honored that! I never cheated on you before that."

Wise quickly disputed that. "Yeah, not with no *dude*. But you cheated. Remember when I caught you out by the pool gettin' your fuckin' pussy eaten by a bitch? When you was like *'run Raven, run!'* Remember *that*?"

Fatima rolled her eyes. She couldn't deny that one because Wise had caught her red-handed. "Whatever. That's not the same!"

"Yes the fuck it is! I should've put a slug in that bitch's ass! And one in your ass too! Hoe ass dyke bitch!"

Fatima and Wise had a very unique relationship. At times they could be pretty ratched. Wise called her names sometimes and sometimes she called him names too. Fatima was okay with that. She knew Wise loved her, so if he called her a bitch every now and then, she let it slide. She knew he was pissed off about her screwing Five, but enough was enough. She was sick of hearing about it. Fatima scowled at Wise. "Are you done, you filthy mouthed, disrespectful piece of shit? I'm your wife, asshole! The mother of your two children! You better not forget that!"

Wise glared at her and left the room. On his way out, he mumbled, "Fuckin' bitch!"

"That'll be *Mrs.* Bitch, thank you," she yelled at his back. "And don't forget I have a doctor's appointment this morning!"

Wise's response was filled with sarcasm. "Get your baby father to go with you!"

Fatima rolled her eyes. That asshole didn't know what to say. She grabbed her cell phone and went to go call Portia. She went out back by the pool so she could talk without Wise eavesdropping. It was chilly out there but it was a bright and sunny day. Portia's phone rang four times before she picked up.

"Hey, Tima," Portia said sadly.

Portia sounded down. Fatima took that as a bad sign. "P, what up? You good, boo?"

"No, sis. I'm *not* good. What the hell happened, Tima?"

"P, I'm so sorry! Wise crept in the house while we were on the phone! And then he left right back out, so I ain't even know he heard me. I should've been looking at the security monitors 'cause this nigga heard everything. His black ass ain't come home last night, and then he gon' come up in here talking all reckless and shit. This dude is real disrespectful. I let him vent because I know it hurt him to hear about me and Five. But he got one more time to call me outta my name. I'ma cut this bastard up in here, P." Fatima got quiet for a moment. "I guess he told Jay, huh?"

Portia sighed wearily. "I guess so… Yo, Jay straight flipped, sis! Shit, I thought he was gonna kill me! The kids woke up and they were hollering and shit. Girl, Jay was so mad he punched through the fuckin' wall in the bathroom. I know he did that to keep from bashing my brains in, but he probably fucked his hand up. I hope it ain't broke or nothin'. He left the house right after we got into it, so I don't know." The situation had Portia dismayed. "This is messed up, Tima. What if Jay gets into it with Vino behind this? I'm scared, sis. I can't believe this shit came out after all this time."

Fatima felt horrible that she had stirred it up. "Damn, my bad, P. Did you admit or deny it?"

"Bitch, I denied it! You crazy? Jay was mad enough to kill me!"

Fatima shook her head. That was all her fault. She apologized to Portia again. "P, I swear I didn't mean for this shit to happen. I'ma fix this, boo. Don't ask me how, but I promise I'ma fix it."

"I dunno know if this can be fixed, Tima." Portia was on the verge of tears. "What if it's too late? What if I lost my husband behind this?"

Fatima could've kicked herself. Empathy for her distraught girlfriend sent her pregnancy hormones into overdrive and made her eyes tear up as well. If she had destroyed Portia and Jay's marriage, she would never forgive herself. She had to figure out a way to make things right.

CHAPTER SIXTEEN

Fatima sat in her obstetrician's waiting room ensconced in a plush red mommy-friendly chair. As she waited on her name to be called, she thought about Wise. She couldn't believe he had refused to accompany her because she had messed with Five two years ago. Wise was being a hypocrite. He had cheated on her numerous times. Fatima felt like he should just get over it, especially because of the circumstances. At the time she thought he was dead and gone.

Fatima was upset with Wise as much as he was pissed at her. He had been missing the night before. She knew he was with that bitch and it ate her up. Fatima tried not to think about it because every time she got upset, the baby got upset. She could feel her little man inside of her kicking up a storm. Fatima rubbed her belly soothingly and coaxed him. "Everything's okay, lil' man. Mommy's sorry. It's all about you now, papa." It was as if the baby heard her. He quit kicking and settled down. Fatima smiled to herself. She and her son were already in touch.

Despite an attempt not to, Fatima thought about her selfish ass husband again. Regardless of what had happened, he should've come with her to the doctor. Wise was on some bullshit. "Fuck him too," Fatima mumbled to herself. After she was done at the doctor's, she was heading over to Portia's place to see about her. To hell with Wise.

Wise being absent gave Fatima the opportunity to do some research on something she had been contemplating for a while. She didn't want Wise to know, but she wanted to have her labor induced early to avoid anymore damage to her figure. Fatima didn't want to gain anymore weight than she already had. She also did not want to be judged about her decision, so she had kept it to herself.

Fatima made no secret about the fact that she'd had some work done. Everyone close to her knew about her plastic surgery. Portia had even teased her about it before. She called her Nip & Tuck. Fatima had gone under the knife because she was self-conscious about her weight. The premise of being overweight bothered her, especially when her homegirls had it so together. She didn't want to be the fat one in the crew.

Fatima reminded herself that Portia and Laila had worked hard to lose their post-baby weight. They worked even harder to maintain their figures. Pilates, aerobics – All the shit Fatima hated. That's why she cheated her way to perfection. Having money made being fabulous a lot easier.

Fatima rubbed her belly. She was ready to drop that load and get it over with. Wise was acting up, so she needed to get right so she could fight for her husband. He had run to the arms of another woman for solace. That was something Fatima would not make light of. She had gone to hell and back with Wise, and she loved him enough to do it all again. She couldn't lose him to some bitch. Wise was a part of her.

Fatima didn't plan on being pregnant any longer than she had to. She was glad she was having a son. That knucklehead Wise would have the boy he'd always wanted. She just needed to speed up the process. She decided to speak to her doctor to see about having her labor induced.

Before she could think about it any further, she heard her name being called to see the doctor.

An hour later, Fatima was done with her sonogram and examination. She left the doctor's office armed with adorable 3-D pictures of her baby and the knowledge she needed to make her decision about the labor induction she was contemplating. Fatima's doctor was against it but she admitted she'd seen it done before. Her exact words were, "But not without complications. So I suggest you let the bun in the oven brown a little longer." Fatima appreciated the doctor's professional opinion but she decided she would do some research online.

She exited the building and didn't realize she was being watched. The same car that had followed Wise home earlier that morning had tailed Fatima to the doctor. Sitting at the wheel was a disgruntled woman that hated her for reasons she believed were justified.

Lily had been with Wise the whole night before. He had shown up at her door unexpected and wound up staying over. She had taken the surprise visit as an indication that he was coming around. Lily believed Wise had come because he wanted to be with her. That assumption gave her the courage to have the talk. She stared off into space and replayed the scenario in her mind

After a few drinks, Lily switched off the hip-hop she'd been playing and put on something soft. The slow jams mixed tape she had created exclusively for the occasion kicked off with the song "I Want You" by Marvin Gaye. She swayed her hips to the beat and sauntered over to Wise and wrapped her arms around his neck. She put her lips to his ears and started the conversation with lines she had been rehearsing for weeks.

"Baby, nothing feels better than being in your arms. I am so in love with you! You're the soul mate I prayed for God to send me. I wanna take care of you and grow old with you. I know what you need, baby, and I wanna be there to make sure you always have it. Boo, let's get outta here. I purchased some land on the beach in Puerto Rico – so we can build our dream house. I already put things in motion. It won't be long before we can just frolic on the beach by day and make love under the stars all night." After she had offered him the opportunity to escape with her to paradise, Lily smiled at him expectantly and waited for him to agree.

It was obvious that Wise didn't buy into the bohemian fantasy she'd tried to sell him. He had looked at her like she was crazy. He said, "Lily, we not about to run away together. I can't just run away and live carefree. I have a family! I'm about to have a son soon. So, I'm sorry but that's just not something I can give you."

Lily felt like he stabbed her in the chest. She detested his loyalty but she told herself he just needed a bit more convincing. She had smiled and played if off and then attempted to sex the thoughts of his wife and kids out of his head. Wise had stayed with her all night but he didn't seem so convinced the following morning. Before he left, Lily had hugged him and asked him to reconsider going with her to Puerto Rico.

Wise had gotten annoyed that time. He shook her off and responded, "Stop fuckin' stressing me about that! You know I can't go with you to no Puerto Rico!"

Lily had recoiled in disappointment. She realized then that his mind had been across town with his wife all night. She wondered what that bitch had over her.

When Wise left her house that morning, Lily had jumped in her car and followed him home. She told herself that she just wanted to see where he lived, but for some reason she hid out by his house for hours. She'd even considered knocking on Wise's door, but she didn't know what would come of it. She doubted he would appreciate that.

Lily had spoken to Wise's wife the day before, when the bitch had answered his phone. She had told Lily to give up and move on. Lily had thought about taking her advice, but then Wise showed up at her door wanting to have sex. She had believed she had the sexual prowess to make him leave home, but realization dawned on her and showed her otherwise.

As Fatima walked out of the doctor's office, Lily sat in the parking lot watching her through binoculars. She was overcome with envy when she saw exactly how pregnant Fatima was. Fatima felt fat and out of shape, but in Lily's eyes she was beautiful in her voluptuous, with-child state. Lily wished she was the one about to pop with Wise's baby. She stared at his wife and was reminded of the child Wise had forced her to abort. The child they had conceived in love.

Lily hated Fatima simply because she was married to the man she loved. The big belly she had only made matters worse. Lily was crushed and determined to change things.

CHAPTER SEVENTEEN

Jay opened his eyes and squinted at the sunlight shining through the blinds on the window to his right. He slowly sat up and looked around the strange room he just woke up in. He was unaware of his surroundings, and his head hurt something terrible. He realized he was in a hotel room. And for some reason, his right hand was throbbing in pain. He wiggled it and noticed that his knuckles were bruised and swollen.

Jay's stomach was upset too. He burped, and was grossed out by the aftertaste of the alcohol he had consumed the night before. He had really overdone it. Jay yawned and stretched, and then he got up to go take a piss. His body ached like he had been jumped and stomped out by a crew of angry, steel-toe-shoe wearing midgets.

On the way to the bathroom, it all came back to him. Jay remembered he got drunk and grilled Portia about an alleged affair Wise came through and informed him about. When she denied it, he got pissed and punched clean through the bathroom wall. That was why his hand hurt so badly. After that emotional dummy move, he drove to Vino's house to confront him about Portia. He had seen Kira come out of Vino's building, and had changed his mind and broke out. Then he decided to check into a nearby hotel.

The W Hotel was a nice elite spot. Jay had rented a suite fit for a king, but the situation was a royal pain in the ass. After he had checked in, he'd spent the remainder of the morning sleepless and miserable. Jay had pictured himself hurting Vino over and over. He had a bad temper, so it was good that he'd given himself time to cool off. Seeing Kira was a blessing in disguise. There was no telling what he would've done if he hadn't seen his sister. He didn't want to kill that boy. Definitely not over no woman. It wasn't that serious.

Jay was too classy to go out like that. What did he look like banging on some dude's door at three in the morning and accusing him of sleeping with his wife, two years ago? There was no way he'd ever let a nigga see him that far off his A-game. He was a boss. He wasn't pressed. If he had a wife that was that easy to get in the sack, he didn't need the bitch.

Jay had barely slept a wink. Although he was still tired, that morning he showered and checked out of the suite. Cas was supposed to be released from the hospital that day. Jay had high hopes of it coming to pass, so he made tracks across town to see about his right-hand man. Along the way there, he made some important business calls.

When Jay got to the hospital, Cas's room door was closed. Instead of just barging in, he courteously knocked three times.

A woman's voice called out, "Come in."

Jay grinned and pinpointed the voice immediately. That was Laila. He opened the door and walked in the room and greeted his main man with a pound and a man hug. Next, Jay hugged Laila.

Jay stood at his recovering crony's bedside beaming. "You look good, man. You look like yourself again. Word.

Are you ready to go? Or have you gotten a little attached to this place?"

Cas made a face and shook his head. "Absolutely not, man. I'ma do back flips and moonwalk out this mothafucka when they release me."

Jay imagined Cas doing acrobats and Michael Jackson dance moves as he left the hospital, and laughed out loud. Laila was tickled by the notion as well. She cracked up and joined Jay in the hilarity.

When the mirth quieted down, Jay looked sort of sad. Cas peeped the sudden mood change but he didn't comment. He could tell Jay had something heavy on his mind.

Laila had gotten to know Jay pretty well over the years. She sensed that as well. Concerned, she asked, "Jay, are you okay?"

Jay shook his head and didn't respond. He didn't want to talk about it. He had already stressed about that shit so much he didn't have the energy.

Laila saw that Jay didn't want to discuss it, so she left it alone and gave him space. She gathered Cas's belongings while they waited on the doctor to come by.

Dr. Sanji showed up a few minutes later and informed them that all of the test results had come back good. The doctor wrote Cas three prescriptions and then he presented him with his discharge papers.

Cas was a free man. When he was dressed warm enough, the trio got ready to make moves. Cas refused to ride down to the lobby in the wheelchair the nurse offered him. He opted to walk instead. Laila kissed her macho man on the head and then put a hat on him so he wouldn't catch a cold.

$$$$$

The same time Cas was getting released from the hospital, a young man was being released from a Pennsylvania state prison. The young man had been incarcerated for some time and had fantasized about getting out. But now that the day had finally come, he was a little hesitant. He was glad he was going home, but he had nothing to go home to.

Rodney was better known by his street moniker, Hot Rod. He had been christened Hot Rod by the streets due to his burning passion for stealing foreign cars. Hot Rod had been arrested at fourteen and detained as a juvenile delinquent for the majority of his teenage years. A day after he was old enough, he was sent to state prison to finish out his sentence. After he had served a total of eight years and seven months for charges that included multiple counts of auto-theft and a gang-related playground stabbing, he was finally released back into society.

Hot Rod had been caged before he got a chance to do a lot of things in life. That list included having sex. He had never made love to a woman before, so technically he was still a virgin. Getting some pussy was in the top five on his to-do list, but it wasn't his number one priority. Hot Rod had been pleasuring himself since he was fifteen, so a few more days wouldn't kill him. He'd done his time like a man and emerged from the system with one main objective. He wanted the heads of the niggas that had killed his big brothers, Powerful and Mike. Powerful and Mike Machete, AKA the Scumbag Brothers, were the only living relatives he'd had. They had both been shot dead in the streets by some Brooklyn niggas. Rumor had it they had died in two separate but related heated gun battles.

Hot Rod's brothers had been his mentors. He was left alone in the cold world to fend for himself. He didn't have any family now, and he knew who was responsible. So he was a villain with a vendetta. Hot Rod hit the bricks set out to avenge his brothers' death. It didn't get any more serious than that.

$$$$$

After Jay and Laila got Cas settled in at home, Laila noted that Jay still seemed a little glum. He smiled outwardly but ever so often a hint of sadness showed in his eyes. Jay and Cas were like brothers, so Laila knew Jay was in high spirits because Cas's homecoming was a celebration-worthy occasion. But something was pulling him down. Concerned about Jay's melancholy mood, Laila questioned him once more. "Bro, you're not yourself today. Is everything okay with you?"

Cas had been thinking the same thing. "Word, son. How come you so low? What's the deal, my nigga?"

Jay figured there was no point in hiding the news from either of them. He felt like everyone knew anyway. The whole town was probably laughing at him like he was some fucking joke. He looked at Laila and spilled the beans. "Laila, your homegirl is a hoe. Our marriage is over."

Laila's eyes popped in shock. That was some disrespectful shit. She knew Jay wasn't *that* guy, so there had to be some reasoning behind it. Prepared to defend her girlfriend at all costs, Laila stuck her nose in. "Jay, why you say that? What the hell is going on?"

Equally surprised, Cas wondered what had happened while he was hospitalized. "Son, what do you mean by that? How the fuck is your marriage over?"

"I meant just what I said. This *bitch*... Yo, ain't no turning back from this one. Portia fucked Vino!"

Cas and Laila looked at one another in disbelief. "*What*?" Laila asked. "Where you get that from?"

"From Fatima! So I *know* it's true."

Laila was confused as hell. "Hold up, lemme get this straight. You try'na tell me that Tima told you Portia screwed Vino? Jay, are you *sure*? I never heard nothin' about this. And I'm willing to bet money that that's not true. Portia would *never* do you like that!"

Jay shook his head dolefully. "I didn't wanna believe it myself. But why would someone just waste time making this up? That doesn't even make any sense."

Laila couldn't dispute that. "You right, bro. But still... There has to be some type of misunderstanding, or something. There's *no way*. I'm telling you, Jay."

"Laila, you think it's easy for me to admit this shit? You think I want it to be true?"

"Well, did you at least ask P about this?"

"Of course I did. And of course she lied." Jay shook his head in disgust. "I'm done with that broad."

"Nah, Jay, my gut is telling me there has to be a mistake."

"Well, my gut is telling me it's true! That's my *wife*! I know her."

"I know Portia too! And she *never* cheated on you, Jay! So why would she now?"

Jay sighed. He was running out of patience with Laila. "When Portia and Tima went to L.A. me and her were split up over that Ysatis bullshit. The bitch did it to get back at me! Don't you get it?" Jay shook his head angrily.

Laila just sighed. Her best friend's marriage was on the rocks and it saddened her deeply.

Jay took a deep breath and calmed down. He reminded himself that Laila wasn't the enemy. She was just worried. He sat down and dropped his head, and then confessed about his behavior in front of his children. "I got so mad last night I fucked around and played myself in front of my kids. I ain't been home since." Jay paused and exhaled the guilt he'd been harboring about the way he had exploded. "I'm not proud of that shit, man. I snapped. Now my kids probably gon' be lookin' at me sideways, like I'm a maniac and shit. But all of this shit is Portia's fault!"

Laila was adamant about helping them work it out. "Jay, I don't mean to butt into your business, but I know what y'all got. You and P are perfect for each other. Bro, please just let me try to get to the bottom of this."

Jay sighed and shook his head. "Laila, no disrespect, sis, but you really blowin' mines. It is what it is. I'm *done*." He looked over at Cas and changed the subject. "Cas, you a'ight, man?"

Cas nodded. "I'm good, son. Are y*ou* a'ight?"

Jay just shrugged like he was tired. "You need me to help you get upstairs, or anything?"

Cas laughed and joked to lighten the mood. "Nah, man, I didn't get shot in the legs. I'm okay. And don't forget about the elevator I had installed when we went through Laila's situation. Son, I'm up outta that hospital, so I'm good."

Cas pulled a smile out of Jay with those comments. He hadn't meant to be such a killjoy. He was really happy Cas was home. He just had a lot on his mind at the time.

Cas understood. He and Jay had been best friends for about thirty years. Jay needed to be alone so he could think. "Just holla' at me later, man."

Jay nodded sincerely. "No doubt, son. I'ma come back through." He gave his man some dap and told him and Laila he'd see them later. As an afterthought, Jay added, "That meeting is tomorrow. I'ma head over to headquarters to make sure the projections and stuff will be ready."

Cas nodded. "That's what's up. I been thinking, too. I have some ideas, man."

Jay said, "You can join us on Skype, my nigga. I'll have them set up a webcam in the morning." Cas looked pleased when he said that. Jay thought about asking him for some advice about something, but decided against it. Partly because Laila was standing right there, but mostly because he knew there was no point in speaking on it. He was still going to confront Vino, but he would do so like a man. Jay gave his crimie Cas another pound and made his way to the door.

Cas stopped him before he walked out. "Son, do me a favor. Tell your sister I want my son to stay with me this week, man. I miss my kids."

Jay nodded to assure Cas that he would take care of that. He made a mental note to call Kira when he got in the car.

Laila locked the door behind Jay and then she looked at Cas. "Baby, what you think about him and P?"

Cas shrugged. "Call Portia and check on her," he suggested.

Laila gave him a little smile. "Boo, that's exactly what I intend to do." Just then, her cell phone rang. She looked at it and saw that it was Portia calling. "Wow, P gon' live a long time," Laila said, and answered the phone. "Hello?"

"L Boogie, what's good? Is my brother doing okay?" Portia asked.

Laila knew Portia was a wreck but she sounded pretty good. "Hey, P, everything is good. My baby sittin' right here. My man is home!" Laila beamed at her husband.

"That's what's up! God is so good! Put me on the speaker."

"Hold on." Laila switched her mobile phone to speaker mode. "Go 'head, boo. He can hear you."

Portia said, "Cas, our prayers have been answered! Welcome home, brother! God is *so good*!"

Cas laughed and agreed with her. "You can say that again, P! All the time! Your boy still here, so I'm a'ight, baby girl. How are you?"

Portia paused for a second because she almost broke down. She decided not to burden Cas and Laila with her grief. They were happy. Portia sighed. "I'm okay, bro. Or I will be, God willing. We all will."

Cas said, "No doubt, P. God willing." He noticed how Portia had danced all around the issue. Cas didn't want her to know he'd already heard about what went on between her and Jay because he didn't want her to feel uncomfortable. He wasn't the dude to judge, so he was staying out of it. He didn't even know the whole story yet anyhow. "Portia, I ain't in the hospital no more but make sure you get by here to see me. I guess I'ma be in the crib for a few days."

"Yes, please take it easy, Cas. You're still healing."

Cas smiled. "No doubt, P. Thanks again for keeping Skye for us. I'll be sending for her in a little while."

"She's good, Cas. Skye ain't no problem. That's my baby cakes. I don't mind watching her. You need peace and quiet right now."

"I know you don't mind, P. Thanks, baby girl. I had enough peace and quiet in the hospital. I just wanna see my kids. I miss hearing them laughing and running around."

Portia was touched. "Aww, that's so sweet. I know that's right, bro."

Cas chuckled. Portia always had to get mushy. "Take care, P."

"You take care too, baby. Love you, bro."

"Love you too, baby sis."

Laila smiled and rejoined the conversation. "P, are you home?"

Portia sighed. "Yup, I'm home. I'm about to feed the baby. Skye and Trixie are taking a little nap right now."

Cas and Laila both smiled. Portia was truly a gem for keeping their little one for them. Macy had been staying over there as well. It was good to have family.

Portia said, "Tima just called and told me she was gon' stop by on her way home from the doctor. She should be here soon. I guess I'ma chill with her for a little while."

Laila knew Portia. She could tell she was keeping something from her. They agreed to talk later on and then got off the phone.

Laila wanted to check on Portia in person. She also hadn't seen Fatima in a few days. Laila asked Cas if he would mind if she went over Portia's for a minute.

Cas didn't protest. In fact, he insisted that she go. He assured her that he would be fine until she came back. He wanted to get to the bottom of that mess between P and Jay as well. Laila could also bring his baby girl, Skye, back when she came home.

Before she left, Laila and Cas headed for the kitchen to make one of the healthy concoctions of super-healing foods that Cas was convinced would accelerate his recovery. Cas had always been a health food enthusiast. He was fanatical about eating right and no one could dispute his theory because he was a pretty healthy guy. Even his doctor had co-signed that. Cas talked Laila into joining him for a power smoothie that contained raw spinach and some things she never thought she'd ingest. Laila managed to drink the smoothie without throwing up, but she made some faces that really cracked Cas up.

About ten minutes later, Laila helped Cas get comfortable and brought him everything he would possibly need in her absence. Cas laughed and assured her that he'd be fine. "Just hurry up and get back here with my girls. Skye *and* Macy. I wanna see my kids, man."

Laila loved that Cas loved and accepted both of her daughters. She bent down and kissed him on the lips. "Boo, I promise I'll be back in an hour."

After Laila left the crib, Cas sat there for a moment and reflected on his journey. It was good to be home. He got up and looked around at the fine art that adorned the walls. Cas took a moment to appreciate his collection, and then he gave himself a little tour around the bottom floor of the house to get reacquainted with things. Cas had been so close to death when he was shot, he looked at things from a different perspective now. He'd learned to count all of his blessings, big and small, and give thanks to God.

The words of a gospel song Laila had played in the car on the way home, "I'm Still Here" by The Williams Brothers, came to Cas's head. He was no gifted vocalist. but he sang a few words from the chorus. *"I made it through another day's journey. God kept me here, so I'm still here."*

He thought about the mindboggling visit he was paid by the devil. Cas was all brass neck and balls, but that incident had broke him. That was the scariest shit he had ever encountered. He had never fought a battle like that before. Without God, he would've been easily overpowered. Cas was grateful to still be there. He looked up at the ceiling and said it out loud. "Thank you for your mercy, God. Thanks for givin' me another chance."

Chapter eighteen

As Laila drove the short distance to Portia's house, she was super careful as usual. It hadn't been long since she had regained the courage to drive again. She had been involved in a terrible car accident that had left her temporarily paralyzed, so she never navigated off point.

Laila checked her mirrors again and thought about her girls. God had blessed her with three beautiful daughters. Her Pebbles was deceased, so now she was an angel in heaven. Her baby had been brutally murdered in cold blood. That reality of that was oftentimes crippling. Laila glanced up at the sky. She would never recover from her loss but she thanked God for the time He'd given her. To know Pebbles was to love her. "Thank you, Lord," Laila said.

Reminiscing had choked her up a little. Laila smiled to herself and thought about her other two daughters. Macy and Skye were alive and well, thank God. Her darling baby and her princess on the verge of womanhood were the joy of her life. Laila couldn't wait to see them. She had to get her some sugar from Skye. She missed her little juicy chocolate mama.

Laila was flooded with shame every time she thought about the way she had shunned Skye when she first gave birth to her. She'd refused to hold her and nurture her the way a newborn baby needed their mother to. Laila had been messed up in the head at the time because she was paralyzed

153

and going through severe postpartum depression. Cas had spent a ton of money on therapy and professional counseling, but Laila had her girl Portia to thank for actually getting through to her. Now Skye was one of her most prized possessions.

Macy was Laila's prize as well. She was at school that time of day. Laila was proud of Macy because though she was pregnant, she was still doing what she had to do. Laila was grateful that Macy had been so mature and accepting about her absence lately. Laila had been by Cas's side every day since he was in the hospital. She knew her kids were in good hands at Portia and Jay's house, but she also knew they had missed her. It seemed as if Macy understood though. Her daughter was a Godsend. Macy was holding up good but Laila wouldn't make light of the fact that she had seen her father get killed. Macy needed her attention as well.

Laila thought about her foolish ex-husband, Khalil. He had actually sneaked into her wedding and singlehandedly destroyed it. Khalil destroyed himself in the process. What an idiot. Strangely, when the wedding pictures came back, Laila saw him in a couple of photos smiling as if he was an invited guest. She couldn't believe Khalil had actually posed for pictures before he opened fire on her and her new husband. That was so creepy.

Laila got to Portia's house and parked out front. She shut off the radio and then she got out and rang the bell. A minute later, big bellied Fatima opened the door.

Fatima grinned and hugged Laila. Then she snatched her inside like there was some top-secret emergency business at hand. Fatima shut the door and pulled Laila's coat about the current catastrophe in their clique. "Girl, we got big problems! It's a code-ten, bitch! Get in here so we can fill you in."

Portia walked up and joined them in time to see how alarmed Laila looked by Fatima's come-off. Portia was sad but she couldn't help but chuckle. Fatima was always so animated. "Hey girl," Portia greeted Laila. They exchanged air kisses and then she seconded Fatima's motion. "Laila, that's the code for 'my marriage is ruined!' All because of this bitch running her damn mouth." She looked at Fatima sideways.

Fatima sighed like she felt terrible. "P, I told you I'ma fix this."

Portia rolled her eyes and made a face. "Yeah, yeah, yeah."

Laila had heard Jay's side of the story. Now she wanted her homegirls' version. She feigned ignorance. "What the hell happened? What y'all talkin' about?"

Portia sighed like she had the world on her shoulders. "Girl, come on in and let's get comfortable. We gotta start from the beginning."

Laila followed her girls inside so they could brief her on the situation. They all had a seat on the sofa in the day room, and Portia proceeded to fill her in. Speaking in a low voice because Jaylin was asleep right there in his playpen, Portia revealed the latest drama in her marriage. She told Laila how Jay had flipped and disrespected her in front of the kids. Portia led her homegirls upstairs and showed them the hole that Jay had punched in the bathroom wall. Fatima and Laila realized the depth of his anger and looked sympathetic.

When they went back downstairs, Portia cracked open a chilled bottle of Moscato and then she took out two wine glasses for her and Laila. Fatima's pregnancy wouldn't allow her to indulge. The girlfriends sat around talking and evaluating the situation. Fatima and Laila disapproved of Jay's behavior but they both understood. They advised Portia to maintain her innocence no matter what and pray to God it all passed.

Laila stopped at two glasses of wine but Portia kept on sipping. After about five glasses, she was pretty tipsy. Out of the blue, she started crying. Laila and Fatima were surprised at first. They just looked at her.

Portia leaned back on the chair and grabbed her head. She was so frustrated she blurted out, "I'm so fuckin' mad right now! How could this shit happen?" She zoomed in on Fatima through teary eyes. "This is all your fault, bitch! You the one who talked me into that shit!"

Fatima looked like she'd been slapped. "What? Seriously, P? Don't even try it. Boo, I know you lookin' for somebody to blame, but you know you wanted to fuck him."

"Only because yo' ass was out there being loose first. You're a *terrible* fuckin' influence!"

Fatima breathed deep and tried not to get offended. She knew Portia's anger was misguided. "Word, P? A'ight, I'll hold that. Whatever!"

"I shouldn't have never went out there wit' yo' ass." Portia rolled her eyes in disgust.

"We went out there because Callie stole my shit, remember? The sex was just a bonus."

"That *bonus* ruined my fuckin' marriage!" Portia spat.

Laila intervened before Fatima could say another word. "P, come on. Woman up, bitch. Fatima didn't force you to give up no pussy. Get a grip, because that shit happened in the past. Now you just better focus on your future. It's true, your marriage is at stake, but I know Jay loves you. And you love him too, so you better figure out a way to get through to him."

Portia knew Laila was right. She sighed. "I know, sis. I have to." She looked over at Fatima and apologized. "My bad, Tima. I'm sorry, baby girl. I'm just scared to death. I can *not* lose my husband."

Fatima nodded sympathetically. "You won't, P. Don't worry."

"No, you *won't*," Laila cosigned. "Now twist something up, because your emotional ass needs to smoke and chill the fuck out."

Portia didn't bother to deny it. She looked at Laila and laughed. "I know, right? That damn wine got me all spilling over and shit. Lemme go get some trees. I'll be right back, y'all."

A few minutes later, Portia returned with a freshly rolled blunt. She led her homegirls into her office so they could puff. Fatima insisted on taking "two little pulls" from the el after Portia fired up.

When the ladies were done smoking, they woke the babies up from their too-long naps. Skye was ecstatic when she saw Laila. She hugged her and wouldn't let go of her. Laila laughed and loved it. She showered her baby with kisses.

While they were all together, Laila suggested that they discuss plans for their annual Simone dedication at AIDS Walk New York. Their homegirl had been gone for a while but she was still missed. They'd made it a tradition to keep Simone's memory alive and so far they'd kept it up.

In the midst of them talking, Macy walked in. She'd left school a little early that day because she felt kind of sick. When she saw her mother sitting there she was surprised and happy as well. "Mommy!" she yelled, and ran into Laila's arms like a little kid.

Laila laughed and hugged Macy tight. She was thrilled to see her as well. Her big baby was having a baby now herself. She smoothed her daughter's hair out of her face and noticed there were blonde streaks in it. "Hey, pretty girl. How you feeling?"

Macy grinned. "Much better now." She walked over and greeted her aunties with hugs. Portia and Fatima were all smiles.

Laila felt some type of way about not being involved in Macy's hair-color change, so she spoke on it. "I like your hair, Mace. Although I didn't know you had dyed it. I wish you would've talked to me first… But it still looks healthy."

Macy giggled. "I didn't dye my hair, Ma. These are extensions. They're just blonde clip-on pieces. Look." Macy parted her long tresses with her fingers and showed her mother one of the hair clips.

Laila was glad to see that was just pieces. "It blends in so well! Good job! It looks professional."

"It is. I went with Auntie Portia to the hair salon the other day. I just wanted to try something different."

Laila smiled, "I ain't mad, boo. It's cute."

"Thanks, Ma."

Laila ran her hand over the nape of her neck. "Shoot, I need *my* wig piece done. I have a hair appointment this evening too. I gotta get my cut tightened up."

Macy smiled and exaggerated, "Umm hmm! I thought you were growing it out or somethin'. Ma, how's Cas?"

Laila beamed and then did a little two-step. "He's at the house, boo. He came home this morning!"

Macy's eyes lit up. "That's what's *up*!" After she heard the good news, she was genuinely joy-filled. She looked at the evidence of her mother and aunts' afternoon cocktails, and joked, "You Steel Magnolias ain't got no business up in here drinking this early in the day. This is what y'all do when we go off to school, huh?"

The three girlfriends all laughed and tossed sofa pillows at Macy. That girl had a smart mouth. Macy had been a riot ever since she was small.

Laila looked at the clock and noticed the time. She had been there for a while. She told her girlfriends she had to be going. Then Laila told her daughters what Cas had said. "Cas wants to see you girls ASAP, so we gon' head on home."

Macy and Skye were both delighted. They were ready to go. Macy looked at Portia and said, "Auntie P, darling, please don't cry because I'm leaving. You know I'll be back soon."

Portia grinned. "I don't know how I'll manage without you, sweet cheeks. I'ma miss your lil' pretty self, but you know you have a room upstairs. You're welcome any time. You and Skye both. I love my nieces to pieces."

Macy knew Portia meant that. "I know, Lady P, I know." They shared a little smile. Macy started to give Portia a message for Jayquan but she decided to contact him directly. Macy looked at Laila. "Ma, I have Skye's car seat in my car, so y'all can ride to the house with me. I insist. You've been drinking, anyhow."

Laila only had two glasses of wine so she started to protest. She gave in and agreed to leave her car parked over there until later. Laila handed her keys to Portia, and she and Skye hopped in the red Mercedes that Cas had given Macy for her sixteenth birthday.

$$$$$

When Laila and her girls got home, she took Skye inside while Macy parked her car in the garage. When Skye saw her daddy, she grinned and got excited. The baby ran to Cas and jumped in his arms.

Cas smiled from ear to ear and made up for all the hugs and kisses he'd been missing. Skye was his little chubby cheeked chocolate star. His baby was adorable. Cas pretended to bite her and she laughed out loud and loved it. Then she was ready to box.

Laila laughed but she told the baby to take it easy because her daddy was hurt at the time. That was Cas's fault because he'd always played so rough with Skye. He had their baby running around acting like a little boy.

Just then, Macy came inside. She stood in the doorway for a moment staring at Cas holding her baby sister. Without warning, Macy looked at her mother and burst into tears.

Concerned that his stepdaughter was boohooing her heart out, Cas put Skye down and stood up as fast as his pain would allow him. "Macy, come here."

Laila got worried. She assumed that Macy broke down when she saw her baby sister with her father because she missed Khalil. Macy had not only lost her father, she had witnessed his murder. The poor girl had every right to be traumatized.

Cas was thinking the same thing. He had made the same assumption Laila had. As he watched Macy in tears, he felt horrible. He figured she blamed him for her daddy's death and hated his guts. Cas and Macy had a great relationship before all that mess happened, so that was heartbreaking for him. He called her once more. "Macy."

Macy timidly walked over to Cas and stood in front of him with tears streaming down her pretty face. She had her head down as if she couldn't stand to look at him. Cas felt like the scum of the earth. He prayed that she would learn to love him again.

Macy spoke and surprised Cas with her words. "Cas, I'm so s-s-sorry," she stammered.

Alarmed, Cas asked, "Sorry for *what*? What's wrong, lil' mama?"

Macy sobbed, "F-for what my father did to you."

Cas couldn't take it any more. He grabbed that girl and held her in his arms. Macy hugged him back tight and cried her heart out. Cas was choked up but he found his voice after a moment. "Macy, what happened had nothing to do with you. You don't have to apologize for *anything*. I feel like *I* should be saying sorry to *you*."

"It wasn't your f-fault either. All you did was love my mother and treat us nice. You just wanted us all to be happy. You did everything you could."

Cas raised Macy's chin and wiped away her tears. "Stop crying. Everything I ever did was done out of love. I love your mother and I love you too. You hear me, Macy? I love you just as much as I love the rest of my kids. I need for you to understand that. I know I'm not your father, but I'm here. I'll *always* be here for you, okay?"

Macy nodded and managed a little smile. She hugged Cas again. "I'm so happy you're okay, and I'm *so* glad you came home. I'm ready for us to be a family again."

Cas swallowed. Damn, his eyes watered up when she said that. He smiled and planted a little kiss on the top of Macy's head. He'd never been the type that cried easily but she hit a soft spot. He really loved that little girl. Macy didn't know what her forgiveness had done for him. Cas had been carrying a lot of guilt around ever since she had lost her father. She didn't blame him for it. He needed to hear that.

Cas and Macy's emotional encounter had Laila choked up as well. She stood there quietly and watched with tears brimming. It took everything she had to stay out of it, but she gave her husband and daughter space to have their moment. She had the feeling that they would all be fine.

Macy had hit it right on the head. Laila was ready for them to be a family again too. She and Skye joined Cas and Macy for a group hug. Love was definitely in the air.

A Dollar Outta Fifteen Cent 4.5

CHAPTER NINETEEN

That afternoon, Jay sat in his office in a meeting with a gentleman named August "Auggie" DeVaul. Auggie was a retired NBA player who had his hands in quite a few profitable endeavors. Auggie also had an inner-city youth basketball league that Street Life Entertainment had donated a ton of money to. Jay was in the process of signing another check. It was a worthy charity. Jay loved the kids.

His company was also the proud new owners of a team in the youth league. Team Street Life was officially called the City Slickers. They had hired a coach and were currently recruiting players. Playing ball kept those kids off the streets. It could save their lives. Jay put his John Hancock on the check and passed it to Auggie. Afterwards, he stood, indicating that their meeting had come to a close.

Auggie grinned when Jay handed him the check. His smile widened when he saw the amount. "Alright, alright!" he said, and stood up and towered above Jay. He stuck the check in his inside pocket of the expensive merino wool jacket he wore. "You ain't got to kick me out, man. I gotta be going anyhow." He laughed.

"Nah, man, I gotta take a piss," Jay laughed.

"Whatever, mothafucka." Auggie shook Jay's hand firmly. "Mr. Mitchell, I thank you very much for this handsome donation. On behalf of my organization and on behalf of the children whose lives this money will change, I

163

offer our sincerest appreciation." Auggie winked at Jay and adjusted his necktie and lapel. The huge diamond pinky ring and studs in his ears sparkled from the sunlight shining through the office window.

Jay said, "We're helping to save kids, so that's money well spent. Thank you for all the updates, man. And please let Minister Fontaine and his fellow clergymen and board members know that we extend our gratitude for the opportunity to give back." Jay walked Auggie to the door and shook hands with again. "Take care, man. I'll be in touch."

After Auggie left, Jay opened the blinds and stared out at the city line. He had a great view from his office. He remembered he had promised his mother he'd call her. Mama Mitchell had ringed him a little earlier to see how he was doing. He'd told her he was in a meeting, and would call her back. Jay stared down at a motorboat floating down the East River and decided to do his mother one better and head out to Brooklyn to see her.

Twenty minutes later, Jay drove across the Brooklyn Bridge. While en route to Mama Mitchell's, he made a phone call to an associate about some investments. The business talk wound up lasting the duration of the trip. The conversation ended just as he reached his destination. Jay pulled up outside of his mother's house and, out of habit, checked his mirrors and looked around before he hopped out. The freshly waxed Bentley shone in the sun. Jay knew it commanded attention so he locked the doors and headed toward the house.

Jay opened the gate to his mother's yard and jogged up the stairs and rang the doorbell. He had keys to the house but always alerted his mom that he was there, so he wouldn't startle her. He used his key to let himself in.

"Hey, Ma, it's me," he called out. Jay didn't want to mess around and get shot upon entering. His mother owned a licensed gun and she would certainly use it. Mama Mitchell had refused to take the throw-away pistol he gave her to protect the house a while back, so he had insisted that she get a gun permit. Jay said she needed something to protect herself since she lived alone, and she didn't argue with him. She believed in the right to bear arms just as he did; she just wanted to do it the legal way. Jay didn't have any beef with that. He'd helped her with the process. Attending target practice at the range with his mother had been hilarious.

"I'm down in the kitchen, son," Mama Mitchell yelled down the hall.

Jay followed the sound of his mother's voice. The closer he got, the more his spirits rose. When he entered the newly remodeled kitchen, the sight of his mama standing there did something to him. She wore a gray and melon colored Nike warm-up suit and sneakers, and a headband that matched. She smiled at Jay like she hit the number.

Jay grinned back at her. "Hey lady, how are you feeling?" He gave her a big hug and a kiss on the cheek.

Mama Mitchell beamed at her only son, whom she loved dearly. "I'm fine, son. What a pleasure to see you. Sit down and join me for some tea."

Jay sat down on a bar stool. "Oh yeah, Cas is home, Ma. He came home this morning."

Mama Mitchell nodded happily. "I know, son. Praise the Lord! I called and spoke with Caseem just a while ago. He sounded well. And *strong*."

Jay nodded in agreement. "Thank God."

Mama Mitchell put a tea kettle full of water on the burnerless touch stove and turned it on medium-high. "I'm glad you came over, son. There're a couple of things I wanted to talk to you about."

Jay raised an eyebrow. "Like what, Ma?"

"First, I have something to tell you."

Jay swallowed and prayed that it wasn't bad news about her health.

When she saw the worried look on his face, Mama Mitchell said, "Don't worry, your mama's fine. This is about *you*, not me."

Jay exhaled and relaxed. "What's goin' on, lady? Spit it out."

She didn't know how Jay would take it, but she gave it to him straight. "Your father contacted me the other day. He asked for you."

Jay was totally unprepared for that one. He screwed up his face in distaste and said the first thing that came to his mind. "Man, I thought that nigga was dead."

"Your father's *not* dead, Jay."

"Hell, he might as well be."

"Son! That's not a nice thing to say."

Jay grew agitated and sighed. "I'm just being honest. I'm not interested in seeing him, Ma. For *what*? I'm almost forty years old. So what do I need him for *now*?"

Mama Mitchell didn't know what to say. Growing up fatherless had left her son with some issues. Jay was certainly entitled to feel some type of way, but she didn't want him to miss out on the opportunity to meet his father. He needed to bury the animosity he harbored towards the old fool. "Son, carrying all that negative baggage around isn't healthy."

Jay didn't respond. Mama Mitchell decided to leave it alone for the time being. "Well, I have his contact info if you change your mind."

"Don't worry, I won't," Jay snapped. When he saw the look on his mother's face he softened his tone. "I'm sorry, Ma. Pardon me. It's been a long day. I do not wanna see that dude, but I can't speak for my sisters. So run it by them. Laurie and Kira can make their own decisions."

Just then, the tea kettle began to whistle. The steam shooting from it matched the steam Jay had let off. Mama Mitchell turned the stove off and fixed two cups of chamomile tea. She understood his hesitance on the matter. She loved Jay and supported whatever decisions he made.

She sat a tea cup in front of Jay and brought up the other issue she wanted to address. Her sources had confirmed that there was some trouble in paradise. "So, what's going on at home, son? Wanna talk about it?"

Jay shook his head sadly. "Nope. Not at all. How are *you* doing, Ma? I'd rather talk about that."

"I'm alright, son. What happened with you and Portia?"

Jay just swallowed and remained silent. Was his mother reading him, or did she know something? "Why you say that?"

"Well, I heard there was some ruckus between you two last night."

"If that's what you wanna call it. I think me and her are done, Ma. I'm walking away."

His mother looked surprised but she remained cool. "Walking away from the family you love so much? And why is that?"

"Because ..." Jay couldn't even bring himself to say it.

"Just *because*?"

He sighed. "No, Ma. Portia cheated on me, okay?"

Mama Mitchell raised an eyebrow. "Are you *sure*?"

Jay nodded. "I'm sure."

"How are you so sure? Was you there to hold the light?"

"No, I wasn't there. But ..."

"Exactly! So how do you even know that mess is true?"

"I got it from a pretty credible source, Ma."

"Oh, so you have proof?"

"I ain't got no proof, but ..."

"But *what,* Jay? Son, let me give you some advice. You ending your marriage over some *alleged* infidelity will affect more than just the woman you're upset with. What about your children? And Jay, you know you have a good wife. I believe Portia has already proved that to you. Right or wrong?"

Jay was scowled, and was forced to agree. "You right, Ma."

"Son, you know better than to act a fool in front of your children. Have you taken the time to think about how all this mess has affected them? They called me, you know."

Jay had the dumb face. "They did?"

"Yes, they did."

"Which one? Lil' Jay or Jazz?"

"Does it matter, Jay?"

"I just wanna know."

"Why, so you can chastise them?"

"No, Ma. I ain't mad they called. I know I scared them. They've never seen me like that before. I'ma have to have a talk with them. I gotta apologize. They shouldn't have to go through that."

Mama Mitchell eased up off Jay because she could see that he felt it already. She knew her son was a good man. She had raised him that way. She trusted that Jay would do the right thing, and left it alone.

An hour later, she walked Jay to the front door. Her last words of advice were, "Talk things over before you go jumping the gun. You hear me?"

Jay nodded. "Love you, lady. Call you later."

"Love you too, son. Take care of yourself."

"I will." Jay sealed that promise with a kiss on the cheek.

He had to admit that he felt better when he left his mother's. He wasn't over that Portia/Vino shit yet, but he owed his children an apology. He had frightened them when he stepped out of character.

Jay was no hypocrite. He led his family by example. The behavior he had exhibited was the opposite of everything he stood for. He made up his mind. His next stop was home where his kids were.

As Jay drove along to New Jersey, he imagined what he would say to Vino when he saw him. The more he thought about it, he knew his approach had to be subtle. He wouldn't give a nigga the satisfaction of knowing they had caused him grief.

Jay's thoughts shifted back to his kids. He was only a few miles from the house so he decided to put all that bullshit on a backburner. A record he liked played on an XM station he'd been listening to. It was a pretty song called "Daughters" by John Mayer. Jay hummed along with the chorus.

"Fathers, be good to your daughters. Daughters will love like you do. Girls become lovers - who turn into mothers. So mothers, be good to your daughters too."

Jay dug that song but that day it had a different effect on him. He thought back to the night before, when his little girls had cried in the bathroom doorway watching him manhandle their mother. Jay felt like an ass. That just wasn't cool. If his little girls grew up with issues because he had scarred them, he would never forgive himself. Jay cringed at the thought. His father had fucked up his childhood on so many levels he couldn't count them on one hand.

CHAPTER TWENTY

Jay stood at his house door and punched in the four-digit code that deactivated the security alarm. He stuck his key in the lock and let out a little sigh of relief when it turned. The way he had showed his behind the last time he was home, he was glad the locks hadn't been changed.

When Jay got inside, the first thing he did was locate his kids. Lil' Jay, Jazz, and Trixie were up on the second level in the rec section. He assumed the baby was upstairs with Portia. Jay greeted his heirs heartily but he didn't exactly receive a warm welcome. The kids were clearly Team Portia. It was written all over their faces. Jay figured he wouldn't be on their "favorites" list at the time, but the lackluster reactions hurt.

Jayquan was clad in a wife beater and basketball shorts, playing a video game. He just nodded at Jay with a straight face and barely looked at him. Jazmin had these pretty French twists in her hair and wore a cute purple sweater and skinny jeans. She crossed her arms and looked at Jay as if she wanted an explanation. She looked like a smaller replica of Portia. Jay's baby daughter, Trixie, wore a little pink sweat suit with matching barrettes in her hair. She looked hesitant, as if she was reading him. Trixie said, "Still you mad, Daddy?"

Trixie was going through that stage when children mixed up their words. Though she sounded adorable, her words broke Jay's heart. He smiled and shook his head. "No, baby girl. Daddy's not mad anymore. I promise not to get that mad again. I'm sorry, sweetheart. Okay?"

Trixie paused, as if she was making sure he was being sincere. Jay stifled a laugh. His daughter was vigilant and on point just like her father. After a moment, Trixie said, "Otay, Daddy."

Jay started cheesing. "Come 'ere, girl!" Trixie grinned back at him and rushed into his arms. Jay picked his baby up and swung her around. She laughed out loud and loved it. It seemed like she was delighted to be in her daddy's arms. Jay felt good about that. One down, two to go.

He got Trixie to smile pretty easily, but the others were not so forgiving. Jazz tried to play hardball but Jay grabbed her and showered her face with kisses. She couldn't help but giggle. Then Jay literally saw her eyes light up. Her love for him shone again. Jay's smile was so big he showed all thirty two teeth. Little things like that look were the things he needed to get by.

Jazz said, "Daddy, we should go to church so God can fix you and Mommy. Like that time on Mother's Day, when you came in the church and told Mommy you were sorry in front of everybody. Please, Daddy, do that again. Mommy's so sad. I want us *all* to be happy! Don't you?"

The way she looked at him, Jay knew he didn't have a choice. "Of course I do, baby." Jazz acted just like Portia sometimes.

Jay was grateful for the breakthrough with his girls, but his crowned prince was on some nonchalant shit. Jayquan just continued playing a game on Xbox like he wasn't even standing there. Jay walked over and gave his son the special attention he knew was in order. "What up, Lil' Jay? How you doin', man?"

Jayquan just shrugged and wouldn't meet the eye contact his father initiated. Jay touched him on the shoulder to get his attention. The boy moved out of his reach and still wouldn't give him any eye contact. Jay could see that he was pretty upset with him. He knew Jayquan was hurt by his poor choice of words the previous night, so he couldn't blame the little dude.

Jay had a seat across from his son and stared at him for a moment. Both his daughters scrambled into his lap. Jay held his girls tight and addressed all three of them at once. "Listen, guys, I wanna apologize for what happened last night. I was upset and out of character. I promise y'all that will never happen again."

Jazz said, "Okay, but you have to apologize to Mommy also. She's upstairs giving Jaylin his bedtime bath."

Jay nodded and looked at his watch. "Isn't it your bedtime too? It's a school night, Jazzy." Just then, Portia yelled downstairs for Jazz as well. *"Jazmin, come on up here so you can take your bath!"*

"I'm coming, Mommy!" Jazz responded. She hopped off Jay's lap and gave him a kiss on the cheek. "Good night, Daddy! Remember what I said!"

When Jazz ran off, Trixie jumped up and ran behind her. Jayquan got up and followed them and left Jay sitting there all alone. Jay felt stupid. He also felt disrespected. He was the parent and he demanded revere from his children. He refrained from going after Lil' Jay and elected to give him a pass, only because of the situation.

Jay was determined to have a man-to-man with his boy, so he headed upstairs as well. When he got to his son's bedroom, the door was locked. He knocked and waited for the angry little dude to answer.

Jayquan came to the door a moment later. "What up, Pop?" he asked.

"I need to holla at you, man. We need to talk." Jay entered the room without being asked. The first thing he noticed amongst the usual teenage boy-clutter in Jayquan's room was the neon pink scarf hanging on the arm of the chair in the far left corner. Jay figured it belonged to Macy, who had gone home to see Cas when he got out of the hospital. Jay knew it was only a matter of time before Macy came back. She and Jayquan were very close.

Jay had a seat and looked his son straight in the eyes. "Look, man, I'm not feelin' you throwing me all this shade. You're upset with me. I get it, okay? But don't *ever* walk away from me like that again."

Jayquan sighed impatiently. "Yeah, a'ight. You got it."

Jay studied him. He was still resentful. "Son, what are you huffing and puffing for? Lose the attitude. If you got something to say, then say it. I raised you to speak your mind."

Jayquan straightened his shoulders and looked his father in the eye. "That's true, you did. Are you ready for the truth, Pop? Can you handle it? Because the rules always seem to change when it comes to you."

Jay knew where that was coming from. He sat there and took it. "Son, I owe you an apology…"

Jayquan cut him off. "I'm not done, Pop. I need to say this."

Jay shut up so he could hear him out. "My bad, son. You got the mic. Speak."

"A'ight, I'm just sayin'… You keep flip flopping, Pop! It wasn't that long ago since you promised us that we was gon' be a family again, and then you do this! Portia just came back, and now *you* wildin'. Am *I* gon' have to be the mature one around here and raise these kids? Somebody has to be sane!"

Jay couldn't believe his son came at him like that. He felt like shit. He hung his head in shame and searched for the right words.

Jayquan saw his father's reaction so he turned it down a little bit. "Look, Pop, I'm speaking for my sisters and Jaylin too. No disrespect, but all this bull crap is affecting us too. Are you and Portia gon' be together, or not? Stop playing with our emotions and just tell us what it is!"

Jay cleared his throat. "Son, first let me start by apologizing. I taught you to be respectful and never put your hands on a woman, and then I showed you the exact opposite. I'm not proud of what I did, but I'm human. I made a mistake. Man, I'm sorry for disrespecting your mother in front of you. And I'm sorry for disrespecting you and your sisters as well. I was completely out of line, and that only happened because I reacted out of emotion. Son, try not to *ever* make that mistake. Don't react out of emotion. And *always* think before you speak."

Jayquan just nodded and didn't say anything. He didn't look so mad anymore. Jay saw that he was getting through to him, so he continued to school him. "Lil' man, you gotta be mindful of your thoughts, because your thoughts become your words. And be mindful of your words, because your words become your actions. Be very mindful of your actions as well, because your actions become your habits. Your habits become your character, son. And that determines who you are and what you stand for. Character is everything."

Jayquan listened and absorbed the wisdom like a sponge. He was no dumb kid. He appreciated the jewels his father often dropped on him. Jayquan decided to throw it back on Jay. He wanted to see if he would walk the walk about the talk he talked. "Pop, if character is so important, don't you think you should apologize to Lady P too?"

Jay just looked at him. Lil' Jay put him on the spot. He'd made up with his kids but he wasn't ready to make nice with his wife yet. Jayquan had taken the conversation on a detour.

Jayquan sensed his old man's hesitation. "I think you should apologize because you said some pretty harsh things. I'm just sayin'... Regardless of whatever happened between you two, she's always been good to you, Pop. Was that really necessary?"

Jay was on the verge of telling Jayquan to stay out of grown folks' business. He didn't know the half. Jay knew deep down inside that he'd gone into defensive mode because he wasn't ready to face Portia. He could tell from the way his son looked at him that he didn't have much of a choice. If he wanted to teach his boy to be a man, he certainly had to act like one. Respect was everything. He had to be a positive role model. He wasn't just raising a son; he was raising a young father. Jayquan was having a kid himself. The things Jay taught him would carry on for generations. "You're right, son. That wasn't necessary at all. I was in my feelings at the time. I'll apologize to Portia because it's the right thing to do. Are we good?"

"We good, Pop. I accept your apology. You still my man." Jayquan stuck out his hand so they could shake on it.

Relieved, Jay grinned and stood up and gave him a pound. He couldn't resist the urge to steal himself a hug in the process. He grabbed Jayquan and kissed him on the top of his head. Jay expected him to protest but he didn't. "Lil' man, I'm going to check on Cas. You wanna go see how your uncle doing?"

"No doubt, lemme put on some clothes, man. You go in there and talk to your wife. I'll be ready in a few."

Jay nodded and felt like he was the kid. He made his way down the hallway to the master bedroom where Portia was. When he walked in, she was putting the baby to sleep. Jaylin was lying on a pillow on her lap.

It was hard to face Portia. Jay felt bad about what he'd done, but she had cheated on him. He was filled with guilt and contempt. He coolly averted eye contact, and said, "What up?"

Portia peeped that Jay wouldn't look at her. His greeting was empty and phony. Her response to that bullshit was, "Hey."

Jay walked over and leaned down for what she thought was a kiss at first, but wasn't. Not for her anyhow. He kissed the baby on the forehead. Jaylin's eyes were closed, but when Jay kissed him, he opened them and peeked up and smiled. Then he shut down again. Jay grinned and rubbed his curly hair. Jaylin was a handsome little dude.

When Jay smiled, Portia was ready to forgive him. Surely her kiss would come next. She sat there looking cool and composed but her heart raced with anticipation. There was so much nervous energy pumping through her veins, you'd have thought she was running from the police. Portia didn't know what to expect from Jay. The last time she'd seen him, he had been pretty out of control. She wanted a sincere apology.

Portia had always been a sucker for Jay's smile, but that one wasn't for her. When Jay looked at her his expression was stone cold. The apologetic kiss on the forehead never came either. Portia just sat there quietly and watched Jay go in the bathroom.

When Jay took a look at the new artwork he'd punched in the bathroom wall, he shook his head and wondered what he was thinking. No wonder his hand hurt. Jay went back in the bedroom and told Portia his intentions. "I'ma get somebody to fix the wall tomorrow. Me and Lil' Jay about to go over Cas crib for a minute." After he said that, he walked out of the room. He had come home to make up with his kids, not to reconcile with Portia. He got angry just looking at her ass. He went to say goodnight to his daughters. Then he would wait for his son downstairs.

Portia watched Jay leave and listened as his footsteps echoed down the hall. She realized that was as good as it got. Jay was not feeling her. He had never before handled her so indifferently. Her marriage could be over. As the truth set in, a lone tear rolled down Portia's cheek. She wished for the millionth time that day that she could rewind time. She had fucked up when she had sex with Vino. That incident had come back and given her a black eye worse than the one she'd dodged when Jay punched through the wall.

Portia would go to her grave denying the infidelity Jay assumed she was guilty of. But she felt like he owed her a pass. Hell, Jay should give her a pass on just about anything. She had stuck with him after he made a baby on her with a younger woman, and now she was taking care of the child like he was her own. Portia would never throw that in Jay's face, but he couldn't be serious. All of that stuff had to account for something.

Jayquan assumed that his parents had made up, so he had cheered up considerably. He worried when Jay and Portia were on the outs. Before he headed downstairs, he went to check on Portia. He walked in the room and said, "Lady P, me and Pop goin' to check on Uncle Cas. We'll be back in a little while. Are you okay?"

Portia put on a synthetic smile. "Yup, boo, I'm good. I'm about to lay this boy down. Do me a favor, baby, drive Laila's car over there. She left it when she was over here earlier. The keys are on my dresser right there."

Jayquan said, "Okay, I got you." He walked over and kissed Portia on the forehead. "I'll be back. Love you."

Portia smiled. That was the kiss that she had longed for. "Love you more, baby. Be safe."

Jayquan nodded and winked at her. He picked up Laila's car keys off the dresser and headed out. When he got downstairs, he told Jay what it was. "Pop, I'm driving Laila's Lexus over there. She left it here earlier 'cause she rode with Macy home. I'll follow you, and then later I'll push the Bentley back here."

Jay shook his head at him. "Yo, you stay frontin'." Jayquan was always trying to call the shots. He was quite a character.

Lil' Jay continued trying it. "I'll be turning sixteen real soon, so I need as much driving practice as I can get." He winked at his father to make sure he got the hint.

"Look at you, you so thirsty." That boy was on him about his first car like tires on rims. Jay laughed and followed his mini-me outside. Jayquan's silliness had cheered him up. Jay didn't say anything but the truth was, he looked forward to car shopping as much as Jayquan did. He would be sixteen in no time.

CHAPTER TWENTY-ONE

Across town, another father and son were reuniting. Kira had just arrived at Cas's house with Jahseim. When Cas saw his son, his grin was as big as day. Jahseim ran into his arms like he was thrilled to see him. They hugged one another tight. Cas could tell he missed him because he wouldn't let go for a minute. He hugged his boy even tighter.

"Daddy, I'm so glad you're okay!" Jahseim looked up at his father. "I was praying for you everyday!"

Cas kissed his first-born on the top of his head and whispered a prayer of thanks that he was alive to see him again. "I appreciate that, son. Don't ever stop praying for me, okay? I pray for you too. Before I pray for myself."

Jahseim hugged him again. "I love you, Daddy."

"I love you more, man!"

Kira stood there trying not to cry. She was glad that their bond was so strong.

Cas stepped back and sized his son up. "Is it me, or did you get taller?"

Jahseim grinned and stood up taller. "It's not you, I'm growing. That's what everybody keeps saying."

"You right, you are growing. How have you been, Jah?"

Jahseim nodded. "I'm good. How are *you* doing? Are you still in pain from the bullet that was in you?"

Cas was surprised by his son's forwardness but he gave him a straight answer. "I'm in a little pain but I'll manage."

"I'll help you with the stuff you gotta do. Okay?"

Cas smiled. "Thanks, I would really appreciate that. Go on inside and see your little sister. Skye's been asking for you all day."

Jahseim grinned and then he looked at his mother. Kira smiled and opened her arms. He gave her a hug and kiss, and said, "See you in a few days, Mommy. Love you"

"Love you too, baby. Call me." After he ran off, Kira turned and faced Cas. "So how are you, Cas? Really?"

"I'm good, Kira. Thanks. I'ma just take it easy for a few days."

Kira nodded. "You look good. Don't push it too hard. And lemme know if you need anything. Okay?"

Cas nodded. He appreciated that. "A'ight. How *you* been?"

Kira smiled. "I'm actually pretty good. Take care of my baby, Cas. He's all I got."

"That's my little man. Come on, Kira."

Kira smiled again. Cas was a great father. "He's really been worried about you. He kept having these moments when he'd get real sad and depressed. He didn't even wanna play football with his little league team no more."

Grateful for the rundown, Cas nodded. He realized that was the first time Kira had been inside of his new house. She usually just dropped Jahseim outside and waited until he got in, and then kept on going. Cas had to admit that Kira looked nice. She looked happy as well. Cas was glad that they were finally in a good place with their parenting relationship. It had taken them a while to get there. "Listen,

I appreciate you coming inside to see about me, and thanks for bringing my son over. I missed that little dude."

Kira grinned at her baby daddy. She was glad they were in a good place as well. It had been a rocky road with obstacles that had included her doing prison time. "Cas, I had to come and make sure you were good. Regardless of whatever, we family first. Take care of yourself, babe." Kira looked at the time on her phone. "I gotta be going 'cause I got a studio session." She gave Cas a brief hug and headed on out.

Cas yelled out the door behind her, "Yo, lemme hear the new music! Can I live?"

Kira looked back and laughed. "Most definitely! Lemme just make sure it's fire first. Then I'ma send it to you."

"Make sure you do that." As Cas watched Kira leave, he thought about the favor she had done for him when he needed her assistance cleaning up that Jay and Ysatis situation. Ysatis had been threatening to go to the police with some old dirt she had on him and Jay, just because Jay wouldn't leave his family and be with her, so Cas had been forced to get involved. Kira had befriended Ysatis and took her down to Miami so he and Wise could put his plan into action. Cas couldn't have done it without Kira. He and she had been through some things, but she was alright with him. Kira was right, they would always be family. Cas wished her well and hoped that she would find love and happiness again, just as he had.

$$$$$

That evening Laila left and went to her appointment at the hair salon, so Cas spent some quality time alone with his kids. Jay and Lil' Jay came through to check on him and Wise and his little girl, Falynn, stopped by too. Cas and his cronies got to talking and laughing, and then so much for the rest and relaxation the doctor had prescribed. Cas was glad to see everyone and touched that they had thought about him.

His mother also came over that night. Ms. B arrived right after Laila returned from the hair salon. Laila was in a pleasant mood and answered the door with a smile. She greeted Ms. B politely and let her inside the house. But Stevie Wonder could see that there was tension between them. It was as thick as London Fog. Both women were curt and phony as three dollar bills. The funny thing was Laila didn't even know what the problem was. She hadn't done anything to Ms. B. Not that she knew of. Laila decided to be adult and air it out while they were alone.

Before they went inside where everyone was, Laila addressed her mother-in-law. "Ms. B, can I talk to you, please?"

Ms. B. raised an eyebrow and stuck her hands in the pockets of the full-length mahogany mink she wore. "Yes?"

"I was just wondering why you've been so different toward me lately. Why are you throwing me shade? Have I done something to you?"

Ms. B sighed and didn't bat an eye. "Okay, we're adults, so I might as well say what I gotta say. You on my shit list, Laila. I don't think my son married the right woman. He needs somebody to take care of him, not bring drama into his life. I don't like you for my son, dear. I want you out of Caseem's life. And that's that." Ms. B scowled. "That little *love triangle* you had going on almost cost my son his life. I don't find it cute, honey. In my opinion, he was better off with his first wife, Kira."

That was a hard slap in the face. Ms. B was on some other shit. Laila bit her tongue and stood there until she was done stabbing her. She was grown and had birthed three children of her own, but she'd been raised to respect her elders at all times. Cas's mother was reaching but Laila took it without bucking back. She couldn't disrespect her mother in-law. Laila would sew her lips shut and cut them off before she sassed Cas's mother. However, she was a woman just like Ms. B. was. She had the right to defend herself.

Laila cleared her throat and chose her words wisely. "Pardon me, Ms. B, but you have the wrong idea. There was never any *love triangle*. I was divorced from that man, and free to move on with my life. Cas was divorced and free to move on too. We *both* started over. There's no crime in that. I'm *very* sorry about what happened and I thank God everyday that my husband is alive and well. My crazy, deranged ex-husband snapped and showed up at our wedding. No one could predict that."

"Yeah, but if that ain't a sign that a marriage isn't meant to be, then I don't know what is. God gave Caseem another chance. God forbid, my son may not have the same luck next time."

Laila made a face. "Now, wait a minute, my ex-husband is *dead*. Remember? God bless his soul, there won't *be* a next time. And I hate to take it there, but let's not forget that Kira, Cas's ex, tried to kill me and my baby. She torched my house in the middle of the night! When I was paralyzed! When me and my *baby* were *sleeping*! That was *atrocious!* But did I leave Cas because of Kira's actions? No! That wasn't *his* fault, Ms. B."

Ms. B just stood there with her arms crossed and looked at her. Laila knew she was a tough lady who didn't take any shit, so she toned it down a little. "Pardon me for raising my voice. I was just trying to get my point across. I'm not justifying your son getting shot, I'm letting you know that's how strong our love is. We got pass that mess with Kira, and we gon' get pass this too. I *love* your son. Caseem and I are married, we have a beautiful family, and we gon' be together. I hope you can accept that."

Ms. B's was unmoved by Laila's testimony. Her reply was snide. "Well, I won't make any promises, hon."

Just then, Skye appeared. When she saw her grandmother, she yelled, "Gamma!" She grinned and ran over and hugged Ms. B. tight.

At the sight of her granddaughter, Ms. B's whole demeanor changed. She grinned and picked Skye up and gave her a kiss. She loved her grandkids and nothing would ever change that. They had her blood running through their veins. There was no need to question Caseem's paternity because Skye looked just like him. Both of his children did.

Cas came out behind Skye to see what the women were up to. His mother greeted him with a smile and a kiss to the cheek. "Hey, baby!"

Laila put on a fake smile like nothing was wrong and headed upstairs to give Cas some time with his mother. She'd had enough of Ms. B that night.

Cas said, "Hey, Ma, how you doin'?"

"I'm doing just fine, son. How are *you* feeling?"

"I'm good. Come in and have a seat, Ma." Cas led his mother to the red living room. He didn't bother to disclose the fact that he was kind of tired. His body let him know he wasn't quite at a hundred percent yet. Cas also didn't bother to disclose the fact that he'd heard the bulk of his mom and Laila's conversation. He wasn't going to address it at the time because he didn't have the energy, but he would certainly address it. His mother and wife were the two most important women in his life. They couldn't be bickering with one another. He wasn't having that.

CHAPTER TWENTY-TWO

That night Melanie and Eighty were sprawled across the queen-size bed in her condo. For the last hour they had been creating a to-do list for the adult entertainment company they had decided to partner on. The couple brainstormed about money-making ideas until Melanie changed the topic.

She wanted to get to know her man better. Mel lay on Eighty's chest and sweetly inquired about his past. "Baby, tell me why they call you Eighty. How you get that name?"

Eighty laughed. "You already asked me that before, Mel. Why you wanna know so badly?"

Melanie smiled. "Because, boo ..."

"If I told you, then I'd have to knock you off. I don't wanna do that because your head game is too good."

"Oh, word? I'ma do it like this next time." Mel laughed and bit him on the shoulder.

Eighty pushed her and popped her on her ass. "Cut that shit out, Mel."

Melanie giggled and placed her lips to his ear. She seductively murmured, "I'ma guess how you got that nickname."

Eighty looked amused. "A'ight. Go 'head."

"Okay. They call you Eighty 'cause you got eighty bodies."

Eighty laughed out loud. "Damn, Mel, I ain't the Son of Sam! Where you get that from?"

Melanie stared at her man with adoration. Eighty was about ten years older than her but he was boyishly handsome and had a great smile. "So *why*, baby? Tell me," she whined.

Eighty playfully spanked her on the ass. "Why you so fuckin' nosy? Huh?"

"*What*? I told you all my deepest, darkest secrets!"

"Mel, you did porn. Everybody done seen your deepest darkest secrets."

She rolled her eyes at him. "Whatever, asshole. You ain't about to hold out on me. Not no more, nigga!"

"Word?" Eighty her challenged, amused. "You sure about that?"

Mel looked at him and didn't back down. "You heard me. If you *don't* tell me, I'm never gon' suck your dick again!"

Eighty looked shocked. That was blasphemy Melanie was talking. "*What?* Yeah, right. You love that shit more than I do, wit' your freak ass!"

Mel grinned because she was guilty as charged. "You right, I *do* love that shit. But real talk, baby. How'd you get that nickname?"

Eighty shook his head and laughed. "You mad thirsty. Chill, man. It ain't no big deal. I used to take money for a living, and my weapon of choice was a .380. So my mans just started calling me Eighty." Eighty would always be a thug at heart. He recollected his crime-filled past and chuckled to himself. "Shit, I still keep me a .380 close by."

Mel stared at him as if she was mesmerized. She loved herself a bad boy. "So, tell me more, baby. What did you do with that .380?"

Eighty laughed and shook his head. He refused to talk about dirt that was already swept under a rug. He had gotten away with a lot of shit, so that was absurd. "Mel, you got the wrong one. I don't do that. You ain't fuckin' with some lame ass wannabe nigga. I ain't *never* been the type to boast about toast. That's nothin'. I keeps heat, Mel. It's apart of my everyday uniform."

Intrigued, Mel whispered, "Can I see it?"

Simply to show her that he wasn't bluffing, Eighty leaned over and retrieved his gun. Mel was surprised to see that he'd stashed it under her bed. Shocked, she stared at him openmouthed. "Eighty, you had that over there 'cause you don't trust me?"

Eighty told Mel the gospel truth. "I don't trust nobody, baby. Not even myself sometimes."

Mel was fascinated and fixated on the weapon. "Boo, can I hold it?"

Eighty thought about it for a moment. He removed the clip to avoid any accidental discharge. After he made sure there was nothing in the chamber, he handed it to her.

Melanie beamed and took the gun from him. Eighty laughed as she fronted like she knew what she was doing. She got up and aimed at her reflection in the mirror. Mel just wore underwear at the time; a red lace bra and panties. She looked like she was impersonating one of the actresses in a seventies blaxploitation film. Eighty asked, "Who you supposed to be, Foxy Brown or Cleopatra Jones?"

Mel blew on the tip of the gun sexily and looked him square in the eye. "How 'bout I'm *both*, sucka!" She did this cool ass seventies walk to look the part more.

Eighty shook his head at Mel's exaggerated hip-shaking bebop. She had that thing down to a science. The lovers looked at one another and erupted into a fit of laughter. Melanie's silliness turned Eighty on. She could be a lot of fun when she wanted to be. She looked sexy in those lace panties too. Watching her rotund rear end swaying back and forth, he became fully erect. He walked over and grabbed her around the waist. "Get yo' ass over here, girl. You ain't tough."

Mel looked down and saw his dick standing straight up. She giggled in delight and pressed her butt against him.

Eighty said, "You like playin' wit' guns, huh? I'ma show your ass some gunplay." He took the burner from her. "Lay down on the bed," he commanded.

Mel stood on her tiptoes and pecked Eighty on the lips, and then she sank to her knees and tugged at his boxers. Eighty loved head just as much as the next man, but that time he stopped Mel and pulled her to her feet. He picked up the gun clip and reloaded. "Take off everything. Now!" he ordered.

Mel loved when he took charge. She did as she was told. A moment later, she stood before him as naked as the day she was born. Eighty put the gun on safety and traced it along her shoulders. Mel stood there as still as death while he proceeded to take her to another realm. He rubbed the gun barrel around her lips slowly, over and over, and then down her neck. When he traced her breasts with the deadly weapon, Melanie gasped and breathed heavier and heavier. She was electrified. Her nipples stood out like .22 caliber bullets.

Melanie knew better than to play with guns. Strangely, she was turned on and overwhelmed by the danger he subjected her to. It actually made her moist.

Eighty didn't normally fool around with weapons that way. He just wanted to give Mel's freak ass an experience like no other. After that night, she would either run from him or be hooked forever. Eighty placed the gun barrel between Mel's legs and rubbed her pussy next. She sort of recoiled at first, and then she relaxed.

Melanie closed her eyes and moaned. She was delighted by the cold steel on her clitoris. She pressed her pelvis forward to heighten the sensation even further. She realized that grinding on gunmetal was a new forbidden freakiness that drove her wild. Melanie went with the illicit foreplay and lay back on the bed spread-eagled.

Eighty licked his lips. He was pleased that Melanie seemed to be enjoying herself so much. He leaned down, spread her lips apart, and circled her clit with the tip of the gun. Mel closed her eyes. She squirmed and moaned. The look on her face said she surrendered. She trusted him and wanted it. Eighty's dick was rock-hard. A small lake of juices had formed in Mel's valley. He dipped the tip of the hammer inside of the honey. She opened her legs wider, and he inserted it further. She was so wet it made squishy sounds. Eighty stuck it in and out. It aroused him more and more. He rubbed Mel's clit with his thumb and pistol-fucked her until she came.

Melanie was a super-freak. She lay there obligingly and loved every second of it. On the brink of bliss, she threw it back. "Ooh, baby, fuck me!" she begged. It was absolutely wonderful.

Eighty sped up the rhythm and gave her what she wanted. "You like this shit, don't you?"

"Baby, I *love* it," Mel cried. "Fuck me, nigga!"

"Take this gun, bitch! Take it!" he demanded.

The torture was mind-blowing. Dizzy, Mel blurted out, "You black mothafucka, come on and beast fuck me! Right now, Eighty!"

Eighty withdrew the sticky gun and laid it on the bed. He stepped out of his boxers and mounted Mel, and then he penetrated her with his other tool. He slow-grinded and deep stroked that pussy and tore it up. Gradually, he sped up and fucked Mel animalistic like she'd begged him too. When he came, he roared like he was king of the jungle.

Eighty and Melanie's sex was always wild. Especially since they had gone to get tested for HIV/AIDS. They had each proven a clean bill of health, so they went at it no holds barred. They freaked off all the time. Mel was full of surprises. She had spoiled him rotten. Now he looked forward to the special treatment. He informed her that he wasn't fond of sharing. He insisted that certain things be reserved for him. Mel took heed to that, so they were exclusive now. Eighty had that on lock. What he liked most about Mel was the fact that she was determined to get some paper. Her proper pussy was just a plus.

CHAPTER TWENTY-THREE

Wise turned off the road from Cas's house on to the main highway. He and Falynn had been over there for a while. She had been busy playing with Cas's kids while Wise, Cas, and Jay got caught up on things. It was a school night, so Wise had broke out before ten o'clock rolled around. It was pass his daughter's bedtime.

Wise drove through the still of the cool night in a black Maserati and thought about his visit with Cas. Being around him and seeing how happy he was to be home with his family had taken a positive effect on Wise. He turned the music down and rode along in silence for a change. His mind raced back over all of the events that had transpired over the past few years. He and his team were blessed. They had each survived life-threatening injuries and got another chance to be with their families. If that wasn't blessed, Wise didn't know what was. Set aside all the riches and cars, they were blessed with life. God was good.

Something Cas said had stuck in Wise's head. He kept talking about changing for the better. Wise understood how he felt. It was good to switch the game up sometimes. A little change couldn't hurt anybody.

Wise slowed down as he approached a red stop light. He looked in the rearview mirror at his angel cake sleeping in the back seat. He and Fatima were on the outs at the time, but that little girl was the best thing that had ever happened to him. Falynn and the new son Wise and Fatima were expecting soon would be Wise's legacy. His children were everything to him.

Wise thought about the time he'd been forced to stay away from them. He'd been hit in the neck in a shootout that he, Cas, and Jay had with this nigga named Mike Machete. He was one half of this stickup team called the Scumbag Brothers. Those niggas had used Hip Hop, this snake that had posed as their ally, to line them up. Hip Hop and those Scumbag Brothers all got what they deserved. Wise had taken Mike Machete out, but he took a bullet in the process. He had faked his own death to avoid the murder charges associated with that extermination.

During his hiatus, Wise had missed his wife and daughter more than anything. He had counted down the days until he was able to reveal himself. He was ecstatic when the opportunity finally came. He had waited until the family vacationed in the South of France. He had popped up on Fatima first, late at night as she stood alone on the beach. When she saw him she was so surprised she literally fainted. That night they were happier than they'd ever been.

Wise and Fatima had gone from there all way to the point where he didn't even want to go home. Wise knew he had been totally unfair but he was disgusted with Fatima. Since he'd found out about her dirty little secret he could barely stand looking at her.

Talking with his mans had rekindled the family ethic in Wise's heart. Now he felt a few guilt pangs. In all fairness, Fatima had been under the impression that he had passed on when she did that bullshit, so he'd been a real asshole lately. He'd been blatantly disrespectful and said things to Fatima that he'd clap a nigga for saying to her. To make matters even worse, he didn't go to the doctor with her that morning. Fatima was pregnant with his child, so that was foul.

During Wise's moment of clarity he realized he had everything he'd ever prayed for. Therefore, he needed to put his family first and live right. In order to do that, he had to make a few changes himself. When God had spared his life, Wise had promised Him he'd live right. After taking inventory of his soul, he knew he had reneged and failed miserably. Wise didn't want to be taught another lesson for playing with it, so he made a vow to put all the negativity aside and be a worthy husband and father. He decided he would forgive Fatima and end the little affair he had been carrying on with Lily.

The closer Wise got home, the more he looked forward to making up with his wife that night. Enough was enough. Wise thought about the things he had done with Lily the night before and felt awful. A stiff dick had no conscious, but he knew he was wrong for sexing Lily and leading her on.

Lily was really into him. It seemed as if she'd been cool with their arrangement at first, but she had gotten rather clingy lately. She had laid it on the line and expressed her feelings for him the night before, so Wise knew he was dead wrong for smashing her when he had no intentions on honoring her wishes.

He knew exactly what the problem was. He had been selfish and enjoyed the fact that Lily had only been sleeping with him. Though he'd never mentioned it out loud, he had developed some feelings for her as well. Wise couldn't front, he cared about Lily because she was a good person. She had helped his mother conspire to fake his death and then she took time off work to nurse him back to health. Lily could also suck a good dick and hook a mean steak up.

He had spent a lot of time with her. How could he not have feelings for her?

As if on cue, Lily called Wise at that exact moment. She was going to live a long time. He was glad she'd called because it gave him the opportunity to tell her it was really over. Continuing to see her would be unhealthy for his marriage. "Yo," Wise answered.

Lily's intentions for calling Wise were quite the opposite. She'd called to let him know she couldn't go on without him. She'd seen his pregnant wife at the doctor's office earlier that day and gotten a serious wakeup call. It was time for Wise to choose. "Papi Chulo, what up, baby?"

"Ain't shit. On my way home with my daughter. What up, you a'ight?"

Lily beamed. "Now that I got you on the phone, I am. Listen, baby, I gotta talk to you."

Wise sighed. "I'm glad you called. I need to holla at you too."

"Okay, baby, you first."

Wise cleared his throat. What he was about to say wasn't easy. "I think we should let it cool off for a while. I'm try'na do the right thing, so … Lily, I'm about to have a son, so I'ma just be about my family for a while."

"What? I don't understand. Where did this come from? We just spent last night together, and it was so beautiful. We made love all night, Papi. So how can you say that?"

Wise sighed. That was the part he hated. "I'm married, Lily. You know that."

"I know, but I want *us* to be together."

"I have a family," Wise said firmly.

"I know, but I could give you the same thing. Let's make another baby together."

Wise screwed up his face. What the hell was she talking about? "Lily, I have a son on the way. He'll be here in a few weeks. Enough of this, baby girl. You're too good for this. You need to find somebody that can make you happy."

"*You* make me happy! You know what you and I have, baby. You know it's special. Wise, we can have a family together. One *better* than the one you got."

Wise was turned off by Lily's last words and grew impatient. "What the fuck you said? Watch your mouth! Ain't nothin' more important than my kids, so don't ever say no stupid shit like that again!"

Tears welled up in Lily's eyes. "Wise, I'm sorry but I love you! I just want us to be together! We can build a mansion in Puerto Rico, in a beautiful place called Arroyo. I already got the land, baby."

Wise lowered his tone but kept steady. "Well, I'm sorry, Lily. I care about you, but that will never happen. We *can't* be together. That's why I'm telling you to move on, because you deserve better."

Confused, Lily stammered, "Wh-what? Wh- what you *mean*, baby?"

Wise got impatient again. She didn't get it. "I meant just what I said! Look, Lily, it's been lots of fun but we are *done*. So that's that."

Wise's words cut through Lily like a sharp blade. Her defense mechanism kicked in and she thought of a snappy comeback. She was a true Latina, so there was a hint of a Spanish accent in her venom soaked response. "Oh, *word*? Now, all of a sudden you care about your family and your kids. You wasn't saying that shit last night when I had your fuckin' dick down my throat! And when *I* was pregnant by you, you didn't give a rat's ass about having no kids. Now you care so fuckin' much."

Wise shook his head. He didn't even respond to that dumb shit.

His complete silence spoke volumes to Lily. She got choked up and didn't know what else to say. Her heart was on her sleeve and she was just pitiful. Finally, she found her voice and desperately went for broke. "I brought you back from the dead, Wise. Doesn't that mean anything to you?"

Wise looked at his phone like it was contaminated with anthrax. He was revolted. He couldn't believe Lily went there. He reminded her about the handsome stipend she'd received for her troubles. "I definitely appreciate everything you did, but you ain't do me no favor, Lily. You got paid very well for that. A million bucks ain't no chump change. And I *still* have been lookin' out for you. You haven't worked since!"

Lily couldn't dispute that part. Wise had been very good to her. But that just wasn't enough anymore.

Wise gave Lily some much needed advice. "You know what, that's exactly what you should do. Go back to work, Lily. Do somethin' with yourself and quit stressing over me. What happened to all that 'independent woman' shit?"

Wise's sudden barrage of recommendations really stung. Lily was crushed. She was also full of envy and scorned. She hung up the phone so she wouldn't give Wise the satisfaction of hearing her break down in tears.

CHAPTER TWENTY-FOUR

Fatima was at home eating cherries, relaxing, and researching. She sat on her recliner with her iPad, surfing the internet for an at-home method for labor induction. So far she had learned that during the past year, it was done by United States obstetricians more than three times as much as it was done ten years ago. Some of the labor inductions were done for medical reasons, but most were simply convenience inductions.

A convenience induction was exactly what Fatima needed. She discovered some interesting methods during her research. Some of the natural approaches she read about were actually entertaining and right up her alley. She knew without a doubt that nipple stimulation was one she would enjoy. According to the website she found that information on, nipple stimulation caused a labor-inducing hormone called oxytocin to be released into the body. Women could stimulate their own nipples or have their partner do it for them manually or orally. Fatima hoped Wise would participate. That idiot knew how to suck some titties.

Sexual intercourse was another effective method of labor induction. The internet source said semen contained natural prostaglandin, which induced contractions. Fatima hoped Wise would be up for that one as well. Ideally, they could combine prostaglandin-filled semen injections and nipple stimulation for an even better chance. That is, if Wise wasn't still acting stupid. If he was, there was a synthetic prostaglandin agent available as well. The website said it worked just as good for cervical ripening as the natural thing.

Another less appealing induction method Fatima read about was castor oil. Castor oil was a laxative, and stimulating the bowels could ripen the cervix and trigger labor as well. That method would be her last alternative. Fatima laughed to herself because she wouldn't need Wise's assistance with that one. She had been shitting alone since the day she was born – literally.

Wise came in the house with Falynn after ten o'clock that night. Fatima knew they'd been at Cas's, so she didn't fuss about it. She just made moves and put Falynn's butt to bed. It was a school night. She and Wise didn't say much to one another, but they teamed up to get their daughter showered and tucked in. Falynn was dressed in purple pajamas and saying her prayers within twenty minutes. She was sleepy so she fell out quick.

After they kissed their daughter goodnight, Fatima went down to the kitchen for a glass of cold water. Wise followed her downstairs and pretended he was thirsty as well. He really just wanted to talk to her.

Fatima wasn't about to kiss Wise's ass after he had played himself and made her go to the doctor alone. She acted like he wasn't even standing there. She got her water and walked right pass his ass.

Wise got it. She was acting like he was invisible. He deserved that. He grabbed her arm and stopped her on the way out of the kitchen. "Wait, come here for a minute."

Fatima turned around and hit Wise with a blank stare. "What?" she asked flatly.

"I just wanna talk to you."

Fatima was surprised but she kept a straight face. She walked over and sat her glass down on the kitchen counter. "Okay, about what? You got the floor."

Wise took a second to get his words together. He decided to just man up. He loved Fatima and wanted to do right by her. "Tima, I just wanna apologize for all the stupid shit I said. When you dealt with that dude, you believed I was gone, so I forgive you. And that was a sucker move I pulled when I didn't go with you to the doctor. I'm sorry, Ma. Word." He nodded sincerely.

Fatima sighed. She had intended to hold out for a while, but she couldn't. She loved that asshole. "Wise, I forgive you, but you were extremely disrespectful. Don't you know the baby can hear all that negative stuff? He feeds off of our energy, Wise. Falynn don't need to be hearing that bullshit either. You think she don't hear us arguing and shit?"

Wise felt horrible. "I'm sorry, Tima. I love the shit outta you."

"I know you love me, baby, but I need for you to show it. *Every single day*. I *need* that from you, Wise. Okay?"

Wise agreed without hesitation. Fatima had loved him before all the riches and fame. Wise knew his wife was true blue. "Okay, I'll show it more. I need you too, Ma. For real." Wise walked over and hugged her tight. "You my queen, Tima. I love you," he whispered in her ear.

It felt good to be in her husband's arms. Fatima's emotions shifted into first gear but she didn't want to cry. She was ready for make-up sex. Wise could assist her with that labor induction, but she had to address the issue that bothered her more than anything – that bitch Lily. "Wise, one more thing. I can't have you staying out all night. I don't want you fuckin' around with that nurse bitch no –"

Wise cut her off right there. "That's dead. I already told her what it is. We ain't rockin' no more." Fatima looked like she wanted to believe him, but didn't. "Seriously, Tima. I'm really try'na do right by you. You deserve that." He nodded reassuringly.

Wise's tone and expression were earnest. The look in his eyes erased any doubts Fatima had. He stared at her like he was in love with her. Fatima needed that. She pecked Wise on the lips and then she traced the scar on the side of his neck. That scar was a product of the bullet wound she thought had killed him. Fatima ran her tongue along its length and inhaled her husband's spicy aroma. She'd bought him the expensive cologne he was wearing. That night it was aphrodisiacal. It tickled her nostrils and sent her pregnancy hormones into overdrive. Fatima wrapped her arms around Wise and exhaled. "Baby, I need you to rub my titties. They're so sore."

Wise looked forward to that. He palmed Fatima's breasts and realized she wasn't wearing a bra. Her titties were so soft his dick got hard. He massaged her nipples, and said, "Damn! I'll play with these tig old bitties all night, Ma. Lemme suck on these shits." Fatima had a nice rack so it was always a pleasure. "Let's go upstairs so I can suck on that pussy too."

Fatima laughed sensually and murmured some more demands. "Okay, baby, that sounds wonderful. I want you to kiss me and caress me and make love to me until you explode deep inside of me."

Wise pressed his pulsating manhood against Fatima's pelvis to show her how ready he was. He enjoyed making love to her. That night he would make sure it was special. They headed upstairs and peeked in on their six year-old. Falynn was asleep, so the expecting couple headed for their master bedroom.

When they stepped in the room, Wise pushed Fatima up against the wall and ripped her pajama shirt open. Two buttons popped off and bounced off the shiny hardwood floor. He was totally unapologetic about it. Fatima loved when Wise got on that aggressive shit. The couple locked lust-filled eyes and kissed passionately as they undressed one another.

Wise leaned down and hungrily took one of Fatima's juicy coconuts in his mouth. He took his time and pleased his wife with the breast play she desired. Her titties were so pretty he sucked on those bad boys for about ten minutes. They were like caramel Milk Duds. Fatima moaned softly and loved every second of it. She called out Wise's name and coaxed him to continue.

Wise knew how his wife liked it. He knew Fatima's body and knew how to please her. He licked and kissed his way down to the pot of gold at the end of the rainbow. Fatima panted in pleasure and spread her legs wider. Wise darted his tongue inside of her and took her closer to bliss each time he invaded her. That pussy was delectable. He swirled his tongue across her clit until it swelled and throbbed. Wise hit the right spot and Fatima's face contorted in lust. She shook uncontrollably and screamed, "Aaahh, baby, yes!" He had her creaming. At the brink of climax, she grabbed the back of his head and grinded on his face. The wave she rode was mind-blowing. Fatima could feel her uterus contracting.

Wise came up for air and didn't waste any time. He wanted some of that so bad he slid in while she was cumming. He felt her walls twitching on his shaft and couldn't take it. That pussy was so hot and wet, Wise barely got off ten strokes. He squeezed Fatima's ass and drove it home. His toes curled as he groaned and shot off deep inside of her. He and Fatima's lovemaking ended just as she'd requested.

Fatima smiled and caressed Wise's back. She loved her husband and enjoyed being intimate with him. It solidified their love. Sex with Wise was always spectacular. If they carried on that way everyday, she would have that baby in no time.

CHAPTER TWENTY-FIVE

Just before dawn the following morning, Macy woke up feeling horrible. Over the past week she'd been having these extreme bouts of nausea. Some days her morning sickness lasted well into the evening hours. She had no appetite and her sense of smell had heightened substantially. Basically, everything stunk to her. Even things she usually loved: Food, perfume, fragrant soaps and lotions, and even Jayquan. He had smoked some weed the other day before he came over. His clothes and fingertips reeked of that mess so bad she couldn't stand to be around him.

Macy realized she wasn't going to make it to the toilet. There wasn't enough time. She leaned over the side of her bed and grabbed the pink garbage pail that had become her bedside buddy lately. She gagged and stuck her face in the pail just in time. Macy threw up her guts for what seemed like an eternity. When it was finally over, she lay there sweating and breathing heavy.

Laila was up using the bathroom when she overheard her oldest daughter coughing. She hurried down the hall to see about her. When she got to Macy's room door she didn't bother to knock. She stepped in the room and saw her baby laying there looking beat. Laila looked at the pail Macy was nursing and knew she'd been sick. "You okay, doll?"

"No, but I pray I will be. This is driving me crazy."

"Aww, you poor baby." Laila gave Macy a sympathetic look. "Girl, I know your pain. I was sick as a dog when I was pregnant with you. It'll soon pass. I threw up almost everyday for the first five months. But look what God gave me." Laila reached over and touched her daughter's face. "One day it'll be worth it, baby girl."

"I hope so." Macy leaned back on her pillow. Laila took the puke-filled pail from her and took it in the bathroom. She dumped it in the toilet and flushed it, and then washed it out in the tub. Laila washed her hands and then she wet a clean washcloth with cold water. She went back in Macy's bedroom and wiped her face with the cool rag.

Macy managed a smile at her mother's concern. She felt better already. She appreciated having her mom by her side. Laila hadn't exactly been thrilled when she got knocked up. Neither had Macy's grandmother, Mama Atkins, but they hadn't ostracized her. Macy made a mental note to call her grandmother later that day to see how she was doing. Mama Atkins had been a pivotal part of her support system. Macy was glad she would have her mother and grandmother's help when the baby came. She looked forward to finishing school and accomplishing her dreams and goals. She knew she couldn't do it without them.

Laila looked over at the clock on the nightstand. "Macy, go back to sleep for a little while. You still have an hour before you have to get up for school."

Macy sighed. "I'ma try to. Lay in here with me for a little while, Ma. Let me go clean up my gross breath first." She got up and went to the bathroom to rinse her mouth.

Laila smiled to herself and sat down on Macy's queen-size bed. When she returned from the bathroom, they both got in bed. Laila held her baby and stroked her hair until she fell asleep in her arms. That was one of life's simple pleasures. Macy had grown up too fast.

$$$$$

Later that morning around ten o'clock, Jay was nicely suited up in a three-piece dark gray number and lavender colored shirt by Tom Ford. He sat in associate's boardroom waiting for a meeting they had scheduled to begin. Jay and a few well-dressed, cigar-smoking business partners had gathered to discuss a joint venture – the reality show they were all vested in.

Alongside Jay sat the star of the show, Kira, who was leaned back in a chair with her legs crossed and seventeen hundred dollar boots kicked up on the table. Kira was texting a list of instructions to the assistant she had hired a few days before. The siblings, Jay and Kira, were joined by Casino, whose upper half appeared on a wall-mounted flat screen via Skype.

The huge office they currently occupied belonged to the gray-haired gentleman sitting at the head of the table, Bertie Shasho. Bertie was a successful veteran in the television business whose name rang bells amongst the "who's who." One of the industry's most influential figures, Bertie was an elderly, friendly-faced, Jew who smoked fine Cuban cigars like they were Newports. Bertie had a thing for fine cigars, aged red wine, and young black women.

Kira was clad in metallic royal blue jeggings and a yellow off-the-shoulder fishnet top. The Manolo Blahnik foot candy she donned matched her outfit perfectly. Bertie stared at her long legs appreciatively and blew out a cloud of expensive smoke. In the thick accent he'd maintained since he came to America dirt poor in 1962, he said, "Princess Kira, why you don't look so happy, beautiful?"

Kira smiled. Bertie was a likeable guy. "I'm okay. I just have some things on my mind that I wanna address."

Bertie nodded at Kira as if he was interested, and then he looked at his ringing cell phone. "No problem, my dear Kira. I will give you the floor in just one minute. I have important telephone call to take now from Israel. Okay, Miss America?"

Kira nodded and smiled politely. She waited patiently while Bertie answered his phone and had a brief conversation in Hebrew, which his native language. Kira had been looking forward to a sitting down with the bosses. Though she was the star of the show, Jay, Cas, and Bertie were the executive producers, i.e. the money men. Bertie could stare at her legs all he wanted, as long as he continued to cut those big checks she needed.

Jay watched Kira and wondered what she was up to. Why hadn't she informed him of what was on her mind? Jay knew his sister well. Kira had some type of agenda. Jay also wanted to ask her why she was at Vino's house that late at night. He decided against the latter; his sister was grown.

Cas was at home in his office thumbing through some paperwork. He waited patiently for Bertie to get off the phone along with the other attendees that were seated at the conference table. In addition to Jay and Kira, the attorneys were also present. Solly Steiner represented Jay and Cas, Phyllis Berg was Kira's legal eagle, and Steven Bausch was Bertie's attorney. That particular meeting was just about financial business, so there were no crew members or production people present.

Bertie got off the phone and they got down to business. First on the agenda was a discussion about the budget. They threw some numbers and supporting information back and forth, and they finally came to a financial agreement. Next, they talked about scheduling and went over a list of things to be done. The last issue they addressed was another budget question, and then everyone agreed with the terms. The investors exchanged well wishes and shook on it. Bertie looked at Cas and threw a hand up to acknowledge him as well.

Cas put his fist forward and extended a virtual pound via the webcam. Bertie grinned and dapped him back. Jay and Kira followed suit, and the attorneys all laughed and respectfully mimicked. Cas's cyber-presence was in no way underrated.

When they were all done, Bertie zoomed in on Kira. "Miss America, before we come to a close, you want to speak something? What you have on your pretty mind?"

Kira smiled and thanked him. Then she got right to the point. "The producers believe I need a love interest on the show. They think that would boost the ratings." She looked at Jay, Cas, and Bertie's reactions so far. None of them really had any. She went on to tell them about her golden idea.

Kira introduced the idea of a romance transpiring with one of her music producers, and everyone got sort of quiet. She has been anxious to get a stamp of approval from the big dogs, so that wasn't the reaction she'd hoped for. She needed the show producers to come to terms with the fact that she had carte blanche. She was tired of going back and forth with them. If Bertie, Cas, and Jay got behind her, they would no longer scrutinize her suggestions.

Kira hated when people, men particularly, didn't take her serious. She was irritated but she remained cordial. She cleared her throat. "I made a suggestion, and I would appreciate being taken serious. This show was *my* idea, remember? It was good enough for you *gentlemen* to turn loose the purse strings, so please have a little faith in me. And in the future, when I have an idea, please don't just look at me like I'm stupid."

Bertie laughed and took out a cigar. He handed Jay one as well. "Calm down, Miss America! Don't upset! The way this works in show business, we make big casting call to find Mr. Perfect for you. We screen hundreds, maybe thousands of handsome guys, all for one special guy for you and America to love."

Kira nodded patiently. "I understand that, Bertie, but we don't need to audition anyone. I already have Mr. Perfect, so let's not waste time or money."

Bertie lit his cigar and calmly dissuaded Kira. "But darling, this something we can not rush. All the elements must be there. It's all about chemistry. How we know there is a chemistry between you two? We have to attract viewers, my dear. This is big numbers game. That's what television is all about."

"Bertie, I know, trust me. I assure you that there's chemistry. I'll even show you." Kira got her new assistant, who was waiting for her out in the lobby, on the phone. "Miranda, please escort my friend in here."

Jay no longer had to wonder what his sister was doing at Vino's. She was clearly sweet on that dude. Jay's ego told him to shut that shit down immediately; right on the spot. But his issues with Vino were personal, so he kept it business for the moment and kept his thoughts to himself.

Seconds later, there was a knock at the door. Kira got up and happily did the honors of opening it. Vino was standing on the other side. Kira grinned and grabbed his hand and pulled him inside.

Jay watched his sister's face light up and frowned noticeably. He reminded himself that they were in a professional atmosphere and relaxed.

Vino walked in the boardroom and felt awkward, as if he was on exhibit. All eyes were on him. He hadn't been in a room with that many crackers staring at him since his last court case. He greeted everyone politely. "Good morning. How y'all doin'?"

Bertie Shasho spoke first. "Hello, my friend. Very well, thanks." The three attorneys mumbled responses that Vino barely understood, Cas said "what up" on the flat screen, and Jay gave him a poker-faced nod.

Bertie said, "You are good looking young man, true, but looks just one fourth the formula. Where is the chemistry?"

Vino got a little nervous and wondered what he had walked into. He didn't know how to respond to that, so he didn't. Kira had got him to agree with the idea she'd pitched him, but he wasn't about to be subjected to that type of scrutiny.

Kira surprised Vino and everyone else and pecked him on the lips. Then she got bold and grabbed the back of his head and French kissed him sensually. She closed her eyes and made it the kind of soft kiss that was shared with someone you loved. Kira slipped Vino some tongue and the whole nine. After the kiss, they just looked at one another for a second, speechless. Everyone else was as well.

Kira snapped out of it and got back into business mode. She turned around and winked at Bernie. "There's your chemistry, Mr. Shasho!"

The kiss didn't last that long, but strangely, Kira had proved her point. Bertie shrugged and coolly continued smoking his cigar. "Okay, my dear. Since I have a big hard-on in my pants now, I vote he's in." Everyone laughed except Vino and Jay.

Kira sensed that Vino felt uncomfortable, and she didn't blame him. She owed him an apology for her spontaneity. "My bad, boo. I ain't mean to put you on the spot like that. Thanks for being such a good sport."

Vino had been caught off guard, although it was obvious he'd enjoyed that kiss. Stevie Wonder could see that.

Bertie refrained from voicing his true sentiments, which were kind of lewd. He had imagined kissing Kira's lips and also feeling them elsewhere, but Bertie knew better than to express that. Kira wasn't the average reality starlet that he could take advantage of. She was connected with some heavyweights. Her brother and ex-husband had clout and were well-respected.

Jay just sat there and looked on. His crazy ass sister never ceased to amaze him. The girl didn't have a shy bone in her body. He didn't enjoy seeing his baby sis plant a juicy one on a nigga he suspected had sexed his wife, but Jay kept his opinion to himself. He was typically not an emotional guy. He didn't let personal feelings govern business relationships and decisions.

Cas was still watching on a Skype video conference. He was so surprised by that kiss, he laughed out loud. It tickled his funny bone but he was otherwise unaffected. He already knew how bold Kira was. She had initiated what he and she had. Kira's aggressiveness had resulted in some late night sex, and then they ultimately hooked up, had a kid, and got married. They were divorced now, so Cas could care less what Kira did in her love life, on or off camera. He wished her happiness. As long as his son wasn't subjected to any bullshit, he was okay with any sensible decision Kira made. Cas had peeped Jay's reaction too. He didn't look so thrilled about Kira's idea. Cas was sure it had everything to do with what Jay told him had allegedly happened between Portia and Vino in L.A.

At the close of the meeting, the executive producers concluded that they would set up a screen test for Vino. The results of that screen test would determine if he'd make the cut. Everyone agreed that was best, and Kira didn't argue. She had faith that Vino would pass the first time around. Her gut told her that he was the one.

They wrapped up the meeting and Jay shook hands with Bertie and the attorneys. He saw Kira and Vino slip out the door. Jay got out of there as fast as he could. He wanted to corner Vino so he could question him. Seeing him at the meeting gave him the opportunity.

As Jay rode the elevator down, he decided that it wasn't the time or place. He was unsure about how to approach Vino anyway. What would he say, *"Hey, man, did you fuck my wife?"* Jay wanted to be upfront and candid, but he didn't want to look like some insecure asshole. He was no bitch. He wondered if Vino would even admit anything. "Only if he got a death wish," Jay muttered to himself. He bit his lip in anger. Just that fast, he was pissed off again. That was why he couldn't forgive Portia yet. Just thinking about that shit fucked up his mood.

When Jay got off the elevator in the lobby, he didn't see anyone. That was probably a good thing. He took a deep breath to let off the steam he had built up and decided he would speak to Vino after business hours.

When Jay got back to his office, he had Robin notify Vino and tell him he wanted to see him. Vino was instructed to meet Jay at the Honeycomb that evening so they could "have a drink."

When Vino got the call about Jay's "request" to have a drink later, he assumed it pertained to the inappropriate kiss Kira had laid on him. Vino didn't need the drama in his life, but he knew better than to turn Jay down. That man was paying him a lot of money. Jay and Cas had offered him an ideal opportunity, so they deserved his respect.

CHAPTER TWENTY-SIX

At seven o'clock that evening, Jay and Vino sat across from one another in the VIP section of the Honeycomb with nothing between them but the honeycomb shaped candleholder centerpiece on the table. Vino was a cognac man like Jay, so Hennessy was their drink of choice. The men sipped shots of liquor and made small talk.

Jay looked over and saw that chick he had conversed with the last time he was there, Breylan. She sat with her girls a few tables to the right. Breylan looked nice that evening too. Her hair was styled differently that time. She caught Jay's eye and waved at him, so he smiled and nodded at her.

Jay focused back on Vino. Now that he had the chance to question him, he wanted to do it right. He waited until they ordered their third round of drinks. He wanted to ensure that Vino was relaxed and not so calculated with his responses.

Vino was one step ahead of Jay. He felt a different from usual vibe from him that night, so he expected him to come at him with some concerns. He stayed on point and waited until he brought it up.

Jay was tired of lollygagging. He looked his young friend in the eyes and began the interrogation. "Vino, you spent some time with my wife out in L.A. I sent you some spread to look after her. Remember?"

Vino recollected, and nodded. "Yeah, no doubt."

"Lemme ask you somethin'. Man to man. During the time she was out there, did anything happen between y'all?"

Vino almost choked on the Henny he was sipping. He'd been anticipating something from Jay, but was in no way prepared for that. That shit with Portia happened so long ago, Vino had sworn it was water under the bridge. He pretended to be baffled by the question. "What you mean? Anything like what?"

Jay kept his eyes trained on Vino's and read his reactions like a polygraph machine. "Did you and Portia get... *close* out there?"

Vino shifted uncomfortably. He was on the hot seat. "Pardon me, man, but exactly what are you asking me?"

Jay folded his hands on the table and didn't blink once. "Did you smash my wife? Just answer me, man."

Vino made a face as if he was appalled. "Hell no! Jay, man, what would make you ask me something like that?" He wasn't generally a liar, but his response had been prompted by both fear and revere. He had too much respect for Jay to look him in his face and cop to something like that. He was also understandably afraid of the consequences of such an act. He wasn't stupid, nor did he have a death wish.

Jay heard Vino loud and clear, but he wasn't satisfied yet. "A'ight, so what type of contact did you have with her? I already know y'all spent the night together." Jay stated his last sentence like it was a fact but he was only bluffing. Wise had furnished him with the only information he had, so he didn't know anything. He was trying to get Vino to crack.

Vino was as nervous as a three-time felon on the stand, but he had every intention on sticking to his story. He just prayed he came off convincing. "Yeah, man, I'll admit that I fell asleep on the couch in her hotel suite, but all we did was talk that night. We smoked a couple of els and just kicked it. All your wife talked about was *you*. She was upset, and said you and her was goin' through some things 'cause you cheated on her. Portia cool peoples, so I lent her an ear and a shoulder to cry on. She told me she was praying y'all would make it, but she was real hurt. Man, then we puffed another one and dozed off on the sofa. That's *all*, Jay." Vino nodded sincerely. "That's the only reason I stayed. That loud had me so damn high, I got sleepy. I apologize about that, bro. I was in the studio for a long ass session the night before, and it came down on me. Jay, you da big homie, and you done looked out for me on numerous occasions. I would never disrespect you, man."

If Vino was lying, that nigga was good. If he was telling the truth, Jay still had his doubts. He stared him down for a moment. Jay didn't appreciate the fact that he'd taken the initiative to comfort his wife. Who the fuck was he supposed to be? "Look, when I paid you to look out for Portia, I meant her safety. Not all that extra Dr. Phil shit."

Vino nodded humbly. He certainly couldn't argue with that.

Jay mulled it over for a minute. The little devil version of him sitting on his shoulder said late-wait that nigga and clap him. He bodied dudes for violating him. The last nigga that messed with his wife, this lame named Wayne-o, was a dead man. Jay reminded himself that he had killed him for breaking in his crib and raping Portia. With Vino, it wasn't that serious. And Portia had interacted with him voluntarily.

Jay told himself that she was replaceable. He didn't want to kill that boy over no bitch. He had to teach Vino a lesson, but there was more than one way to skin a cat. Jay had the means to hurt him without laying a finger on him. He could end that nigga, just like that. He could be spiteful if he wanted to, and cut off the financial lifeline to his production company. He could also have it blacklisted and cut off Vino's legs and have him blackballed, so nobody in the industry would ever fuck with him. Not being able to make any bread would hurt him more than anything.

Annoyed, Jay sighed. The stress about the situation was getting to him. He would never know exactly what had happened, so maybe it was easier to believe Vino and leave the past in the past. Being that Vino and Portia had both denied it, he didn't have much of a choice.

The more Jay thought about it, he had to take Vino's word for it. He had looked him in the eyes when he answered him. All a man had was his word and his balls, so he'd give the dude the benefit of a doubt.

Vino knew Jay was sitting there analyzing him. He was deciding whether he believed him or not. He was probably also wondering if he should do something to him. If the shoe were on the other foot, Vino would've scrutinized Jay's story just as hard if it was his wife. He really felt fucked up about the situation. He had lied to that man's face. But had he not denied it, there was no telling how things could get out of control. Vino was no sucker by any means, but the reality was that he had sexed that man's wife. That was a serious violation, so that wasn't the time to G up. He knew niggas that had died for less. Hell, he had two brothers that did.

Vino wasn't proud of himself one bit. Jay was a dude he had tons of respect for. He had only tried to help him get on, so that wasn't a good look. He was out there on Jay's coast, so he knew he could probably snap a finger and end his life if he chose. Jay and his teammates were some real ass niggas. Vino was about that life as well, so real recognized real.

Jay made up his mind. He decided to let that shit go and give that nigga a pass. Vino was just a little dude trying to come up. Jay didn't see him as a threat. The more he thought about it, he knew he had bigger things to focus on. He was a move-making mothafucka. A multi-millionaire. Jay gave Vino his ruling. "A'ight, man, we ain't got no beef."

Vino maintained a poker face and didn't express the relief he was flooded with. He summoned the hostess to refresh their drinks, and then he reached across the table to give Jay a pound.

Jay relaxed and gave the nigga some dap. Fuck it, they had business together. Now that he had squashed the personal shit, there was something else Jay wanted to address. He was curious about the business between Vino and his sister. After their drinks were replenished, Jay brought it up. "So, what's the deal with you and Kira?"

Vino shook his head and sighed. "Man, your sister somethin' else. And that little kiss earlier was her idea. I ain't know nothin' about it. That was Kira all day."

Jay wasn't surprised. Kira was audacious like that. He thought about her coming out of Vino's building that night. "So, what, y'all two startin' somethin'?"

Vino shook his head. "Nah. She cool, but I know her and the homie, Casino, was together. Cuz, that's a formula for drama, and I ain't wit' that."

Jay said, "Cas and Kira turned it off a long time ago. Cas probably don't even care."

Vino shrugged. "Maybe not. But I ain't try'na start nothin' out here, cuz. Ya' boy just in this here city lookin' to capitalize. I'm try'na put my mama in a nice house, so I don't wanna take no chances."

"My nigga Cas is pretty approachable, believe it or not. If you ain't sure, you should just ask him. It would be a good idea to holla at him anyway, especially if you gon' do the show."

Vino smiled and shook his head. "Nah, man. He might get offended."

There was something about Vino's smile that gave Jay the indication that he dug Kira more than he'd let on. Judging from that passionate kiss they'd shared earlier, the possibility of them two hooking up was pretty strong. Jay knew how his sister was. She went hard and sunk her claws into everything she wanted. It appeared that Vino was her latest prey. Jay decided he would mind his business. "What up with Five?"

Vino shook his head and sighed. "My nigga still jammed up. They try'na pin this body on him. They won't give him no bail yet. He good otherwise, though."

Jay shook his head. He was a reformed street dude, so he sympathized with Five's plight. He sent up a quick prayer for him. "Man, I hope he be a'ight. Keep me posted, and lemme know if he needs anything. Y'all gotta get him a good lawyer."

Vino nodded earnestly. "We lookin' for the best we can find."

Jay said, "Good." He was glad he and Vino had talked. He was reminded what a likeable dude he was. But even if he didn't have sex with Portia, Jay doubted he would be able to trust her again. She was supposed to be his leading lady. Seeking comfort in the arms of another dude was completely unacceptable. In any shape or form.

CHAPTER TWENTY-SEVEN

That night Melanie had stepped out dressed to kill. She wore a shiny blue mini-dress and five-inch red YSL pumps. Her hair and makeup were flawless and she was in classy mode. Mel sat with her legs crossed at a table in the Honeycomb VIP section. She sipped Korbel chardonnay and bobbed her head to the music.

Her motive for being there that night was the fact that her boo, Eighty, was there. He worked there as head of security, so she came through sometimes just to check on him. She secretly did it to make sure he was behaving himself. Eighty was an attractive dude. Chicks paid attention when he entered the room. Mel was no idiot.

Mel spent most of her time at the Honeycomb alone, because Eighty was working. He checked in with her in between making his rounds, so she had time to sit back and observe what the others in the spot were up to. That night she saw Portia's husband, Jay, seated at a table on the other side of the VIP section. He was sitting with that new west-coast producer cutie, Vino. They appeared chummy, as if they had just stepped out for a few drinks that night.

Seeing Jay made Melanie think about her cousin Portia – her American idol. Portia lived a fairytale life. She had encouraged Mel to get it together. There was a time when she would've only been in a spot like the Honeycomb trying to be in the mix, but she was no longer some mixie chick. Melanie had matured. She looked at life differently. The new Mel was determined to have something. She admired the lifestyle that her cousin Portia and her girlfriends lived. She wanted a castle-like crib and a garage full of fancy cars too.

The settlement Melanie had swindled out of Wise for allegedly beating and raping her was the first real money she had ever seen. It was long gone, and the meager funds she had at the time were evaporating. Mel's last gig was being a low-budget adult film actress. She didn't want to go back to that. She was getting older. She didn't want low-budget cameos in porn; she wanted to be the HBIC of the company that made the movies. Day and night she fantasized about the lifestyle change she knew would follow when she and Eighty brought her ideas to life.

Just then, Eighty walked up behind her. "What up, Ma?" He sat down across from Mel.

She perked up and smiled at him brightly. Melanie was tipsy and bursting with bright ideas. "Hey, baby, I been thinking. We have to do this now! We need to start building our empire, boo. We could be a super-power couple. The sex industry is a *billion* dollar industry! We could be huge! Baby, look at me." She looked in his eyes with the serious face. "I guarantee you, if you put your money on this you will *not* regret it."

Eighty liked the sound of that. But as Mel stared in his eyes sincerely trying to get him to invest in her porn production endeavors, he got the impression that she believed he had some serious bank.

Mel continued trying to persuade him. "Babe, I want you to check out the budget I been working on. I estimated all the production costs." She fished in her purse and pulled out a folded up sheet of paper with some writing on it.

"Boo, this is what we gonna need." She passed Eighty the paper.

Eighty looked it over and saw a figure at the end that was over two hundred racks. He whistled and said, "Damn!"

Melanie smiled and countered his hesitation. "Boo, we gon' need like a quarter mil' in startup capital to do what we gotta do, but later on you gon' see. The return on your investment will be ridiculous. To start out with, baby, just put up a hundred thousand dollars. I'll make it work, I know this business."

Eighty had made the transition from the streets to the legit side successfully thus far. He was no broke nigga, but he was far from a major player yet. He knew this about himself and aspired to establish himself enough to change that. However, at the time it was just unrealistic that he could fund a project so immense.

Mel looked so hopeful; he didn't want to burst her bubble. She actually had a great plan. He just needed to get the scratch to finance it. A quarter million was no chump change, but Eighty had touched it before, and he would touch it again. In the past he had taken larger sums than that. But these days he was trying to live right, so he told himself he would get that money the right way. He just had to stall Melanie in the meantime. "Look, this is what you need to do. Put all that on paper, the right way. Devise a *real* business plan. *Then* lemme see the numbers. No offense about your little hand-written budget here, but this is business, Mel."

Mel nodded. She didn't have a problem with that. "A'ight, I can respect that. I want you to take me serious, so I'm on it." She smiled and got up and sat on Eighty's lap and hugged him like he had just said yes.

Eighty grinned at Melanie's enthusiasm. He loved her energy. He was getting older, but with Mel by his side, he envisioned himself aging like Hugh Hefner. He had to get that money up. He had thought about asking Jay and Cas for a loan, but he figured that would be pretty tacky, considering the fact that Cas was recuperating from a bullet to the chest. Eighty really wanted to do it on his own. He would figure out a way, even if he had to go back to his old ways.

Melanie planted a kiss on Eighty's cheek. His cologne smelled so good. "Ummm, damn baby." He laughed and slapped her on the butt. Mel knew he had to get back to work, so she got up off his lap. "Boo, I'ma finish up my drink, and then I'm going home to start working on that business plan. I'll see you at the house." She smiled as he got up walked away.

Melanie hadn't been focused on what Jay was doing, but when she stood up she happened to see Vino get up and leave the table. Mel sat back down and drank the last of her chardonnay. When she was done, she looked over and caught a glimpse of this chick standing at Jay's table laughing and talking with him. Then the woman had a seat and she and Jay continued the conversation they appeared to be enjoying so much. Mel's female instinct went off. She wondered if her cousin Portia knew where her husband was.

Melanie sat there a little longer then she'd planned to, so she could investigate. She didn't know that woman from a can of paint, but she had seen her there a few times. She had to give it up; the bitch carried herself like she had her shit together. Mel had Portia's best interest at heart, so she felt that the right thing to do was to notify her about the possible competition sniffing around her man. Melanie opened up the camera on her Galaxy phone and casually zoomed in on Jay and his lady friend. The pair appeared rather chummy. Mel snapped a few photos and then picked out the best one. She texted the photo to Portia with a comedic caption underneath: *"Harpo, who dis woman?"* Mel chuckled and considered that her good deed for the day. Satisfied, she got up and headed home.

$$$$$

That night Portia was at home helping Jazz with her homework. They were in the process of wrapping it up when her phone sounded off and alerted her that she had a message. She checked it and saw that it was some type of picture mail from her cousin, Melanie. The MMS text had a caption on it that read: *"Harpo, who dis woman?"* That was a line from the movie "The Color Purple" so Portia assumed it was a photo of something funny. She decided to finish checking Jazz's math homework before she opened it up.

About an hour later, Portia tucked her little girls in bed and kissed them goodnight. Trixie had her own bedroom but she was afraid to stay in it by herself. On the nights she didn't sleep with Portia, she slept in the room with her big sister, Jazz. Portia turned on their night-light and then she walked down the hall to her bedroom to check on the baby. She peeked in and saw that Jaylin was still asleep. She continued making her rounds and headed downstairs to check on Jayquan in the studio.

When she got down there, she saw that he was down there with some boys she didn't recognize. Portia said hello to them and asked for their names. Two of the three young men smiled and politely introduced themselves. The third was a little prick. You could tell he thought he was tough from his body language. And his pants were sagging way too much. The wanna-be stuck out his chest and said, "They call me Tracks – 'cause I run shit."

Portia couldn't believe he'd said that. She looked at him like he was crazy. He had the nerve to stare her down. That boy was rude as hell. She wondered who he belonged to.

Tracks boldly sized Portia up and eyeballed her breasts. When he saw the shocked look on her face, he gave her a little cocky smirk.

Portia could see that Tracks was an obnoxious little bastard. Under no circumstances would she accept such insolent behavior from a boy her son's age, especially not in her house. "What's your real name?" she demanded.

Tracks sucked his teeth like he was annoyed. "Pardon me, ma'am, I'm Tom Dickerson," he said sarcastically.

Portia knew he made that up. She decided she didn't like that little asshole. She was seconds away from sending him home. "Well, do me a favor, little Tommy. Stay in a child's place." After she warned him, she didn't wait for his response. Portia decided she'd let Jayquan get rid of his little friend. "Lil' Jay, baby, I need you in the kitchen for a moment." Portia said goodnight to the other boys and left.

Jayquan told his friends he would be right back, and followed his mom. When they got in the kitchen, Portia came right out with it. "Who the hell is that little rude bastard? What are you doing hanging with somethin' like that?"

Jayquan was silly. He had the nerve to laugh. "Lady P, chill. Tracks cool, he just be playin' around all the time. That's my man."

Portia made a sour face. Her gut told her that boy was no good. "Be careful who you call your friends, son.

Choose them very carefully and make sure they have your best interest at heart before you become loyal to them."

Jayquan nodded. "I got you. I was gettin' ready to say goodnight to them niggas anyway, so they 'bout to break out. I got a game tomorrow, Lady P. You gon' try to come through?"

Portia smiled proudly. "I'll be there front and center, baby. Wouldn't miss it for the world." She thought about what Jayquan said, and got stern on him. "That being said, don't you think you should tell your friends good night, so you can get a good night's rest?

"It's mad early, what you *mean*? You act like I'ma little kid. I ain't Jazz and Trixie. I got this. Relax." Jayquan winked at Portia and grinned, and then he went back to the studio.

"You heard what I said," Portia yelled after him. She looked at her phone to see what time it was, and realized she hadn't looked at the text she got from Melanie yet. Portia opened the message, prepared to be tickled by Mel's wacky tacky sense of humor. Her last text had put her in stitches. But when Portia saw the picture Mel had sent her, she didn't laugh one bit. She stared down at Jay sitting with another woman, and almost cried. That shit wasn't funny.

Portia tried not to think the worse. Jay was a businessman, so it could've been completely innocent. But he and his lady friend seemed so well-acquainted, Portia had her doubts. She couldn't wait to question Jay about that shit. She knew that wouldn't be easy, considering the fact that he was upset with her and barely speaking to her. Maybe she should just lay back and see if there was a reason to be alarmed.

That was easier said than done. Fuck that. Portia's intuition told her to call her husband and see where the hell he was. She had to call Melanie first to see where she had taken that picture. Then she would know if Jay was telling the truth about his whereabouts. She dialed Mel and got her on the fourth ring.

"Hey, what up, cuz? I knew you'd be calling me before the night was over."

"Thanks for the detective work, Sherlock Holmes. Where were you?"

Mel giggled. "At the Honeycomb. Jay was with a dude first. That fine ass producer, Vino. Then he left, and that chick went over to Jay's table. They was talkin' for a minute and then she sat down with him. P, I ain't see no groping going on or nothin' so I'm not accusing Jay of anything. I just thought you might wanna know."

Knowing was half the battle. "Thanks, Mel. Good looks," Portia said sincerely. If she had a fight ahead of her, she would rather be prepared. She didn't have a war strategy planned or anything. She just wasn't about to let no bitch steal her husband.

Melanie said, "We family, boo. Now, I hear yo' ass thinking hard over there, so lemme answer them questions I know you got. I've seen the bitch around a couple of times. She ain't no spring chicken either, she's a *woman*. Like late thirties – but *good* late thirties. I bumped into her in the bathroom one time. She carries herself nicely, shoe game was on point. But you know somethin'? It might not even be shit to that, so don't go jumpin' the gun, P."

It was too late for that. Portia rushed Mel off the phone so she could locate her cheating ass husband. "Thanks for the rundown, boo. You good, right?"

"Umm hmm, I'm good. Don't small talk me, chick. We'll catch up later." Mel laughed. "Go 'head and call your hubby. I know you fiendin' to know where that nigga at. Just don't say *I* told you. You gon' get me in trouble with Eighty. Love you, pretty girl. Talk to you later."

"Love you too, sweetie pie. Smooches."

Portia dialed Jay at the speed of light. His voicemail picked up. She frowned and wondered if he was somewhere sexing that bitch. She called his phone again, and again. Jay picked up the third time. Portia sighed in relief, but she kept cool. "Hey, I was just checking on you. Are you okay?"

Jay was curt with her. "Yeah. Why?"

Portia could tell he was still angry with her, so she lied. "Trixie keeps on crying and asking when you coming home. Where you at?" She wondered what he and Vino had talked about.

Jay frowned at the phone. She had the nerve to question him. He'd only answered Portia's call to make sure his kids were okay. He was on his way home, but he thought about doing an about-face just to spite her. Jay only dismissed the option because he was beat. He needed to get some rest. "Tell my daughter I'll see her soon," he said snappishly. Jay hung up on Portia without another word.

On the other end, Portia stared down at the phone and thought about calling Jay back and cursing him out for hanging up on her. She wasn't normally a passive bitch, but she let it ride. In the back of her mind, she knew she was guilty as sin. She couldn't blame him for hating her, because she had done some foul shit.

When Jay got home about forty minutes later, he stared right through Portia and didn't say a single word to her. Jay kissed his three sleeping children and then checked on Jayquan. He and Jayquan stayed up talking for a while. Then Jay took a shower and crashed in one of the spare bedrooms.

Although Portia was sad that she had to sleep alone again, she was glad Jay was home. He was in another bedroom but he could've been out with another woman. As long as they were under the same roof, they were still a family.

CHAPTER TWENTY-EIGHT

The following morning, Lily was in her recently remodeled bathroom applying eye shadow in the mirror. When she was done, she applied a little mascara and then styled her freshly dyed, shoulder-length tresses. Going blonde was a drastic change, so she hoped they really had more fun. Lily stepped into her shoes and slipped on a black blazer. She had a job interview that morning at eleven o'clock. She wanted to get there a little early.

Wise had suggested that she had too much time on her hands. He believed that working would occupy her idle time and be good for her. Lily had taken the advice he had so coldly given her, and decided to go back to work. Luckily, she had left her job at the hospital on good terms. She had a stellar record during the six years she'd been employed as a nurse there, so they had assured Lily that they'd keep a position open for her, in case the arrangement with her "new private client" didn't work out. Lily was ready to go back to work, but not at the hospital. She was taking her résumé and credentials to apply for a job at the doctor's office Fatima attended. She'd done some research and learned that they were hiring, and then she'd called and set up an interview.

Lily shared her two-story home with a pet Yorkie named Trista. She was under her and craving some attention. On Lily's way out the door, she reached down and rubbed her head for good luck. "Mommy's gotta go, Trista. See you in a little while. Smooches!"

That afternoon, Lily left the doctor's office feeling good. On the way to the parking lot she did a little salsa-influenced happy dance. She had nailed the interview. She got the job, and started on the following Monday. As she drove to her favorite café to celebrate, she thought about her next move. Now that she had gotten hired, she had to figure out what she wanted to accomplish. Lily didn't exactly have a plan. She just wanted access to Wise's wife and baby's medical records. Having that information could turn out to be the leverage she needed.

$$\$\$\$\$\$$$

Wise had made a conscious effort to be a better husband and he was sticking to his guns. He'd been staying close to the house to make sure Fatima was okay. They had been getting along great and their sex life was on fire. Fatima's sexual appetite had been voracious lately. She wanted it all the time.

Wise was getting pretty drained but he gave Fatima all the loving she wanted. He conceitedly figured he'd put it on her so good she couldn't get enough. That was partially true, but he didn't know the whole story. Fatima was trying to induce her labor. Though she loved being intimate with her husband, she had a bigger picture in mind. She was ready to have that baby.

One day Fatima got excited because she thought she felt labor pains. She had Wise rush her to the hospital, but it turned out to be just Braxton Hicks contractions. They sort of hurt but they weren't actually the real deal. The doctor put her on bed rest and ordered her to report to her office twice a week.

Another mandatory doctor's appointment rolled around, so Fatima and Wise got ready and headed for the women's health center she attended. They arrived right on time for her 11:45 a.m. appointment. They checked in at the front desk and were told to have a seat in the waiting area.

The waiting area was comfortable enough, with its' purple painted walls, plush red chairs, and huge HD television, but Wise was a little restless sitting there. He kept glimpsing at his big-faced Rolex and counting the minutes. He endured the torturous boredom of the how-to breastfeeding video currently playing, and waited for Fatima's name to be called. He had a few questions for the doctor, so he looked forward to seeing her.

Wise was thumbing through a car magazine when he looked up and saw a girl going into an office down the hall. From behind, her resemblance to Lily was uncanny. He did a double take. The girl walked like her and was also shaped like her. Wise saw that the girl was a blonde, so he ruled it out because Lily's hair color was dark. Just then, the doctor's assistant called Fatima's name and took his mind off of it.

Minutes later, Fatima's examination revealed that her cervix had started dilating. When the doctor told her the news, she almost jumped for joy. The funny thing was she didn't even really have any pain yet. She smiled, because she knew her do-it-yourself induction methods had paid off. She asked the doctor what the plan was from there.

The doctor told her to go home and go for a walk. Then she would dilate a few more centimeters. She said it would probably be hours before anything happened, so he arranged for her to be admitted to the birth center she was scheduled to deliver at the first thing the next morning. She had her personal number, so if anything changed she was to contact her.

The instructions Wise received were simple. He wasn't to leave Fatima's side and had to pay close attention to her. He was a little nervous, but he was happy nonetheless. He and Fatima left the doctor's office with big smiles on their faces. It was official. The baby was coming the following morning. They rushed home to get things in order.

Fatima was glad she had time to go home and get prepared. She already had her maternity bag packed, but she had a few more things to do. The main thing was getting Falynn situated with a family member who would look after her. Fatima knew her parents wouldn't hesitate to step up, and Wise's mom, Rose, wouldn't mind either, but she planned to ask Portia to keep her daughter. Portia's little girl, Jazmin, went to the same school as Falynn, so Portia could get Falynn to school with no problem. Wise's mom and Fatima's parents lived in New York; therefore they would have to commute to Jersey everyday. None of them would complain, but that would be a huge inconvenience.

When Wise and Fatima got home, Wise ran around taking last-minute inventory to see what they needed for the baby.

Fatima laughed. "Boo, relax." She assured him that they were fully-equipped and baby-ready. "Wise, the baby's nursery has been ready for three months. It's filled with enough stuff to last until he's a year old; from a bassinette to a walker. We got stuff that we will probably never even use."

"Okay, Ma." Wise laughed and reminded himself that it was their second time around. They got through it the first time. He willed himself to relax.

Fatima walked around the house for a little while, as the doctor had instructed. Then she settled down and called her besties. When Portia and Laila got wind that she had already dilated two centimeters, they both got in auntie mode and promised they would be by her side the following day. An addition to the family was always a celebratory occasion.

Wise called Jay and Cas, and the upcoming birth of their nephew affected them similarly. They looked forward to having another man in their clan. They were outnumbered by the women in the family, so that would level it off a little bit. Wise also called his mother to tell her the good news. Everyone was ecstatic and said they would be present for the birth of his son. All hands would be on deck.

Wise couldn't front, the family support was comforting. He was so thrilled he couldn't stop smiling. He whispered another prayer for his wife and child's wellbeing. He didn't underestimate the perils of childbirth. A woman was in a vulnerable state while she was in labor. Wise had an aunt who had died in the process of giving birth, so he knew better than to take it lightly.

$$$$$

As Jay drove home that evening, he thought about Wise and Fatima's new blessing. He was genuinely overjoyed for them. Wise would finally have his namesake. For some reason, Jay thought about his father after that. His mother had informed him that his "sperm donor" had asked for him. He thought about meeting with that chump and asking him where the hell he'd been throughout his life. Jay dismissed the idea as quickly as it had popped into his head. He didn't need that mothafucka in his life complicating shit. He had enough problems.

His mind drifted back to Portia. Jay got angry because he couldn't talk to her about his father. She was usually his go-to when he had something he was struggling with. He needed to ask her if he should consider sitting down with his father. He wished he could confide in her about it, but he couldn't because she had betrayed him.

The issues about Portia and his pops were both nagging at Jay continuously. He refused to let them govern the way he lived his life, but he couldn't stop thinking about either of them. He didn't like the change of heart he was having. He wasn't ready to forgive. Sometimes it was easier not to. He was no good with all those emotions and shit. Jay knew that he had to address both situations, so he could let go of the negative energy consuming him and move on. But he didn't believe he was ready yet.

CHAPTER TWENTY-NINE

That night, Cas was alone with his children in the family room of their home. Laila and Macy had gone to the supermarket for groceries, so Cas was watching Skye, who was watching television, and helping Jahseim with his homework. Cas checked his son's fractions and noted how tired he was. He had gone for a checkup the other day. His doctor said he was doing well, but had warned him not to exert too much. Cas should've taken heed to the advice, because the horseplay he'd shared with his kids a half an hour ago had let him know he hadn't fully recovered yet.

Cas checked Jahseim's social studies assignment next, and he thought about his promise to be there for Wise and Fatima's baby's birth. He was happy for them, but he decided he would sit that one out. He wanted to get back on his feet, so he had to take it easy. He had stayed in the hospital so long after he was shot; he wasn't ready to see one again yet anyway. He would volunteer to babysit the kids so everyone else could go.

When Cas was done checking his son's homework, he told him about the new cousin and sports buddy he would gain the following day. "Jah, Uncle Wise is having the baby tomorrow."

Jahseim grinned and nodded. He looked pretty pleased. "Good, I can't wait. I'm a boy, so I can teach him and Jaylin all kinds of stuff." All of a sudden Jahseim got real serious. "Umm, Daddy, I gotta tell you something. I don't wanna play football no more."

Cas looked up, surprised. "I thought you loved football, man."

"I do, but I don't like my coach. Not anymore." Jahseim paused for a moment. "Is *dick* a bad word? Can I say dick, daddy? Mommy said that's a bad word."

Cas figured Jahseim wanted to call his coach a dickhead for getting on his nerves, or something. He held back a laugh. He wanted to keep an open line of communication with his boy, so he skipped the censorship. "I'll let you say it this time. But you can't say it around mommy, or any other girls or ladies. Go ahead and speak, lil' man."

Jahseim looked cross. He didn't respond for a moment, and then he put his head down. "I don't like my coach because he tried to touch my dick. I don't feel right when people try to touch my private parts. So I don't wanna play football no more."

Cas's first instinct was to run and get his gun. He had to contain himself. He was ready to kill that fucking coach. It was a good thing he was home alone with his kids, or he probably would've gone to find the perv that second. He swallowed and took a deep breath. For the sake of getting the full story, he collected his temper and looked in his son's eyes. "What coach did this to you? Tell me what happened, son."

"Coach Perry. He told me I was his favorite player, and said he wanted to have a secret meeting after practice. He said he wanted to teach me some stuff the other boys didn't know. We were in his office, and I told him I had to use the bathroom. He said he was gon' come go with me."

Jahseim stopped talking and looked at his father. He wondered if he had said too much.

Cas almost grabbed him and shook him and yelled, "Finish the story!" The suspense was killing him so bad, he had to stop himself. Careful not raise his voice, he said, "Go on and tell me, son. Don't worry about nothin', I'm your father."

Jahseim nodded confidently. "Okay. Coach came in the bathroom with me and was lookin' when I was trying to pee. He followed me in the stall, so I tried to turn away like this." Jahseim reenacted the way he'd attempted to shield himself from his coach's eyesight as he urinated. "Then Coach smiled at me all weird, and then he leaned down and looked my dick."

Cas was boiling hot. He fought to maintain self-control. He wondered how he had allowed that shit to happen. This was a father's nightmare. His son had been molested by a man. "Then what happened? What did you do?"

"I zipped up my pants and moved away from him. He stood there while I washed my hands and said I was the best on the team. He said he was gonna treat me real special, but we had to share secret special time together. He said that's what special buddies did sometimes. Then he said he didn't want me to say anything to anyone about our secret, and then he asked me what special present I wanted. I asked for one of the war games Mommy won't let me play. For my Xbox. He promised me he would get it. Then we left the bathroom. I went home after that. So then, the next time I went to practice…"

"Tell me the whole story. What else happened?" Cas probed.

"After practice was over, Coach told me he had a game for me. He said he got me *Call of Duty: Modern Warfare 2*, but it was in his office. I told him I didn't wanna go with him to get it."

"And what he say?" Cas asked.

"He said if I wanted it, I had to come get it. So I went with him."

"And?"

"When we got in the office, and he gave me the game. Then he said he would get me all the games I wanted, but it was my turn to do something special for him. He said he had a game *he* wanted to play. The tickle game. We had to tickle each other until one of us surrendered. So we started playing, and I gave up first 'cause I was laughing so hard I couldn't breathe. We was playing, then he stopped tickling my ribs and grabbed me in a bear hug from behind. Then he started rubbing on my dick!" Jahseim made a face that implied that he didn't appreciate that.

Cas felt sick on the stomach. He thought about the promise he had made God. He had vowed to live right, but now he was faced with the ultimate test. He visualized himself loading the bullet that he would put through that coach's forehead the first chance he got. "What did you do then, Jah?"

"I told him to stop touching on me like that! He laughed and told me it was okay for boys to touch each other. Then he showed me this magazine with pictures of all these men doing nasty stuff to each other. Real nasty stuff. One man was kissing another man dick! I said 'ugh, that's nasty!' Coach said that wasn't nasty because boys made the best buddies. Then he said I was his best buddy, so we could play like that too. Then he asked me what video game I wanted next. Somebody knocked at the door, so I went back to the locker room to get my stuff. Then Mommy came and got me. I didn't say nothing because I was scared to tell Mommy. I don't want her to go back to jail."

Cas was going to kill that mothafucka. "When did this happen, son?"

"A few weeks ago, Daddy. While you were in the hospital."

"You been back to practice since then?"

"No, I told Mommy I was sick one time, and then I said I didn't wanna go."

"Good. You won't be playing for that coach ever again." Cas wanted to make it clear to his son that boy-on-boy relationships were unacceptable, so he skipped the politically correct explanation. Not that he had a problem with gay people, or anything. He had nothing against them. He would never make any public anti-gay statements, but Jahseim was his son, so he would raise him the way he wanted to. "Jah, that was a homosexual magazine that sick fuck showed you. That's not what real men do. That's wrong. God didn't make boys for boys, son. When you get old enough, you'll marry a woman, just like I did. You hear me?"

Jahseim nodded and screwed up his face. "I don't like no boys, Daddy."

"Good. Are you okay?" Jahseim nodded, so Cas asked, "Why didn't you tell me sooner?"

Jah said, "Because I knew you would be mad. I don't want you to go to jail either. I was scared."

Cas hugged his son tight and assured him that he was safe. "I wasn't there to stop what happened that time, but I swear to you, I promise, I will never let anyone hurt you again. I'm sorry I let this happen, lil' man. I love you more than anything."

"I love you too, Daddy. It's not your fault Coach Perry is a faggot."

Cas was surprised by his boy's forwardness, but he couldn't have said it better himself. Now Coach Perry was a dead faggot. Cas kept picturing that cocksucker's bloody murder. He had never said a word to anyone about it, but he was once fondled as a child as well. He was groped by a friend of the family's older son when he was just five years old. He'd been too ashamed to tell his mother. He never told a soul, but as a result, he had developed a defense mechanism that was tougher than kids' twice his age. That was one of the reasons Cas had taken to boxing when he was a young teen. That was also the main reason he walked with a hammer. He refused to be pushed around.

Cas thought about calling Jay, but he changed his mind. He would speak to him about it in person. He figured Kira also had a right to know. First, he wanted to rectify the situation. He had to come up a clean extermination plan. He also held back because he didn't want to ruin the moment about Wise's new baby coming. Everyone was in such high spirits; he didn't want to destroy the festive mood.

$$$$$

That evening Fatima lay on her bed with her legs propped up in the air. She was on the phone with Portia while Wise's freshly deposited semen marinated on her cervix. When she and Wise came in from the long walk he had accompanied her on, Fatima had demanded that he have sex with her, and then made sure he ejaculated inside of her. Wise preferred to shoot off on her ass, but he didn't complain.

Fatima had literally been a cum dump, but she was one with a cause. She believed Wise's semen was the antidote that would make her labor easier. She swore it was the reason she had started dilating in the first place.

On the phone, Portia told her to take it easy and pay close attention to her body that night. Fatima promised her she would head to the hospital if she needed to. They made arrangements for Falynn's care while she was hospitalized, and the girlfriends called it a night.

When they got off the phone, Fatima called for her husband. "Wise!"

He came running to make sure she was okay. "What's wrong, Ma?"

"Wise, what the hell did you tell Jay about Portia? They still on the outs behind that shit."

Wise shrugged. "I dunno, I was mad that night. I told him she messed with Vino. Jay told me he approached that lil' nigga too. But he said the nigga Vino denied everything. He said he just *comforted* Portia when she was upset and shit."

Fatima kept a straight face and silently thanked God that Vino hadn't admitted to having sex with Portia. She was sure he had his reasons as well, but she sure was glad. She looked at Wise and shook her head. "See, bigmouth, I told you nothin' happened. You started all that shit for nothing."

Wise shrugged. "Well, better safe than sorry. Don't nobody want no hoe for a wife. Fuck outta here!"

Fatima rolled her eyes. Wise and his damn mouth. Suddenly, she felt a contraction coming on. Her eyes popped. "Oh shit, Wise! These contractions are getting harder!" She leaned back and took a series of deep breaths until it passed.

Wise got nervous and began to sweat. That wasn't a fire drill. They were live and uncut. He stood there confused and wondered what to do. "Should I boil some water or somethin', Tima?"

Fatima held back a laugh because it was too painful at the time. Wise didn't have a clue. "No, fool. That's not necessary."

CHAPTER THIRTY

That night, Laila cooked a hearty meal for her family: sautéed chicken breasts, garlic mashed potatoes, and vegetables. Everything was good earlier, but Laila noticed a change in Cas's mood since she'd gone to the supermarket. When they ate dinner together, she noticed he acted like something was on his mind.

After the kids went to bed that night, Laila asked her husband what was bothering him. Cas was gruff with her and blew her off. That really surprised Laila because he had never spoken to her that way. She decided not to make a big deal out of it. She backed off and gave him his space.

About five that morning, Cas and Laila were in bed when she felt him get up. Laila thought he got up to use the bathroom, but he went in the closet and started pulling out clothes. She grew concerned. "Baby, what are you doing? You okay?"

"Yeah, go back to sleep. I gotta make a little run."

Laila looked over at the window and saw that it was still sort of dark outside. She wasn't on Cas's back, but she had to ask where he was going at that hour. It was before dawn. "A run where, babe? You need me to go somewhere with you?"

"No," Cas said firmly. "Go back to sleep."

"Cas, I'm starting to get worried. Where you goin'?"

"I just gotta take care of somethin'. I'll be back in a little while."

Under regular circumstances Laila would've backed off, but Cas was still healing. He still had staples in his chest. "I don't think you should be out in that night air, baby. You're still very infection-prone. The last thing you need is to catch pneumonia or something. God forbid."

Cas knew Laila cared, but she was annoying him. He ignored her, because he figured that was a better alternative than snapping at her.

Laila watched him continue to move about as if she hadn't said anything. She realized that he flat out ignored her. She told herself that this new rude side of Cas wasn't for her. Her senses told her that whatever he was up to was something dangerous. When Laila saw him get bullets for his gun, her suspicions were confirmed.

Cas didn't say another word. He went in the bathroom to shower. When Laila heard the water running, she got up and grabbed her cell phone from the nightstand. She was so scared about Cas's unexplained behavior, she went down the hall and called Jay on his cell. As the phone rang, she prayed he picked up.

Jay was asleep when he got the call. He saw Laila's number on his caller-ID and got worried. He looked at the time and prayed everything was okay. "Hello?"

Relieved, Laila blurted out, "Sorry to bother you, Jay. Cas is up in here all mad at something, and he gettin' ready to go do something crazy! Can you *please* come over here and stop him? He's not listening to me."

Though Jay didn't quite understand what Laila was talking about, he sensed the alarm in her voice. He wondered what the deal was, but he got out of bed in the guestroom he'd been sleeping in and didn't ask any questions. "I'll be there in a few, Laila. Just try to stall him."

"Thank you, Jay. I'm sorry I had to wake you. Please hurry."

Jay went in the bathroom and freshened up. After he brushed his teeth, he walked down the hall to him and Portia's bedroom, where his walk-in closet was located. He stepped inside the closet and pulled out a pair of black Polo sweats and a matching hoodie. He slipped into the clothes and stepped into a pair of white and black Concord Jordans. Jay headed downstairs and grabbed his Bentley keys, and then he hurried to Cas's to see what the deal was.

As he turned down Cas's driveway, motion detection lights lit up the property like a football stadium at night. When Jay got in front of the house, he called Laila to let her know he'd arrived. A moment later, she opened the door.

Laila was so relieved to see Jay, she hugged him. "Thanks for coming, bro. Come on in."

"No problem, baby girl." As Jay walked inside, he asked, "Where is he?"

"He's upstairs getting ready. I don't know what's wrong with him, Jay. Cas is up to something. I don't be on him like that, but he's not well enough to be doin' no crazy shit. Not yet."

Jay shook his head. He agreed. "Nah, you're right. He's not."

"I know," Laila sighed. "He won't talk to me about it, so I'ma stay out of it. I'm sure he'll let *you* know what's bothering him."

"I hope so," Jay said. "I'ma go up there and holla at him."

"By all means, bro. Please do."

Jay jogged up the winding staircase two steps at a time to Cas and Laila's master bedroom. He tapped on the door and then walked in.

Cas was sitting down tying his boots; a pair of black suede Timbs. He looked up at Jay, surprised.

"What up, man?" Jay asked.

"You serious? No Laila didn't call you over here this early." Cas sucked his teeth and shook his head. "Sometimes that chick be bug – "

Jay cut him off with a quick lie. "Nah, man. I was just up early."

Cas made a face at him. "Yeah right."

"Son, what are you up to? Where you headed this time of morning?"

Cas sighed as if something was really troubling him. "I couldn't even sleep thinkin' about this shit. Man, you don't even know. I gotta go handle something."

"Like what, man? You barely healed up yet, Cas. Lemme take care of whatever it is for you. What's goin' on, man?"

Cas shook his head and took a deep breath. He looked Jay in the eyes and spoke with pain. "Man, this homo nigga touched my son. Jah just told me a little earlier today. It was his little league coach, this cracker nigga named Coach Perry."

Jay stood there in shock. He was repulsed. Now he understood Cas's persistence. "Son, don't tell me no shit like that." Jay loved his nephew like he was his own son. That coach was a dead man walking.

Cas nodded. "I'm 'bout to go finish that nigga."

Jay cosigned that immediately. "I'm wit' it. What's your plan? You got this perv mo'fucka address?"

"Nah, I don't know it. Not yet. I ain't gon' front, I ain't got no plan yet. I'ma just be waitin' for that nigga when he get to work. He has an office at the school, because he's one of the gym teachers."

"Cas, that 'no plan' shit could get us killed, man. They would consider that a school shooting; and we'd be gunned down before we make it back to the car. The pigs don't play with shit like that. I know you mad as hell, but don't react out of emotion, man. You can't go up to the schoolhouse buckin'. You smarter than that. Let's get the info on this nigga and do this shit the right way."

Cas's anguish showed on his face, though he couldn't argue with Jay's reasoning. He wanted to kill that creepy ass coach ASAP, but he didn't want to get done in the process. He had just survived an ambush, so he'd be a fool to walk back into the frying pan. "A'ight, man. You dead ass right. Shit gotta be done the right way. But word on my kids, this sick ass, freak mo'fucka gon' pay."

Jay nodded in agreement. "Hell yeah, that slimy piece of shit is dead."

$$$$$

It was only the crack of dawn, but Portia was at home wide awake. She was up wondering what Jay was up to. She had seen him go in his closet and get dressed at five o'clock in the morning. Then he just left the house. Jay still wasn't really speaking to her, so Portia had fought the urge to chase him down and grill him. He probably wouldn't have told her anything anyway. Jay had developed this horrible attitude toward her, and she hated dealing with it.

Portia had visions of him sleeping around floating through her head. It was sickening. Her stomach was literally turning. She couldn't stop thinking about the picture Melanie had sent her.

"He comes home every night, P, so there's nothing to that," Portia reassured herself aloud. She spoke the truth, too. Jay wouldn't really say shit to her, but he did come home.

Just then, Laila called and eased Portia's worries by filling in the missing puzzle pieces for her. "Portia, I just called to let you know what's goin' on. I called Jay and asked him to come over here. Him and Cas are upstairs talking right now." Laila lowered her voice to a decibel above a whisper. "I stood at the door and eavesdropped on part of their conversation, P. I heard Cas say Jahseim was touched by his coach!"

Portia gasped. "What? When?"

"Recently, I guess." Laila sounded sad.

Portia was also saddened by the news. "Oh my God!"

"I know, that's crazy. But, physically, Jahseim is okay, thank God. He seemed fine earlier at dinner."

Portia sighed. "But mentally is another issue. That baby could wear the scars of molestation forever. God forbid."

"God forbid," Laila prayed too. She and Portia were both mothers, and equally disturbed and disgusted. They were silent on the phone for a moment as they thought about what had happened to Laila's daughter, Pebbles, who was killed by a very sick pedophile.

After a minute, Laila kept on. "I heard their plans, P. They're gonna 'take care of it.' You know what I mean?"

Portia sighed again. "Yeah, I figured. I know they are. But what if they can't pull this one off, Lay? Now this is something *else* for us to worry about." She shook her head and looked up to heaven. "God, please watch over our husbands. Touch them, Lord, so that they will learn to let go, and let *You* handle things. In your Holy Name I pray, Father. Amen."

"Amen," Laila said. "I was thinkin' the same thing. But please don't say nothin', P. I'm not supposed to know yet. When they want us to know about this, they'll tell us."

Portia agreed to keep quiet. "Don't worry, I ain't gon' blow it up. Laila, me and Jay ain't speaking no way. So I'm definitely not gon' say nothin'."

Laila didn't like to hear Portia talk that way. She gave her girlfriend the best advice she could think of. "P, he's gonna come around. Just keep the faith. And don't be passive, sis, fight for your marriage. Your husband is a prize, baby girl. You're married to the money. Don't forget that."

Portia thought about what Laila just said. "You right, sis. Thanks." She was far from passive. Deep down inside, she knew the only thing stopping her from spazzing out was the fact that she was actually guilty of what Jay had accused her of. She was ashamed of herself for sinking so low.

Laila's pep talk also made her think about the picture Melanie had sent her of Jay with another woman. Portia started to mention the fact that she thought he might be cheating, but she didn't want to talk that bullshit into existence. She didn't have accurate proof, so she decided to sit on that info until she had a little more to go on.

At that point, the only thing Portia was sure of was that she was willing to fight for her marriage, by any means necessary. If her family was incomplete, she had absolutely nothing.

$$$$$

Just a few miles away, in Philadelphia, Hot Rod lay on a thin lumpy cot that made the old bunk he'd slept on in prison feel like a Sealy Posturepedic mattress. The decrepit cot was covered in faded, threadbare sheets. It sat in the corner of an even sadder looking grungy room. The fifty dollar a week shithole he called a residence came equipped with the cot that doubled as a sofa he lay on, and an old rabbit-eared television set that sat on a dusty wooden stand in the opposite corner. The filthy, once-white walls were bare, except for a calendar Hot Rod had thumb-tacked up, so he could count down the days.

He lay there awake, just staring at a candle burning. The old-school antenna covered in aluminum foil turned him off so bad; he hadn't even bothered to switch on the TV. The way Hot Rod saw it; he didn't have time to watch television anyhow. He needed to make some serious changes.

He needed a little change for his pockets, too. Hot Rod had been broke since he came home from prison. It was easier to catch a case than to catch a come-up. Everybody around him seemed to be doing bad, so he didn't even know anybody worth robbing.

Being that broke upset Hot Rod tremendously. It reminded him that his big brothers, Mike and Powerful, were not there. They would've made sure he struggled a lot less, but his only living relatives were gone. The Brooklyn niggas that had gunned them down were going to pay for that, too.

Hot Rod had been told that the niggas his brothers were slain by owned a record label – Street Life Entertainment. It was all over the news how his brother, Mike Machete, had killed Wise, the popular rapper, in a gun battle. His brother was killed in the same shootout, and Hot Rod blamed his death on the surviving members of Team Street Life. Them niggas owed him big time. He was deciding how he wanted them to pay.

That's why he didn't have time for TV. He had to make moves. Hot Rod had been selling scented oils, shea butter, and incense for a Muslim brother named Akil. He appreciated the help the good brother had extended to him, but he'd been barely making it. At the end of the day, he hardly had two nickels to rub together. He'd hung in there for a couple of weeks, but it was time to move on. He needed some real paper. He had to get on it like his brothers were. They'd been married to that money.

Hot Rod decided that the following day, he would use the little bit of change he had scraped up to buy a fresh pair of sneakers and a one-way ticket to New York City. He didn't know a soul in New York, but when he left, he wasn't looking back. All he had to go on was the gossip and banter he'd overheard from these two dudes he'd been jailed with. They had mentioned this organization called T.B.G., which supposedly had the whole borough of Brooklyn sewed up. T.B.G. was said to be ran like the military. There was allegedly a real chain of command.

Hot Rod figured that a determined young man such as himself could enlist, and then start from the bottom up. Once he got in, he was confident that he would move up in rank in no time. He had no one or nothing else to gravitate toward, so he was stepping out on blind faith. If he could get affiliated with an organized crime clique like T.B.G., he would surely gain the ability to finish the niggas responsible for his brothers' demise. One thing he had learned in his short life was that there was strength in numbers.

$$$$$

Later that day at work, Lily grabbed a quick bite on her lunch hour, and hurried back to the office to do some filing. She had volunteered to do the extra work, but her motivation wasn't to keep the office more organized. She'd been sucking up to the boss so she could gain access to all of the medical records.

Twenty minutes into her task, Lily came across the papers she was looking for. She smiled mischievously. Now that she knew Fatima's birth schedule, the sky was the limit on her plans for retaliation. Since Wise wanted to play unfair and dis her like she meant nothing to him, she wanted to take away the things he cherished most.

Lily looked at Wise's family as nothing more than an obstacle blocking his and her love. With nothing else to cling to, he would finally be free to love her. Though her ideas were a bit farfetched, she believed the end results of her scheme would be them living happily ever after.

What Lily had up her sleeve would change the lives of everyone involved forever. But the helpless romantic in her believed the connection she and Wise shared would cause the stars to line up in her favor.

$$$$$

If you have unanswered questions and need to know what happens next in this addictive series, tune into *A Dollar Outta Fifteen Cent 5: A Little Bit of Change*, where the saga continues. When the drama building up finally explodes, who will be left standing?

Stay tuned …

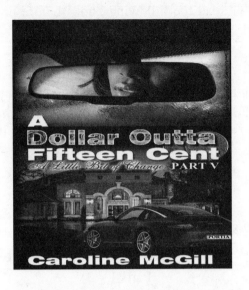

A Dollar Outta Fifteen Cent 5:
A Little Bit of Change

Coming Winter 2014!

Attention true *ADOFC* heads!!! Join us in our new Facebook group, ***Caroline McGill's A Dollar Outta Fifteen Cent***, to leave comments and suggestions, and also to play *A Dollar Outta Fifteen Cent* trivia for a chance to win contests and special prizes.

Also join Caroline McGill on …

Facebook at facebook.com/caroline.mcgill.142

Twitter at twitter.com/CAROLINEMCGILL

"Like" Synergy Publications' page on Facebook today!

Excerpt from "Take It to the Grave"

A packed church was filled with mourners gathered to celebrate the life of a loved one, lost to the streets. The preacher looked down at the dead young man lying in the coffin before them solemnly, and then he made eye contact with the funeral attendees and spoke to them passionately.

"I heard a lot of people stand up and say how good this man was! He helped a lot of people, and touched a lot of lives! See, God judge us by the things we do. He say "let the works I've done speak for me-e." So to the family, I say don't worry! You see, it's alright...Don't you weep no mo'! Lord, don't you mourn. Let not your hearts be troubled, 'cause Brother Jeff don' gone on to another place! A better place! A place where the thunder don't roll, and the rain don't pour. Good God almighty! Where troubled winds no longer blow! Glory hallelujah! I'm talkin' 'bout heaven, ya'll. Do y'all wanna go to heaven? 'Cause *I* wanna go. And if you get there before me...When you get there – tell my mother, and tell my father... That one day... I'm comin' home! I said I'm comin' home! Glory be to God! Hallelujah!"

Jeff's bereaving mother threw up her hands in the air, and cried out, "Rejoice! Hallelujah! Praise God! Rejoice!" Two of the church ushers dressed in white stood over her and fanned her.

Suddenly there was a loud thud. The church doors flew open, and a crew of thugs entered menacingly with big guns drawn. They were all dressed in black, with matching black boots, hats, and guns. At the sight of the intimidating looking crew, parishioners began to panic and look for a way out. Everyone knew that there were slim chances of a happy ending in this situation. That posse's intent was clear. They meant business. It looked like they came to kill.

They walked down the church aisle and further intimidated everyone by ice grilling them threateningly, and pointing guns at their faces. Amidst the thugs was one female, dressed in black army fatigues, black Timbs, and a black hat just like the rest of them.

The last man of the bunch entered the church, and the others in the crew respectfully parted, allowing him to pass. They posted up along the aisle on both sides to make sure nobody made a move. The last man headed up to the front of the church with two men following close on his heels. His presence was that of authority. It was obvious that he was captain, and the other two were his lieutenants.

The captain gave the command, and his lieutenants sprang into action. Jeff had already been shot before he was thrown from that roof, but they walked up to his casket and coldly opened fire on him again, putting a brand new set of holes in his corpse. The lieutenants, Loc and Fuck-You-Phil, had been briefed and given orders. No mercy was to be shown to anyone at Jeff's funeral, not even the preacher. Whoever didn't cooperate was to be gunned down. It was that simple.

People hovered cowardly down by the pews, and witnessed the desecration of Jeff's corpse in horror. To shoot a dead man in his casket was unheard of - and in the house of the Lord? Them boys had to be out of their minds. The funeral attendees all realized that their lives were in danger. The crew of young criminals in their presence was bold and reckless.

The whole church got down, searching for cover, including the preacher. Everybody ducked except for Jeff's mother. She refused to let her son's memory be disrespected that way. She had to speak up in his honor.

"My God...! What have you done? What kind of people are you? Have you no hearts, and no souls? My child is already dead. You all are nothing but the children of Satan! Get outta here! I rebuke you in the name of Jesus. Get outta here! My son is dead! This is his home going ceremony. You killed him once, and you come to shoot him again? How can he rest in peace? My God, have you no shame?" She threw both hands up to the sky like she was looking to God for answers, and shook her head helplessly.

Jeff's mother was upset, and very emotional. She was a woman of God, but her son's murderers were unmoved by her display of maternal bereavement and holiness. Loc, the shorter one wearing the black Yankee fitted cap, walked right up to her and shot her in the forehead at pointblank range.

The woman fell silent, and her blood splattered on Jeff's grandmother, who was seated right next to her. After witnessing her daughter's murder, the elderly woman's initial reaction was of one of protest. She called on the Lord, and stood up, as if there was something she could do. But her protests were powerless, and in vain. Fuck-You-Phil responded with a slug to her chest. That shot knocked her back in the pew. The poor old lady clutched her chest in disbelief, clinging to her life. Two seconds later, she was dead.

The two lieutenants, Loc and Fuck-You-Phil, were a special pair. Neither of them played with a full deck. At the sight of the old woman's demise, Loc started laughing hard as hell. That was the way he had earned his street name. He was just straight loco.

Fuck-You-Phil had his moniker because his name was Phil, and he was known to have told a few dudes who begged for their lives "fuck you" before he pulled the trigger, and took their heads off. Both of the lieutenants were honored they had been delegated the task of shooting up Jeff's corpse, and were delighted to take shit a step further. Fuck that nigga, and his whole family.

To shoot a dead man at his funeral was the highest form of disrespect. That nigga Jeff had fucked with the wrong person's money, so he had to go. The captain, Butch, was so angry about the loss he took behind that nigga, he wanted to kill him again. That was the reason he had rounded up his troops and crashed the funeral. Now they had to find Jeff's partner to retrieve that mothafuckin' money, and kill that nigga too.

Loc had smoked a blunt laced with some powerful angel dust right before they came. He was out of his mind, and in a straight I-don't-give-a-fuck mode. He was already crazy, so the dust made him insane to the twelfth degree. Loc turned to the congregation, and pointed to Jeff's grandmother.

He yelled, "Yo, ya'll think that's disrespectful? I'll show you mothafuckas disrespectful! Y'all wanna see disrespectful? A'ight!"

He unzipped his black fatigues and removed his flaccid penis. He waved it at the congregation with an evil smirk, and then he walked over and pissed on Jeff's corpse. Everyone gasped in horror, each half expecting God to strike him down right there for his despicable act.

After Loc relieved his bladder, he put his dick away, and just stared at everyone. He yelled, "Y'all mothafuckas better act like y'all know! Who else up in here want it? Who the fuck else want it? Nobody move, nobody get shot!"

He raised his gun, and fired twice up in the air. It looked like he was busting shots at God.

"T.B.G. mothafuckas! T.B.G. up in this bitch! Yeah, niggas!"

That was the name of their crew. T.B.G. simply stood for The Bad Guys. Butch was the captain, and he and his team didn't give a fuck. They figured that shooting up the funeral was appropriate. They were all pitiless. There was already slow singing and flower bringing, so it was nothing to body a few more mothafuckas. Jeff's mother had asked for it, and his granny was old anyway. Fuck it!

Butch and his soldiers' hearts were stone cold. That was how TBG got down. They lived up to their name. They were The Bad Guys, and represented that to the fullest.

Synergy + Publications
www.SynergyPublications.com
Books You Can't Put Down!!

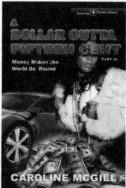

Order Form
Synergy Publications
P.O. Box 210-987   Brooklyn, NY 11221

_____ A Dollar Outta Fifteen Cent 2:
Money Talks… Bullsh*t Walks $14.95

_____ A Dollar Outta Fifteen Cent 3:
Mo' Money… Mo' Problems $14.95

_____ A Dollar Outta Fifteen Cent 4: $14.95
Money Makes the World Go 'Round

_____ A Dollar Outta Fifteen Cent 4.5: $14.95
Married to the Money

_____ A Dollar Outta Fifteen Cent 5: $14.95
A Little Bit of Change

_____ Sex as a Weapon $14.95

_____ Guns & Roses: _Street Stories of Sex, Sin, and Survival_ $14.95

_____   .95

_____   .95

_____   .95

Shipp   .00

  TOT   95

_____

Nam

Reg.

Addr

City:

Ema

930-8818

ons.com